I0661560

Katherine A Forrest

Manx Recollections

Memorials of Eleanor Elliot

Katherine A Forrest

Manx Recollections
Memorials of Eleanor Elliot

ISBN/EAN: 9783337219154

Printed in Europe, USA, Canada, Australia, Japan

Cover: Foto ©Raphael Reischuk / pixelio.de

More available books at **www.hansebooks.com**

MANX RECOLLECTIONS

Memorials of Eleanor Elliott

BY

KATHERINE A. FORREST

" They that be wise shall shine as the brightness of the firmament; and they that turn many to righteousness as the stars for ever and ever."

London

JAMES NISBET & CO.

21 BERNERS STREET

JAMES BROWN & SON

DOUGLAS, ISLE OF MAN

1894

PREFACE.

At the death of Mrs. Elliott some of her relatives expressed a wish that I should undertake a work such as the following ; but I could not then see my way to comply. Years have passed, and I have left the Isle of Man, and distance has made the heart grow fonder of the old home, and its sacred memories. Thoughts and desires revived, and grew stronger, until at last I began to write, and the result is the volume I now present to the public.

The title indicates that I scarcely consider it a biography purely. It is, in one sense, a biography and more. It is an attempt to describe Mrs. Elliott in her surroundings, which, of course, embraced many persons and things. This, it is hoped, widens the interest, and, at the same time, reflects the personality of Mrs. Elliott.

My purpose is to show how a private but powerful Christian life and character, in its hidden influences and operations, and as a centre of moral and spiritual force, is worthy of record. Such lives, for the most part, are lived, and their memory is allowed to fade away ; but surely it were well that some exceptions were made to this rule. To accomplish this, the great difficulty is to blend utility with popular interest. To deduce lessons from a well-known, and from an unknown hero is not the same thing, at least in arresting the attention of men. This has made my naturally pleasant and easy work a somewhat anxious effort.

The sources of information have been, chiefly, the Diary

of Mrs. Weatherell, the mother of Mrs. Elliott, Mrs. Elliott's letters, and those of her friends, together with my own experience of her character and the experience of her relatives and acquaintances.

The two chapters, " Faded Flowers" and " The Seraphim," need a word of explanation. They do indeed break the narrative, but they serve an essential end in furnishing by examples a definition of the style and capacity of Mrs. Elliott for literary work at a comparatively early period of her life.

It is quite possible that my information on some points may need correction ; some things may seem even irrelevant ; but I trust that none of these probable faults are so great as to affect the purpose of the work. I have striven to offend no one, and to refer kindly to all, and to seek on all sides such aids as were deemed by me necessary to illustrate my subject.

K. A. Forrest.

Fraserburgh, *June* 1893.

CONTENTS.

CHAPTER XL

CAPTAIN ALLEN GARDINER, R.N.

CHAPTER XII.

GRIEF UNUTTERABLE.

CHAPTER XIII.

MONA'S CHOICE OF A BISHOP.

CHAPTER XIV.

ASTRONOMICAL STUDIES.

CHAPTER XV.

PHILIP ELLIOTT'S MARRIAGE.

MANX RECOLLECTIONS.

CHAPTER I.

INTRODUCTION.

ELEANOR ELLIOTT!—what associations crowd around that name! It stands alone and prominent beyond almost all others in my heart and memory. It was in 1870 I first became really acquainted with this friend of friends. I had heard of her before this date, for she was well known in Douglas, Isle of Man, where we both lived. I had also met her before, first at the house of Mr. Thomas Cheslyn Callow, an honoured member of the Manx bar; but I remember, on the occasion I first saw her at Mr. Callow's, I felt very shy and half guilty in the presence of one who, I had heard, had passed through much sorrow. Instinctively I realised that my contrasted youth and inexperience, and repute, perhaps, for frivolity and love of pleasure, might cause me to appear a creature out of tune and very contemptible in the estimation of this sedate lady. Consequently, when Mrs. Callow introduced me to Mrs. Elliott as a young friend who had recently returned from school in France, and the daughter of a valued and mutual acquaintance, I felt very sheepish, and glad when the opportunity offered to make my escape from her presence. Yet nothing could have been milder and less awe-inspiring than the appearance of this quiet quakeress-looking gentlewoman.

Another time that I specially recall having met my friend during the early days of our acquaintance, was at a

A

picnic given by the Rev. William and Mrs. Hawley. I do not remember at this time having had any conversation with her beyond the mere commonplaces of social intercourse, yet the impression on my mind was, Mrs. Elliott is my friend, and she will do me nothing but good. There was that about her words and manner which conveyed to the mind the idea that one occupied her thoughts, and elicited her regard.

Again, about this time, I frequently—weekly, I may say—saw her at St. George's Girls' Sunday-school. Her place here, as teacher of elder girls, was at one end of the room, and mine at the other; but from my far-away corner I could see that benign-looking figure, and I could occasionally catch a glimpse unobserved of the absorbed earnest look on that calm, passionless face. I used to watch her when occasionally she spoke to Mrs. Hawley and some of the older teachers, and I envied them the privilege of her notice and words. I was once afraid of—*now* my desire was to *know* Mrs. Elliott, to peer into her heart and share the incentive of her life. But I was still too shy to put myself in her way. Fortunately a circumstance arose that bridged this feeling of separation; but as reference will be made to it elsewhere, suffice it in the meantime to mention one incident which put the seal on my growing interest in, and affection for, my ideal acquaintance.

One Sunday I had been holding forth to my class of juveniles with extraordinary fluency, substituting, I have no doubt, imaginary details for veritable facts, and riveting the children's attention with the glow of my own fervour, making up with emotion for what I lacked in knowledge and true experience. I do not remember what gave rise to it, but I recollect one of the teachers speaking about preparing one's lessons before attempting to teach : "Oh," said I, " *I never prepare.*" " You never prepare, Katie ?" she said, " then *you ought to do so*. I wonder how you can think of sitting down to teach without seriously considering the solemn importance of the work, and without studying the lesson beforehand." The rebuke was honest and well meant, but I was nettled. I thought my wise Mentor very interfering. Mrs. Elliott drew near at this juncture, and noticed, I have no doubt, the vexed colour rise to my cheeks, and my hot retort. "If I were to prepare as you propose I should feel stiff and awkward, and forget everything I had to say—my thoughts *flow*——" I said, indicating by a sweep of my hand the facility of my powers !

Mrs. Elliott smiled. I think I see her now ; it was half an amused, half a conciliatory smile. "You are like me," she said; "if I were to map out my sentences beforehand, I should feel stiff and awkward too." This was, of course, not the point in question ; but what more was said by any one I do not remember; all I remember is, that we trio finally left the school together, and when parting from Mrs. Elliott at her door in Athol Street, she took my hand in hers and held it for some time in a long warm clasp. The other lady noticed the endearing hand-shake, and turning to me as we walked home she said, "Mrs. Elliott seems to have taken a fancy to you, Katie."

If, subsequently, when these two ladies met again, reference was made to the incident of the Sunday-school, and Mrs. Elliott was better informed on the debatable point, I can imagine her saying: "Poor foolish young thing, it would have been too discouraging for us both to have come down upon her; and depend upon it, Miss ——, she will not think the less of your good advice that I did not join issues with you against her—she will weigh your words and act upon them all in good time !"

The Sunday just mentioned was by no means the last that I accompanied Mrs. Elliott to the door of her house after the close of school. It now became almost a habit with me to do so. Usually Miss ——, the lady before mentioned, formed one of our number, but often Mrs. Elliott and I were alone. On these occasions, when we paused at her door, I wished she would ask me to come in and have a little talk with her.

I had so many questions to ask that I felt she, and she alone, could answer; but she never gave me any encouragement to do so; probably, I afterwards ascertained, because she would not countenance anything approaching to Sunday visiting.

One day, however, as our intimacy ripened, I received a note from her, asking me to spend the evening with her and Dr. Elliott, and to bring a volume of Eugène Bersier, that I might read to her one of his sermons.

I well remember that evening; it dated a new era in my life. If I loved Bersier before for the beauty and power of his literary productions, I loved him now for the additional reason that he was the golden link that knit me to the heart of one of the noblest and most interesting of women.

At the hour appointed I made my appearance at 31 Athol Street. What a warm enthusiastic reception I was greeted with! How charming and bright were the words, "Mademoiselle, vous êtes la bien venue!"

Then the introduction took place with the Doctor; but shame be it said, the Doctor, good man! was soon forgotten. I had only ears and eyes for Mrs. Elliott. Yet, strange contradiction, delighted and happy as I was to find myself the guest of my revered acquaintance, I was not altogether at my ease—not at my best. I felt conscious of making an effort to stretch myself to her matured and intellectual height, and of failing miserably in the attempt. Her conversation was so easy, so sustained, so elevated, and yet so sunny; I could in no way cope with its grace, nor respond in any suitable degree to the loftiness of thought and the apparent profundity of the knowledge at my hostess's disposal. I kept thinking in the strength of my desire to please, how stupid and dull I must appear to her—how unutterably insipid must all my remarks be. I virtually bowed before an influence that I felt with my whole being, but could not then wholly fathom, much less define or analyse.

I was in a sense relieved when she asked me to begin and read. Here, I thought, I shall be something more of her match, French being pretty much like my own tongue. What was my surprise, however, to find that she followed me with the same facility as if I had been reading English, and stopped me every now and then to comment upon and discuss the various passages that specially arrested her attention. What clear, beautiful, additional light she threw on those glowing passages; they appeared to start into new life and wealth of beauty beneath the magic of her seemingly inspired thoughts and wonderful powers of expression. She did not speak in French, which led me to ask her how it was she did not do so, when she was able to follow by ear with such ease and correctness. "Oh," she said, "my attempts at speech would be very bungling; you would have no patience to listen to me!"

"Have you not been to France?" I asked.

"No," she said, "I have not, I regret to say, but I purpose to go shortly—there is a special reason why I must go to Germany; and Mr. Elliott's and my intention is to pass through Paris on our way. I am looking forward with intense delight to hear Bersier preach."

The special reason for this journey afterwards transpired. A cataract was forming on one of her eyes, and she had been ordered to consult a celebrated German oculist as to its removal. This calamity to her sight was evidently a sad subject, and she did not care to allude to it.

. . . .

The feeling of restraint that got the better of me in the presence of Mrs. Elliott—a feeling engendered entirely by my own self-consciousness—soon disappeared under the genial simple lovableness of this motherly though accomplished woman. It melted like snow beneath the beams of her ready smile and winning attractiveness of manner and speech. Soon, very soon, I had won my place in her large heart, and she had filled my life with the atmosphere of her individuality. What Mrs. Elliott thought and said I echoed. I had no alternative—I could not fail to bow before a judgment in which I saw no flaw, and to be actuated by a spirit that drank hourly from the fountain-head of Divine love and wisdom. Mrs. Elliott dwelt in the secret presence of the Most High; and everything that she said and did was an offering laid on the altar of heavenly devotion and sacrifice. No heart that had been moved by the impulse Divine, and quickened into life by the Spirit of regeneration, but must more or less come under the sway and gracious influence of this pure woman, who knew no law but that of the indwelling Spirit of God, and the word of His truth! No heart that had in it the essence of the milk of human kindness but what instinctively answered to hers and bowed in sweet accord; no mind enlivened by the gift of a capable and bright intelligence but hailed in hers a superiority that was in most cases absolute, and felt its own vivified and strengthened by contact therewith; no simple, gentle nature but soon learned to rest its shrinking timidity on the heart of this tender, sympathetic friend; no crushed, broken spirit but found solace and restoring health in the breast of one who could point with unerring finger to the Hand that wounds but to heal, to the balm of Gilead that never fails.

Eleanor Elliott! name ever dear and precious!—the synonym of all that was spiritually lofty, morally pure and engaging, intellectually good and forcible!—A star in the firmament of Mona's excellent of the earth!—A crystal dewdrop on the fair cheek of the sunny isle of other days—sparkling and reflecting, as we recall it, a myriad effulgent beams of heavenly and enduring character perpetuated in heart and memory!—A celestial ray—that beloved name—illuminating with chaste brilliancy the history of the past, and flooding with its lingering and beautiful light the path and chequered story of the future!

Such remind us, we too—

> ". . . can make our lives sublime,
> And, departing, leave behind us,
>   Footprints on the sands of time ;
>
> Footprints that perhaps another
>   Sailing o'er life's solemn main,
> A forlorn and shipwrecked brother,
>   Seeing shall take heart again."

CHAPTER II.

OLD DOUGLAS.

ELEANOR ELLIOTT was the elder daughter of William Weatherell, Esq., and Eleanor, his wife. Mrs. Weatherell's maiden name was Lawrence. The Weatherells are an English north county family. They came originally from Durham. Their name, until a comparatively recent date, was spelt *Wetherell.* The noted Sir Charles Wetherell was a member of the family. He was a son of the Dean of Hereford, and learned Master of University College, Oxford, for more than half a century. Sir Charles was born in 1770 and died in 1846. He was an eminent barrister, being the well-known Solicitor-General of the time, and famous opponent of the Emancipation Bill. To use the words of a descendant of his, "He determined to have nothing to do with the scarlet individual, whose seat is on the seven hills!"

The Weatherells past and present appear to partake more or less of the strictly Protestant character of their relation, Sir Charles.

Eleanor Weatherell (afterwards Elliott) was born in 1813 at Salford. When she was three years old, and her sister a year, Mr. and Mrs. Weatherell came with their children to live at Douglas, in the Isle of Man. Mrs. Weatherell had lived there with her parents before her marriage.

Douglas was then a primitive town, with probably less than a quarter of its present population, which at its average rate is something like 20,000, and in summer as much at times as 50,000. In appearance it has also so altered as to be scarcely recognisable with what it was then. There was the old Red Pier with its lighthouse (then *new*, having been completed in 1800), but there were none of the other piers, harbours, and promenades that adorn the place at the present day.

No line of fine steamboats was at that period connected with the island; the only vessels that touched upon its shores with merchandise and occasional passengers were small coasting schooners. Visitors to Mona had consequently a very uncertain kind of access to its remote attractions, the passage from Liverpool, according to weather, being more like a matter of weeks, perhaps, than as now, of hours. It has been stated by old inhabitants that it not unfrequently happened that the Post Office official was suddenly summoned out of church during the Sunday service to be in readiness to receive the mails, a vessel with the anticipated cargo having been sighted on its way to the island.

We may here add, that the Postmaster-General of the island about this period was a member of the fair sex, a Miss Grave, or de Grâve—as she alleged was the correct derivation. This dame was by no means an authority to trifle with. She was cognisant, or said to be, with almost all the "whos" and the "whats" of the insular populace; and it was a very mistaken proceeding to cross the magnate's good opinion, as it soon became transfigured into a sentiment of a very reverse nature, and laid the offender's reputation open to severe and retributive attack. She maintained a wholesome discipline in Post Office Lane, where was situated her abode and office of business. She had a brother, Peter, an estimable and mild individual, who occupied the position of a subordinate clerk to his official relation, and over whom the official right was swayed with authoritative rigour. Miss Grave died some fourteen years ago at an advanced age, the deep depositary of insular family history, a strict Calvinist, and a severe disciplinarian to the last. The demise of this lady and her gentle worthy brother benefited the island charities by a few timely legacies. The Spinsters' Home in Clark St., Douglas, owes its existence to the benevolence of Miss Grave, a useful institution for the housing of eight indigent unmarried women.

What Douglas lacked in primitive times in convenience and man's device, it gained in interest and the picturesque. The fine sweep of the beautiful bay was uninterrupted by breakwaters, iron piers, and artificial contrivances of many kinds to attract the ordinary pleasure-seeker at the expense of the lover of nature; and on either hand the bold promontories of Onchan Head and Douglas Head extended their arms and enclosed seemingly in a jealous embrace the blue expanse of ocean and the quiet insular town set in its background of distant undulating hills, and, nearer, many tinted fields and brilliant foliage. Amid the watery enclosure, sleeping in siren-like beauty, a concealed peril, lay Conister or St. Mary's Isle; and unimpeded over it swept the ocean waves, and at night, with no beacon tower as now, the unwary mariner too often found himself stranded in distress on its hidden rocks, his ship and himself hopelessly doomed to destruction.

But Douglas then, if its population was small in comparison to that of to-day, made up in some respects in quality for what it lacked in quantity. Then, or at least a few years later, was the fair island town the haunt and home of many of the younger scions of noble families, of the gentleman of good old lineage but impoverished fortune, of numerous retired military and naval officers, and of the dilettante in search of literary and artistic quiet. If, as it often happened, the ruined scapegrace of gentle blood and blighted fame thought that, along with immunity* from his creditors' claims, here he could hide his head, and assume an incognito, and none be any the wiser, he soon found that had he chosen a big thoroughfare of the city of London it would have been nearer his purpose, for in Douglas everybody knew every-

---

* At this date the law had not been repealed which enabled a person who had contracted debts in Great Britain and Ireland to be freed from their payment in Manxland.

body; and society there was as select as exacting self-respect and human pride could make it. It was no easy matter for the unknown, or the dubious, to gain an entrance into the privileged circles of social life in Douglas and its neighbourhood in those days. It needed a very clear parchment of evidence as regarded the antecedents and recommendations of the applicant. Gentle blood and an old name were a great deal, but not *all*, that was required; the wild "ne'er-do-weel" found no quarter amongst the *élite* of Man. Would he make sure of a resting-place for the sole of his foot, he had need to fly to the retired glens and hills and remote villages of the beautiful isle.

In 1820, or thereabout, a miniature court might be said to have been held in Douglas, and the Duke of Athol the representative of Majesty; indeed he was styled "king in," and was virtually sovereign of Man. His residence was Castle Mona, a truly regal structure, and situated amidst lovely grounds on the crescent of the bay. The Duke entertained considerably, giving periodical dinners and balls to the gentry, chiefly military and naval officers and their families, especially after the wars of Wellington, when there was a great addition to the influx of military, who settled in Mona for economy, and for the pleasure of each other's society. Wealth was at a discount, and society was so exclusive, that any one ever so remotely connected with trade aspired in vain to gain an entry into the privileged sets.

Sedan chairs at this period were of not uncommon use by ladies of consequence, who were conveyed in them by elegantly bedizened bearers in livery with knee-breeches, when their dameships went to church, or on their rounds of calls.

From 1736 to 1765 the whole island was the property of the Dukes of Athol; previous to that it had been owned by the Earls of Derby and others. In 1765 the reigning Duke of Athol ceded the revenue of the island to the

British Government for £70,000, retaining, however, certain rights.

In 1825 the island was unreservedly given up to the Crown, the Duke agreeing to receive from the Lords of the Treasury, in lieu of his remaining interest in the insular estate, £416,114. Home rule, however, was never abolished, and the island to this day has its own government and laws, the civil government being vested in the Lieutenant-Governor and House of Keys. "The *Council*, which is the upper branch of the Legislature, and corresponds to the British House of Lords, consists of the Bishop, the Clerk of the Rolls, the Water-Bailiff, the Archdeacon, and the Vicar-General. The *House of Keys*, which answers to the British House of Commons, consists of twenty-four members, who are now (since 1867) chosen by the votes of the electors of the island."

In 1830 a small steam-packet company was formed, and once a week a steamer crossed between Liverpool and Douglas. The means of reaching the island thus facilitated, Douglas eventually became a yearly attraction to the inhabitants on the mainland, especially to those of the northern counties.

What a refreshment to the busy citizen and toil-worn mechanic of the English manufacturing districts in past days as now to visit the beauties of this tranquil isle, this gem of the sea, with its splendid coast scenery, its mist-capped hills, verdant vales, and innumerable streams, and all its loveliness enhanced by the interest attached to its ancient laws and primitive customs, its legendary and romantic lore, its old castles with their exciting stories of days gone by, its fairy bridges and weird haunts rife with superstitions infinite, its quaint cosy-looking cottages with their great open fire-places and peat furnaces. Yes, the island was a world of wonder and of charm for the health-seeker and solace-seeker, as well as for the novelist and poet, the dreamer and student of divers colours and degrees.

When the Weatherells came to Douglas to make it their home they took a house on the South Quay. The South Quay in those days was a quiet but quite fashionable locality; now it is completely out of date and its character altered. The Weatherells had, we believe, but at a somewhat later period, amongst their neighbours a certain mysterious Manx official who shall be nameless, Major and Mrs. Tallan and their family of five daughters, and a Captain and Mrs. Jones.

Captain Jones was a very eccentric gentleman. He was usually styled "Count," on account of his haughty reserved bearing. He kept his little wife, who was a great beauty and naturally lively and sociable, in an habitual state of fear and trembling—and everybody else of his acquaintance at arm's length. He made, however, an exception of Mrs. Weatherell, whom he styled "a sensible woman," and to whom he would occasionally stop to speak. The regiment to which Captain Jones belonged had been èngaged in active service in Canada, and he had fought at the battle of Williamsburgh in Upper Canada, where he was severely wounded, and now suffered mentally as well as physically from the effects of his wounds. He was a brave officer and a kind master. He still retained Charles, his servant, who had fought beside him, and had restored his life when he lay for dead on the battlefield. It may here be mentioned that poor Charles, though he never showed the "white feather" in the hottest engagement, died in Douglas of cholera in 1832, which he had caught from the sheer dread of catching it.

Major Tallan had also served in Canada. As for the mysterious Manx official, the first-mentioned neighbour of the Weatherells, it was supposed that he had in some way or other been identified with a murder that had taken place at the Brown Bobby on the Peel Road, but had escaped detection and evaded the law. The story ran that at night he could not rest, and was seen by Mrs. Jones and other neighbours pacing up and down till nearly early morning, in restless disquietude of mind, the garden at the back of his house. The Brown Bobby, where the terrible deed took place, and the incidents of which had never been satisfactorily cleared up, was considered in those days, and perhaps is so still, a haunted spot. Mrs. Jones has been heard to say, that at night her servant Charles never attempted to drive her past that place without the horse becoming restive, and the conveyance in danger of an upset.*

The surroundings of the South Quay at the present day are, to a certain extent, what they were then. There is the outlook on to the upper harbour, generally full of ships and red-funnelled steamboats—minus these, however, as early as 1816–30; the rushing waters of the united streams, the Dhu and the Glas, crossed with the bow-bridge; and, away opposite, the North Quay, with its busy stream of life, vehicles and equipages of different kinds; to the left, in perspective, the hill ascending to Athol Street on one side, and diverging to the Peel Road on the other; to the right, a view of the market-place and St. Matthew's † ancient chapel; and, further along, the Red and Old Landing piers. This part of Douglas, whilst retaining much of its primitive features, has considerably the appearance of a foreign town, so broken is it in outline, so varied in feature, and so rich and profuse in colouring.

To the left of the houses then occupied by the Weatherells and the other families mentioned, is the beginning of the old Castletown Road. A most picturesque bit of road it is now, but how much more must it have been so then, when no modern terraces stole from the background of grassy hills, spangled in the spring-time with myriads of primroses and golden celandine; when, at intervals, trees in patches of woodland decked the emerald bank; and when, further on, the row of primitive white houses that, even at the present

---

* Mrs. Jones died in 1875, aged 85.

† Built by Bishop Wilson—the famous prelate of Man, author of *Sacra Privata*, &c.—in 1708. It is the most ancient church in Douglas.

day, form such a sweet picture were the only dwellings on
this part of the road, and stood out in solitary beauty from
their charming setting of tall trees and brilliant green sward,
commanding in front of them a ravishing view of river,
meadow, and varied foliage. A few paces further on there
is now, as perhaps then, the old mill with its whirr-whirr of
wheel and water, and from it, within a stone's throw, the
first entrance lodge to the romantic grounds of the Nunnery.
The Nunnery House was, in 1816, &c., the residence and
property of Colonel Taubman, grandfather of the present
proprietor, Major John Senhouse Goldie Taubman.

The handsome monument to be seen to the left of the
path soon after entering the grounds is, of course, a comparatively recent structure. It was erected in 1854 in memory
of Brigadier-General Thomas Leigh Goldie, of the Nunnery,
Lieut.-Colonel of Her Majesty's 57th Regiment, who fell at
the battle of Inkerman. Surely nothing could have ex-
ceeded the witching beauty of the Nunnery groves of those
days. Modern alterations have destroyed much of the charm
of past interest, but then nature had in a great measure her
own way; the trees grew luxuriant, and in some parts so
thick that in broad noon it was shadow there. With what
stories were these groves rife! How terrible to walk amid
their gloom when the moon shone pale through the canopy
of interlacing boughs; what visionary shades were, it was
said, seen to flit athwart the semi-darkness—nuns of former
days, unhappy spirits who returned to haunt the scenes of
their earthly woes; what sounds arrested the ear—the sighs
and moans of sorrow or the requiem of the passing bell! It
was with palpitating fear the timorous Manxman in 1816
wended his nightly way through the Nunnery walks. Even
the inmates of the ivy-clad mansion occupying the site of
the ancient Nunnery narrated that they had at times heard
a mysterious carriage and horses drive up to the front doorway and ghostly visitors alight, and then suddenly all become
silent and no one to be seen.

The original building of the Nunnery is said to have been erected in the fifth century, and to have been founded by St. Bridget, who lies buried in the precincts. It was an off-shoot of Furness Abbey in Cumberland.

As to the remains of the once beautiful Nunnery Chapel, renowned for the richness of its architecture and strength of construction, scarcely anything survives the ravages of time, and the injuries offered the sacred fane by the enemies and despoilers of ecclesiastical power and authority, but the eastern gable of the sanctuary, surmounted by the hoary convent-bell, now mute with the history of ages.

Restoration has erected a modern chapel on the site of the old, but in the days of which we write the poet and the artist could with untrammelled fancy contemplate in picturesque and ruined decay the pathetic memorial of a renowned and formidable past.

> He who to Mona e'er hath been,
> And joyed in each romantic scene,
> In fancy oft reviews those shades
> Sacred of yore to cloistered maids ;
> Where once they paced in reverend awe,
> Communing of monastic law ;
> Or where at foot of time-worn cross
> They pensive mused on couch of moss,
> And told their beads when jocund lay
> Of soaring lark hailed forth the day ;
> And where at eve when complines meet
> The refrain stole of anthems sweet ;
> And insect's hum and whispering breeze,
> Soft dropping dews and rustling leaves,
> And faint sheep-bell and purling stream,
> Responded to the hallowed theme.

Such is a brief outline of the fair features of Douglas eighty years ago, such an idea of its personality, those habits and sentiments under which Eleanor Elliott was early trained, and which tended to form and colour her character and life as she grew from childhood to womanhood.

CHAPTER III.

CALL TO CHRISTIAN SERVICE.

WHEN the Weatherells had been about three years in Douglas, a son was born to them. He was named Robert. This son afterwards became the Rev. R. Weatherell, M.A., St. Edmund Hall, Oxon., Rector of Elton, near Nottingham. He is now succeeded by his eldest son and namesake. The young Robert as he grew in years grew in grace, and became the loving and constant companion of little Eleanor, though she was six years his senior. He was a precocious child, old for his age, and the difference between the two was scarcely perceptible, and became less so as time went on. The children were nurtured amidst the beauty and romance of their surroundings. The little brother and elder sister especially delighted in rambling together through the fields and lanes in their neighbourhood, and scrambling in the autumn for blackberries, which grew in wild abundance up the Castletown Road and adjacent hedgerows. They delighted in racing through the Nunnery groves, and in spring and summer time down their grassy slopes, purple with wild hyacinths, to the river's brink, where along its margin the splendid king-cup spread in brilliant clusters of emerald and gold. Here they sported like the butterflies overhead, their young forms sometimes hid in the dense profusion of great flowering rhododendrons, and anon re-appearing, climbing a hedge and over into the expansive meadow, marshy, but fragrant with the cuckoo-flower and odoriferous meadowsweet with its creamy feathery blossoms. Freedom and nature's endless variety of charm filled the hearts and minds,

B

and invigorated the healthy growth of these children. They
early drank at the fountain-head of pure sweet joys, and they
fed upon the daily sustenance till they grew up creatures
of like mould, and endued with the breath and existence of
all that was "lovely and of good report."   Brother and
sister were similar in disposition in many respects, but
Eleanor had a power and grasp of mind and a fund of
effervescing spirits that were all her own. She was intensely original and therefore peculiarly interesting. Her
father died when she was ten years old. About this time
she was sent to school. The school she attended was conducted by two accomplished gentlewomen of the name of
Dutton. It was at 31 Athol Street. Amongst her schoolfellows were Catherine Jefferson, who afterwards married
the Rev. Wm. Hawley (of whom more anon), and Eleanor,
youngest daughter of Major Tallan, mentioned before. Here
Eleanor Weatherell remained until she was fourteen. Her
animal spirits at this time are said to have been extraordinary.
She was the merriest girl in the school, and at times made
the tall house peal with her laughter. Strange was it that
in that very house, then vibrating with her child mirth, she
was in womanhood to pass through the deep shadowland of
grief unutterable, and finally herself to sleep the sleep that
knows no waking until "He come."

On leaving Miss Dutton's, Eleanor was sent to school to
Edge Hill, a suburb of Liverpool. She was at this school
for three years—three years of untold misery. Away from
her home and beloved brother—away from the freedom and
beauty of hills and dales and wild sea-coast, she pined and
pined to such a degree that when her mother came to see
her at the end of the three years she could hardly believe
she looked on her own daughter. Her parents were tall,
and when she left Douglas, Eleanor gave promise of becoming tall too, like them and like her brother and sister.
Instead of which she was diminutive for her age, changed
in the expression of her countenance, and crushed in spirits.

It was a sad disappointing meeting for her mother; and the end of it was Eleanor was removed from school altogether.

To add to Mrs. Weatherell's vexation, soon after she brought her daughter back to Douglas an epidemic of small-pox broke out in the town, owing to the want of attention by the officials to sanitary regulations. Eleanor caught the infection, and was for a long time seriously ill. Fortunately when she recovered, such care had been taken of her during her illness, scarcely a mark remained indicating that she had passed through that frightful disease. And gradually as she recovered her strength, she recovered also to a great extent the buoyancy of her spirits that had flagged so wofully during the time she was at school at Edge Hill. Once more the light of health and lively intelligence shone in her eye, once more a tinge of delicate pink touched her cheeks, once more she could laugh and skip along the country lanes or climb the ocean rocks, rejoicing in a sense of freedom and congenial surroundings.

During these years of Eleanor's life, if Douglas revelled in its gay little dinner parties, balls, and other social entertainments, a large section of it rejoiced in the higher and holier satisfaction of a living spiritual existence. The saintly Rev. Benjamin Philpot ministered at St. George's; and 1832 saw the beginning of the ministry and *reign* of the greatly honoured and beloved Dr. Carpenter. He was Incumbent of St. Barnabas in Fort Street, but his character and spiritual influence were felt in every church in the town. He was a power for God and humanity. To this day his name is held in the highest reverence; and there are those still living who can trace their spiritual birth and regeneration of life to the teaching and saintly example of this consistent earnest man. He was the instigator also of almost every good work that was set on foot in the town and neighbourhood. He cared for the bodies as well as the souls of the community; and by his means the House of

Industry was built, an institution for the housing and employment of the aged and destitute poor.   Visitors to the building may see the Doctor's portrait hanging in the committee-room, as if he presided still over all the delibera-tions held there for the benefit of the institution.   He it was, too, who inaugurated the Hospital and Dispensary in Fort Street, and built and set on foot the schools connected with St. Barnabas Church, where an excellent secular education was given, but subordinate to the teaching and spiritual guidance of the Word of God.   He was a father amongst his people, and from the humblest to the highest was regarded as such.   At all hours and under all circum-stances he was welcome in their dwellings; his counsel was ever needed and as readily given.   An amusing instance of the demand for his advice is that recorded by one who knew of the incident.   Miss Dutton was greatly teased at times by young gentlemen, who for mischief paraded about her house, peeping in at back doors and open windows, to attract the attention of the young ladies under her care; and in desperation at the annoyance, she went to Dr. Carpenter and begged of him to interfere, and have the tiresome youths brought to account for their conduct. "Ah, Miss Dutton," said the Doctor, "believe me, I can do nothing, for where the girls are the boys *will* be!"

The Doctor was an Irishman and could not resist a little fun.   He was said himself to have eloped in his youth with the lady who became his wife, and who was a baronet's daughter; the Doctor having been tutor in her father's house.   Be that as it may, young Carpenter came under the power of the grace of God, and his whole soul henceforth was set on fire in the service of his Lord and Master.

When Eleanor Weatherell was about eighteen years of age she heard Dr. Carpenter preach a sermon from Matt. xxv. 34–36: "Then shall the King say unto them on His right hand, Come, ye blessed of My Father, inherit the kingdom prepared for you from the foundation of the world:

for I was an hungred, and ye gave me meat : I was thirsty, and ye gave me drink : I was a stranger, and ye took me in : naked, and ye clothed me : I was sick, and ye visited me : I was in prison, and ye came unto me." The Doctor had a way of preaching peculiar to himself; it was like a father talking to his children. There was nothing, it is said by some, very learned or exceptionally eloquent in his sermons, but in their appeals to heart and conscience all agreed they were irresistible. His people idolised him, and hung upon his lips as if their souls went out to his. For how long the teaching and indwelling spiritual power of this.preacher had been working upon the heart of young Eleanor Weatherell is unknown; it is possible, as she and her relations attended his church, that the seed had been dropping and perhaps rooting for long, and that the new life born of the Spirit of God had begun. But this particular sermon was as a glorious ray of heavenly light that streamed into the hidden depths of her nature, and caused the leaf and soon the fruit to appear of a healthy vigorous spiritual plant of life. She realised that true faith in and love to the Lord *must* of necessity manifest and prove themselves in works to His honour and praise, and for the good of His creatures. "Peter, lovest thou Me ?" Then, " Feed My sheep, feed My lambs "— was the argument and sum total of the lesson taught and engraven on her heart; and " *Love*," the great commandment, in which all other is included, was from this date forward the keynote of young Eleanor's existence.

As to *where* to begin her operations of service to the Master, the newly-aroused and enlightened disciple went to her own dear brother for sympathy and counsel. His advice was that she could not do better than begin by visiting the Widows' House at the rear of St. Barnabas Church ; it would afford a fine field for the exercise of her devotion and zeal. This house for poor widows is still in Mucklesgate, as the locality is called—a new building on the site of the old. Over the doorway, in the hands of a carved angel, is this inscription :—

" Widows' House, founded by Mrs. Squibbs, 1833 ; rebuilt by public subscription 1868. 'Let thy widows trust in me' (Jer. xlix. 11). Trustees :—Hon. and Right Rev. Horatio Powys, Bishop of Sodor and Man; Rev. J. H. Gray, Incumbent of St. Barnabas ; Rev. Wm. Hawley, Chaplain of St. George's."

From the first date, it is evident the institution was only newly started when Eleanor began her visits there, and for this reason was a very likely place for a youth to recommend as a field of Christian labour, for no doubt the recent in-auguration of the good work occupied the minds of many, and its merits were pretty generally discussed. At all events, there it was Eleanor began her life-service to her beloved Saviour.

From the personal appearance of the subject of this memoir later on in life, one would judge that at eighteen she must have borne a very strong likeness to Frances Ridley Havergal at that age. There was the same style of brow, contour of face, form of head, and the features not unlike—the expression was undoubtedly similar. Now it is possible that there was also a certain similarity of disposition ; and it is quite conceivable that the work of grace having once begun to develop in the case of Eleanor, progressed with a like rapidity and power as in the case of Frances. Miss Havergal's friend, the Rev. Charles Snepp, says to the effect that, having made the start, he never met with any one who advanced with such rapid progress in knowledge and practice of Divine things as did Frances Havergal.

Eleanor Weatherell, it is evident from all that can be ascertained of her life's history and what will follow here, having put her hand to the plough in the work of Christ, matured in knowledge and experience in a very marked way, going from stage to stage in Divine wisdom and its fulfilment in daily life.

"Take my life and let it be
Consecrated, Lord, to Thee,"

was truly the aspiration of her young soul, as it was that of the gifted poetess and Eleanor's twin sister in grace.

At this time she was not only the subject of Divine grace and a living testimony to its power, but her intellect grew proportionately, and outstripped all youthful competitors for learning and general acquirements. The Word of God became her daily and profound study, and the proficiency she attained in Biblical lore and sound theology was very unusual at her age. With the view of assisting herself in Bible study, she set about learning Hebrew, Greek, and Latin. French she had begun at school, but she applied herself to gain a fuller knowledge. German, Italian, and Spanish, as time went on, she added to her studies; but never obtained more than a slight acquaintance with each. She was a voracious reader, and every branch almost of literature came readily to her, and she set herself to its acquisition. Poetry she loved and appreciated with a soul made receptive by the early study and admiration of nature. History she grasped with a masculine understanding, and was able to retain by means of a singular memory for facts and dates. Biography she fed upon, deriving stimulus from the lives of the great and the good for the perfecting of her own character and services to mankind.

About this period also she probably first began to express herself in literary composition, both in prose and verse. In this pursuit there does not appear to have been the faintest desire for distinction. She studied and wrote apparently because she could not help it, or because in both she found a channel to be of further use in the service of her Master, Christ. Humanly speaking, this very unusual lack of ambition in the prosecution of a beloved pursuit is, in her case, to be regretted. Almost everything she wrote and published was anonymous, or never saw the light of day.

It might have been otherwise; she might have devoted

herself far more exclusively to literature, and to good purpose.   But from the date of her call to Christian service, the
love of Christ and humanity bulked so largely in the eye of
her heart that she felt constrained to turn into immediate and
active service all the powers within her.

In addition to her literary ability and acquirements, she
possessed a feature of character that betimes gained for her
access to the hearts and homes of persons of all kinds and
classes, and so enabled her to extend her Christian influence
in a very exceptional way.   The young man of the world
and the dashing girl of fashion were not repelled by the
simpler personality and the higher tone of life of their young
companion in age and social standing.   They owed her no
grudge for her superiority of mind and contrasted seriousness
of deportment, they liked her for her *unlikeness* to themselves, and they drew to her as something dependable as
well as pleasant.   She fortified them with her strength, and
ennobled them with her nobility.   It was without doubt
mainly the result of her being so supremely natural, so
utterly free from self-consciousness, and withal so kind and
sympathetic.   None could feel otherwise than at ease with
her.   She *assumed* nothing, she was herself, and the imita-
tion of no one.   Such persons are a rest as well as an inspiration to meet with.   In writing of this delightful simplicity
of manner which characterised our friend, we are reminded
of a French saying : "Il n'y a rien de si charmant que la
simplicité et rien de si difficile."

CHAPTER IV.

THE CHOLERA.

DURING the years that intervened from the time that Eleanor was eighteen to the time of her marriage, when she was twenty-three, Douglas continued to be favoured with the existence of a degree of spiritual life and enlightenment unequalled perhaps in its history, and propitious to the growth of grace in many a heart besides that of Eleanor Weatherell. Many in after life had to thank God for this privileged time, during which they had been created anew by the Spirit of God, or had received a fresh impetus to the service of Christ, fostered and strengthened by the unwearying and constant ministrations of faithful pastors. There was, as we have seen, at St. Barnabas the godly and beloved Dr. Carpenter, and at St. George's the less popular, perhaps, but equally saintly Rev. Benjamin Philpot, who was succeeded in 1832 by the earnest, true-hearted Rev. Thomas Howard, afterwards Rector of Ballaugh, in the north-west of the island.

Mr. Howard had been at St. George's before as curate in the year 1809. It was during the time of his curacy at St. George's that the early morning services were held in that church for the benefit of working men. On their way to their daily toil at 6 A.M. they could turn into the house of God and have a quiet time of prayer and brief scriptural exhortation. "Sweet hour of prayer"—sweet under all circumstances and at all times, but surely doubly so when the world was still partially wrapped in slumber, or was just awaking to the work of day.

25

It was at one of these services a poor girl—an orphan—by name Nelly Brennan, was brought, through the instrumentality of Mr. Howard, to know her Saviour, and to consecrate herself to His service.

She was the sole offspring of a poor young woman, and a sailor-father, drowned at sea a few months before the birth of his child. Whilst Nelly was still very young, she also lost her mother; and having early been thrown on her own resources to make her way in the world, she acquired habits of self-reliance and diligence that enabled her bravely to fight the battle of life. She was the best mangle-woman in the town (for that was for many years her humble calling), and known by all her employers as thoroughly trustworthy.

Having been brought to a knowledge of Divine Truth, and having vowed her life to God, this worthy creature so contrived to work at her employment that she could at the same time administer of her time and substance to those worse off than herself.

In 1832 a dreadful epidemic of cholera visited the island. People were literally swept away by the hand of death. All day long the dead-cart seemed to be going its rounds from house to house, and the cry heard, "Bring out your dead—bring out your dead!" It was during this time that Charles, Captain Jones' servant, mentioned previously, one day that he had occasion to go from Douglas to Peel, said to his mistress on starting that he had a presentiment that he should die before night. That evening he returned, sickened, and died of cholera.

In Douglas was the greatest mortality; and at night in St. George's churchyard the burial of the dead, as described by eyewitnesses, was a mournful and appalling sight—never to be forgotten. There, by dim lanterns held in the hand, or suspended from the trees, the graves were dug, and in many cases the uncoffined bodies heaped in one after the other, and no stone ever to record more than one word—CHOLERA.

Close to the south-west entrance of St. George's Church, a large memorial stone, railed round, is erected to commemorate the dreadful time. Engraven upon it is a lengthy record of the event, surrounded by a sculptured relievo, illustrating the horrors of pestilence.

This was a period, indeed, to test the philanthropy and devotion of all those who had made profession of love to God and man, and truly many noble instances there were of self-denying efforts on behalf of the sufferers; but one name stands out prominently in the annals of the time, that is the name of the poor mangle-woman, Nelly Brennan.

Where none but clergymen and doctors would dare to venture to alleviate anguish of body, and misery and despair of mind, Nelly would make her way. In seeking not her life, she found it; whilst others who sought to save, lost it. Nelly preserved her health, as if by miracle, all through the continuance of the plague.

None recognised more warmly and sincerely the worth of this heroic woman, who had dauntlessly walked into the very jaws of death in the service of Christ, than Mrs. Weatherell and her daughter Eleanor. One of the first things they did to show their appreciation was to collect a sum of money to offer to Nelly as an expression of their regard for her and her noble work. Little did they know that whilst engaged in their kind endeavour, Nelly. was ill in bed and without the means to get herself even a cup of tea. So neat was her usual appearance, and so comfortable-looking was her little home, that no one ever suspected that Nelly, of all people, knew positively what it was to want; Mrs. Weatherell did not learn the truth until many years after. Nelly's temporary destitution was owing to the fact that when it came to the knowledge of her employers that she visited the cholera hospital, they discontinued to send their clothes to be mangled, fearing infection; and what money she had saved, she had spent it all on the sufferers.

On the occasion that Mrs. Weatherell visited poor Nelly with the purse of sovereigns, lying helpless on her bed, the invalid was wondering within herself—could it be that she should die of want? Suddenly impelled by the thought of the *impossibility* of such a thing, she exclaimed aloud, "The Lord is my Shepherd, I shall not want."

At that moment a gentle tap came to her door, and Nelly calling out, "Come in," Mrs. Weatherell entered with her timely offering.

Acceptable as the gift was, and touching as a manifestation of the faithful care of God for His child, Nelly would only accept a small portion of the amount for herself, and obtained permission to devote the remainder to charitable purposes.

Nelly, though in such humble circumstances, became a power for God in Douglas; not only amongst her poor townspeople, but amongst the refined and wealthy. Young gentlewomen would walk in miles from the country to have the privilege of reading the Word of God in company with this poor mangle-woman.

On young Eleanor Elliott, Nelly's saintly and devoted life had an undeniably strong influence, and the period of her heroic services just happened to be about the time that Miss Weatherell had received her call to follow Christ. Doubly inspiring then was the example of pious Nelly. The good woman's words and deeds were engraven for life in the heart and in the memory of the young and keenly observant disciple of Christ.

From the time she came in possession of it, and as long as life lasted, Eleanor had the portrait of Nelly Brennan suspended in a conspicuous place over her bedroom mantelpiece, enshrined in love and respect, as a memorial of one deserving of all honour.

Another influence also from the very humblest sphere in life was brought to bear on the character of Miss Weatherell. It was the history, as recorded by her mother, of Willie or Bill the Psalmer. Willie was a poor lone man, who lived in an attic with no other window but a little skylight. Through this he used to gaze up at the moon and stars, and fancy, in his simple way, that they were the eyes of God looking down upon him, and watching over him in his poverty and solitude. Willie was such a joyous soul, and he had such a love for singing sacred songs, that he was called " Bill the Psalmer." Mrs. Weatherell used to tell Eleanor that, when she was a young girl, she had so much veneration for saintly Willie, that when he walked on the sea-shore she would walk after him and plant her foot in the print of his.

Mrs. Weatherell was without doubt an earnest Christian, and inclined her family to respect *worth* wherever it was found. The story of poor Willie's happy devoted life appealed to Eleanor's heart exceedingly, and it had its due share in moulding her fine character.

How touching to think that the reflex light of a being so simple, so poor, and so obscure, should have attracted and illumined the path of a young creature like Eleanor Weatherell, highly gifted in mind, and surrounded with opportunities and privileges for self-cultivation and experience unknown and undreamed of by poor Willie. But so it was. And as long as Mrs. Weatherell and her daughter lived, Bill's memory was not allowed to grow dim.

A stone had been erected to his memory, close to the Weatherell vault at the chief entrance to St. George's churchyard, and every year Mrs. Weatherell, and afterwards her daughter Eleanor, had it freshly painted.

During the visiting season in Douglas, knots of people, going to or returning from Divine service, may be seen standing before Bill's head-stone, reading with interest the quaint inscription :—

Here lie the remains
of
WILLIAM KELLY (known by the name of
Bill the Psalmer), who departed this life
the 27th May 1808,
in the 78th year of his age.

Stop, Travler, as thou passest by,
As thou art now so once was I ;
As I am now so shalt thou be,
Fow addloo dy gholl quail dry yee. *

The Widows' House, the first scene of Eleanor Weatherell's ministrations to the poor, continued for long to be her pet scene of operations.

In 1835 her sister, Miss Jane Weatherell, married Lieutenant, afterwards Lieutenant-Colonel, Grier of the 93rd Highlanders ; and her brother was removed from King William's College at Castletown, in the south of the island, to a school in Chester, preparatory to Oxford.

Eleanor, deprived of her sister's companionship and of seeing her brother as frequently as hitherto, had probably more than ever an inclination to devote her time to the poor and needy. The love of her work grew upon her, and soon became an all-absorbing passion.

It was whilst visiting at the Widows' House she became acquainted with Mr. Elliott, a young surgeon who had lately come to practise in Douglas, and whose praises she continually heard sung by the poor suffering women whom he attended. By degrees she began to endow the doctor with all the amiable qualities that her warm heart and lively imagination painted. He, on the other hand, willingly believed that the young lady who had come across his path, and who was so pleasing to look upon, was all and much more than her warmest admirers proclaimed her to be. The end of it was the two young people were irresistibly drawn to each other, and in course of time the doctor declared his affection, which was reciprocated.

* Manx rendering of, "Be ready to meet thy God."

The engagement, it is to be regretted, did not give un-
qualified approval to Eleanor's relatives and friends. The characters and tastes of the lovers were so distinctly divergent,
that it was foreseen that there could never exist between them
the close companionship necessary to a really happy married
life. But Eleanor's strong will, not at this time as subdued
as it afterwards became, asserted itself; and she would listen
to no objections raised by any one in respect to her lover.
He was what her fancy painted him, and he was, we can
infer, the husband she believed God had provided for her.
They had met when and where both of them were engaged
in His work; for though the doctor attended professionally
at the Widows' House, yet he ever evinced in Eleanor's eyes,
and in the eyes of the poor women, a supererogation of
attention and kindness wholly uncalled and unlooked for
in a mere professional.

Eleanor's mind being irrevocably fixed, Mrs. Weatherell
did not withhold her consent; and in due time her daughter
was wedded to Philip Elliott. He made her a truly kind
husband, looking up to her with immeasurable esteem; and
allowing her perfect freedom to follow her own course of
action at home and elsewhere. On the other hand, Eleanor's
noble character and spiritual endowments were equally laid
under contribution to cheer and influence to higher ends the
less exalted disposition and attainments of her obliging
husband.

CHAPTER V.

MARRIED LIFE.

THE Miss Duttons having removed their school from 31 Athol Street to Villa Marina, and the former being the property of Dr. Elliott, he and Mrs. Elliott went to live there. Thus the scene of Eleanor's joyous young school-days became the home-stage of her married life.

Athol Street was a very fashionable locality in Douglas in those days and earlier. It was known for its large houses, and the notability of some of its inhabitants. Amongst these, a few doors removed from the Elliotts', on the other side of the street, was the abode of the Honourable Colonel Richard Murray, nephew of the Duke of Athol. This street had then by no means the gloomy aspect it assumed in after years, when the majority of the big houses were turned into musty-fusty receptacles of lawyers' litter, and all manner of agents' depositories of deeds and mouldering confusion—the arena of red-tapeism and endless bickerings of legal debate.

Every window almost in 1837, and before that period, was gay with sumptuous hangings and floral decorations; and before most doors carriages stopped, conveying to and fro persons of affluence and position.

The claims of home and society, the great attraction for most young brides, only in a minor degree occupied the thoughts and time of Eleanor Elliott. She had, it must be admitted, no decided taste or faculty for household management. Its details fidgeted her, and came as intrusions upon the time she preferred to bestow amongst the poor, and on her studies. She was not, however, averse to company. She entertained with great zest in her own way, and she delighted in conversation and the exercise of social talents generally. She was a born conversationalist. Most subjects interested her, and her knowledge even at the age of twenty-three was so diversified that almost every one found in her a delightful companion.

After her marriage she continued to go out a good deal, and shone in all circles save those decidedly frivolous, but these she avoided.

In every house of her acquaintances where literature, music, and art found congenial soil, there she reigned supreme, asserting her power graciously and irresistibly, all unknown to herself. As for her own little dinner and other parties, one can only imagine from later experience what they must have been. How easy, how spirited, how gay with fine intellectual mirth and deep spiritual piety.

No character is perfect; and it is to be regretted that this young wife, with all her intellectual and winning attractiveness of manner and speech, did not exercise herself to combine with these more of the ordinary female accomplishments of household management. But as a dark spot shows most conspicuously on a white garment, it is possible that this defect in Eleanor's otherwise pleasing character, excited undue notice and exaggerated censure from some who, intent upon the blemish, lost sight of the prevailing beauty and completeness of the whole.

She was a creature of vast powers of concentration and absorption in her favourite inclinations and pursuits. These overwhelmed her with the constraining sense of their importance and need of attention. She strove, there can be no doubt, to do *all* things required of her as a wife and Christian lady, but time failed to enable her to accomplish *the all*. And, what to her were matters of minor and less congenial significance, she handed over to the discharge of those she honestly believed better qualified for their per-

formance. All her life she trusted too implicitly to the
supervision of servants.

Marriage, in a word, did not interfere very perceptibly
with Eleanor's work amongst the poor, and her pursuit of
literature. Indeed, her love for Christian work of all kinds
increased. One religious and benevolent society after
another shared her sympathy and enlisted her services.
Her purse, as well as her heart, was open to all earnest
claims. She was, however, far from being a prominent
religious worker in the community, and her name was
perhaps at no period one often quoted as an authority in
religious and philanthropic circles. She was a power, but
a hidden power, moving in her own orbit, and as the silent
dew, fructifying and beautifying almost all within her
domain. She had an innate and insurmountable distaste
to the public discharge of religious and philanthropic
work; and as for committee meetings of all kinds, she
never in her whole life acted upon them. Herein, it
may be, lay the secret of much of her power: she was a
self-contained force. She was felt to be a reality; and
people loved her and drew to her often without hardly
knowing why. She would have agreed with Spurgeon,
though not with the spirit perhaps in which he said it,
"I believe in a committee of three; one dead, one asleep,
and myself."

As the life of spiritual might and beauty was developing
more and more in this gentle heart, there was also another
life springing into being from hers, and shortly to manifest
itself in the birth of a little son.

A year after her marriage the babe was born. It only
needed this young life to mellow and beautify as never before the character and influence of the mother. She was just
twenty-four when she first dandled her precious child upon
her knee. What joy and thanksgiving flooded Eleanor's
heart! And the gift of this dear child was a bond felt and
understood between herself and her husband. The house

was radiant with sunshine. Everything, even the petty details of domestic duty, were now tinged with the reflection of the prevailing warmth and love. Her woman's nature asserted itself, and home and its claims, if not wholly paramount, were of supreme concern. The boy was christened William, after his grandfather Weatherell. The good Dr. Carpenter performed the sacred rite. Little Willie early displayed an extraordinary likeness to his mother in appearance. He had the same high expansive brow, clear complexion, calm and intelligent eyes; but his were a deep blue, with long lashes, whereas his mother's were brown. He evinced besides, as his little mind developed, the same precocious ability, firmness of will, and pleasingness of disposition.

The like endearing union that existed between Eleanor and her brother when they were children, now began to exist between the mother and her offspring.

Willie was four years old when another child was born, whom they named Henry Oliver. He only lived one year. The death of this boy struck like a knell on the mother's heart. She bowed as a bulrush before the storm of grief. Her bright eye, as it had done once before in her early girlhood, lost its gleam, her features their youthful softness of outline; and the general expression of her face, especially in repose, became pensive and sad.

In 1843 another calamity took place that brought consternation and sorrow into the Elliotts' home, it was the failure of the Isle of Man Joint-Stock Bank. Numbers of families suffered severely, and very many single gentlewomen lost all they had. Amongst those who were nearly ruined was Mrs. Elliott's mother. In consequence of her losses, Mrs. Weatherell was obliged to give up her own house; and, on the pressing solicitation of her daughter Eleanor and her husband, she went and lived with them. This was a heavy trial to the widow, but she bore it meekly and bravely, as became one who had learned in the school of Christ.

In 1843 another son was born to the Elliotts, to take the place of the little translated baby; and once more the parents' hearts were made glad. This son was called Philip after his father, and of the two sons, Philip, in course of time, by far the most resembled Dr. Elliott. More and more little Willie became the counterpart of his mother. He was now six years old—a universal pet and most engaging child.

Mrs. Elliott, if she was not in all respects a model housewife, was a most devoted, painstaking mother. To bring her children up as sons of God was her constant prayer and unwearying endeavour. She conceived that the highest honour had been put upon her when she became a mother; and she watched over her offspring like a gardener over his pet plants—watering their young souls with the Word of life, and training them to the service of God by habits of holy example.

None of this sacred endeavour was lost on the elder boy. It might be said of him, as of Timothy, that from a child he knew the Holy Scriptures, which were able to make him wise unto salvation.

Willie was a most wonderful boy. His mother writes of him when he was five years old: " Our little Willie is an exact mimic; he spends great part of his time in preaching and playing the auctioneer. When he is going to preach he mounts upon a chair saying Mr. Day* is getting into the pulpit, then he covers his face with his hands for a minute and leans forward, then he repeats a few passages from the Lord's Prayer, waving his hands about, and shaking his head in the most solemn manner, and then he concludes with Amen, and comes down from the pulpit. At other times he mounts upon a chair selling things by auction, and waving a chair leg for a hammer, and going through the usual string of phrases, ' No advance; going, going, going, gone!' It is really a most amusing performance."

* The Rev. Maurice F. Day, B.A., then curate of St. George's, Douglas, now Bishop of Cashel, Emly, Waterford, and Lismore.

A friend writes: "At the age of ten he arranged the room as a church; and, attired in a night-shirt for a surplice, called together the servants, and conducted a service, not forgetting the important part—the sermon.

"He used also to go to the shops and speak to the people serving on religious matters. His mother often said his mind was much more like a man's than a boy's—in fact, that few people could enter into her thoughts as he could!"

In another letter of Mrs. Elliott's, speaking of this son, she says that it had been told her by one present that Willie said in a little sermon of his, "The Lord Jesus was a gentle man—I don't mean a gentleman, but a gentle man." Little Willie's thought was brought to her memory when reading the beautiful passage by Decker :—

> ". . . The best of men
> That e'er wore earth about him, was a sufferer :
> A soft, meek, patient, humble, tranquil spirit :
> *The first true gentleman that ever breathed.*"

In another letter the mother says : On one occasion she had to be from home for a short time, and the boys were left in the charge of their grandmother. Willie conceived it would be great fun, and a fitting and graceful thing of them, to express their appreciation of their grandmamma's care when their mother returned to resume the reins of the house, so he and Philip wrote out the following addresses, which they delivered with a presentation of " plate " to Mrs. Weathrerell :—

" WILLIAM ELLIOTT'S ORATION.

"We, the members of this house, do with pleasure witness the return of the mistress of this house. But, notwithstanding, we feel it our duty to give a vote of thanks to the lady who has provided for the happiness and good of this household in such an able manner.

"The perfect satisfaction evinced by all towards the manager might have been remarked by a careful spectator.

"Had we been in the great metropolis our wants could not have been better taken care of, perhaps not so well.

"Among the dishes might not only be seen the good and substantial English, but also foreign reached the table—even from Italy—for there might be seen the excellent maccaroni; and an attentive ear might have heard the table groan under the good things which covered it.

"But these should only be secondary considerations, for what chiefly must be noted is the kindness and good management of the lady to whom the charge was entrusted. Words could not express the praise due to the manager.

"It is therefore resolved and seconded that the thanks of this meeting be given to that lady who has distinguished herself by the able manner in which everything has been conducted."

(Signed) "WM. ELLIOTT."

"PHILIP ROBERT ELLIOTT'S ORATION.

"LADIES AND GENTLEMEN,—I begin by saying that the first thing to be done will be to return thanks to Mrs. Weatherell for all the many savoury dishes which her Ladyship has provided.

"3rd. All the members of the family are sorry at her Ladyship's resignation.

"4th. That when her Ladyship gives up the keys a general chorus of cheers . . . and lastly to present the plate."

The fond mother, who copied and preserved these little speeches, adds in a note that the latter speech was in parts illegible, and that "There was a second part to it (Philip's); and when it was ended, the orator presented the plate to his grandmamma—a *cracked cheese plate.*"

CHAPTER VI.

"FADED FLOWERS."

DURING the years that followed previous to 1852 (a crisis in Mrs. Elliott's life), events of national and individual calamity occurred that threw into shadow and reserve many of the hitherto sunny aspects in her character. They were a formative process, welding her nature into deeper sympathy, wider experience, and more practical piety.

In March of the year 1843, Dr. Carpenter delivered a week-day lecture, in which he alluded to the recent appalling earthquake in the West Indies.

"Ah," he said, "many of you, my hearers, imagine that here in this favoured island we are safe from any such visitation from God. You said the same of the cholera, you believed foreign lands alone were a prey to such things, but it came and swept numbers of your relations and friends into eternity!"

The Doctor's words sent a thrill of awe through his audience, and not a few bent their heads in solemn forethought.

That very night, whilst Douglas slept, the foundations of the isle were shaken, and people were roused from their beds in terror and dismay. The Doctor's prediction had come to pass; the earthquake from which they believed themselves safe had followed them! Happily the shock was of short duration, and the damage done trifling. The voice of God, as spoken by His servant, was, however, heard in the event; and Eleanor Elliott and her household were especially impressed.

On July 10, 1845, Governor Ready, the Lieut.-Governor of the island, died. His death was a truly melancholy one, and one that called forth great and general sympathy for the bereaved widow.

Mrs. Weatherell and her daughter had apparently a deep regard for him who was gone and affection for Mrs. Ready. The Governor was taken ill during the night, and suddenly at 5 A.M. Mrs. Ready was roused from her bed to give him some medicine. In the hurry and agitation of the moment she mistook a bottle containing a mixture for outward application, and gave it to her suffering husband instead of the usual internal remedy. Two hours after he was a corpse.

One evening in November 1846 Doctor Carpenter took tea with the Elliotts and Mrs. Weatherell; and as the conversation insensibly turned from the things of time to those of eternity, the good Doctor alluded to a circumstance which had recently affected him very much. He said only a month ago a gentleman of the name of Hunter came to see him; he bore a letter from a Doctor Tattershall, a Liverpool clergyman, in which Doctor Tattershall asked him to show some attention to his friend Mr. Hunter, who was visiting the island for his health. "Only a few days ago," said Doctor Carpenter, "Mr. Hunter died; and about the same time Doctor Tattershall was preaching in his own pulpit in Liverpool when suddenly he too was called away!"

Doctor Carpenter's story had not time to fade from the impression it left on his friends' minds, when the Rev. Robert Brown, Vicar of Braddan, unexpectedly died. The circumstances of his death were peculiarly distressing. He had been very ill, and some attributed his illness to the great sorrow and anxiety he had undergone owing to his son Hugh having left the Church of his baptism and become a dissenting minister. This Hugh was later known as the famous Baptist, Rev. Hugh Stowell Brown of Liverpool. But on the day Mr. Hunter was buried, the Vicar, having sufficiently recovered, attended the funeral; and the procession passing the Elliotts' house, Mrs. Weatherell remarked how well Mr. Brown looked considering his recent severe illness. On his return from the funeral, a letter was put into the old clergyman's hands; it contained the news of his eldest son's death abroad at New Providence of yellow fever. A few days elapsed when the Vicar's third son died at home, also of fever. One fortnight after, he himself suddenly dropped dead near his own house.

A son of this Vicar of Braddan survives, the Rev. Thomas Brown, late of Clifton College, Bristol, who is the author of the "Foc'sle Yarns," "Betsy Lee," and other Manx poems of peculiar originality, power, and pathos.

What wonder that the wing of the angel of death seemed to hover with threatening plume over the very heads of those who listened to these sad recitals and trembled as they heard. Mrs. Elliott may be said to have kept and pondered all these things in her heart. In after years, so strongly had she been moved at this and subsequent periods to heartfelt compassion for bereaved ones, that she never heard of a death, or witnessed a funeral, without retiring alone with her God to pray for those who wept.

These deaths of familiar acquaintances and friends were in their turn almost submerged in the sorrow of the nation incident to the potato famine that, in 1847, began its dire work in Ireland. On March 24th there was a general fast appointed in the Isle of Man on account of this sad visitation. Prayers public and private went up to the great Disposer of events to avert the calamity and save the lives of a country's population. None exerted themselves more to meet the necessity of the times than Mrs. Elliott. She and her mother and the young Willie were heart and soul in their endeavours to forward material assistance to the poor perishing Irish.

It was at this time that our friend wrote, and published in the *Christian Lady's Magazine*, an article entitled "A Chapter on Faded Flowers." It is a memorial of the fragrant lives of Charlotte Elizabeth and Caroline Wilson, two Christian writers well known in their day.

Charlotte Elizabeth was the Editor of the *Christian Lady's Magazine.* She was a poetess and an enthusiastic lover of poor Ireland. An additional reason why she so much interested Mrs. Elliott was that she threw herself equally heartily into the cause of God's ancient people, the Jews. Of all societies almost for the propagation of the Gospel, the Jews' Society was to Eleanor of supreme importance. Her heart went out to the race of Abraham with a great compassion and yearning desire for their acceptance of the Messiah of God.

Caroline Wilson, the other gentlewoman, of whom she wrote, was the author of "The Listner," &c.

Our friend's article will speak for itself of her power of expression, fervent piety and chaste imagination :—

A CHAPTER ON FADED FLOWERS.

"My beloved is gone down into His garden to the beds of spices, to feed in the gardens, and to gather lilies."—CANT. vi. 2.

Charlotte Elizabeth and Caroline Wilson are dead and gone, like summer flowers. Let us consider these lilies of Eden, for they were lovely and pleasant in their lives, and in their deaths not long divided. We know that they shall live and grow again, clothed with such robes of beauty as Solomon never wore. "Light is sown for the righteous." It was sown when the righteous One, the Light of the world, was buried in the dark earth, and rose again on the first day of the week—a glorious sheaf of first-fruits to wave before the Lord of the harvest. And so the children of light go down to the grave and are hidden for a time, but they shall yet spring forth in the golden splendours of immortality. Therefore we have hope concerning our sisters that they shall return with all that holy family whom the Lord will confess before His Father and the holy angels. He shall stretch forth His hand towards His disciples and say, "Behold my brethren and my sisters—for whosoever will do the will of my Father, the same is my brother and my sister and my mother." Then the Marys and Marthas and Dorcases, and all the blessed women of all time, whose names are written in Scripture and in heaven; who did what they could for Jesus, so that the whole house of God is yet filled with the odour of their offerings; who ministered unto Him, and sat at His feet and waited for His words, and wept for their sins and for His sorrows, shall enter into the joy of their Lord. They shall be gathered together in one sweet society of kindred spirits, of one heart and mind in the unity of one Spirit of love. Now they compass us about as a luminous cloud of witnesses; then they shall clearly shine forth as glorious stars of light, revolving round the Sun of Righteousness, and reflecting His brightness for ever and ever. It is meet and right that we should give thanks unto our Heavenly Father, for those who have departed this life in His faith and fear, beseeching Him to give us grace so to follow their good example, that with them we may be partakers of His heavenly kingdom.

Charlotte Elizabeth and Caroline Wilson now rest from their labours, and their works do follow them. They were servants of the Church and friends of Jesus, loving what He loved, and doing His commandments. They both reflected the same light of heaven, though in varied tints of beauty and of grace. One was like Peter in fervency of zeal; the other rather resembled John in depth and stillness of love. "Go ye to the lost sheep of the house of Israel," said the Good Shepherd. This command was especially fulfilled by St. Peter, it was his peculiar vocation. So, according to her ability, and besides her other works of faith, did Charlotte Elizabeth seek the welfare of the house of Israel. Her spirit was stirred within her for the Lord's heritage, the dearly beloved of His soul. Her last testimony in this magazine was an indignant protest against Gentile coldness towards this ancient people, whose first father was called the friend of God. And her dying voice breathed the same spirit of zeal in a good cause. "Truly she fell asleep in Jesus, and not only so, her last testimony to His faithfulness and truth was a message to her beloved Israel."

Thus the last aspect of her soul was eastward—looking towards Jerusalem.

It reminds us of a sweet passage in the life of Christian. "The pilgrim they laid in a large upper chamber whose window opened towards the *sun-rising;* the name of the chamber was Peace, where he slept till break of day, and then he awoke and sang." So she sleeps in peace, and when the day dawns she will awake and sing. She was not only the friend of the Jews, but of the Gentiles also. The limits of these pages forbid any detail of her works of faith and charity, and so we merely prolong the last breath of her soul, as it still seems to whisper among the leaves of this book. She was not partial in the law; she sought to fulfil all righteousness. Yet we do not unduly exalt our departed friend—we glorify God in her; because it is His pleasure to place burning lamps in earthy pitchers, that the power and the victory may be of Him alone. It is to be supposed that, like other daughters of Eve, she had her faults and her "foolishness," and they are known to God, who remembereth that we are but dust; and they are buried out of His sight in the sepulchre of Calvary, never more to rise. But when the trumpet sounds she will herself arise, disencumbered of the earthen vessel, and clothed with the light and perfection of a spiritual body.

Of that other sweet sister of the Lord who is fallen asleep we need not inquire—" Whence had she this wisdom and this holy love?" Her gentle voice is hushed in death, or she might answer—"All my fresh springs are in Thee, O Lord!" She drank deeply of the well of Bethlehem, the eternal spring of wisdom and truth and love. Like the beloved disciple, she leaned on Jesus, and so her ear caught

the softest whisper of His voice, and her heart answered to
His heart of love, as the calm lake reflects the sunlit sky.
Thus she could respond to the witness of John—"We have
known and believed the love that God hath to us"—"He
that dwelleth in love, dwelleth in God—God is love." The
God of her life, in whom she trusted with such childlike
confidence, having loved His own while she was in the
world, loved her unto the end, and was her guide unto
death. "Till within the last hour, utterance was used to
speak of the love, truth, and faithfulness of God in Christ,
and in terms the most touching. Nothing occupied her
during the latter part of her course in this sickness, but the
joy set before her—so bright, so serene."

> "So gently shuts the eye of day,
> So dies a wave along the shore."

The last book of Caroline Wilson is a transcript of the
"Great Commandment," written in her tender heart by the
finger of God Himself. She was indeed a living epistle of
Christ, and being dead she yet speaketh. It has been said
of our heaven-taught sister that "she manifested in 'Christ
our Lord,' and other writings, the philosophic strength of
'spirits masculine,' combined with feminine grace and tenderness." This union of grace and strength forms what we deem
angelic excellence.

This is true, but we enter not now into any analysis of
her varied gifts and graces. All that we can do is to glance
at the last work of this wise-hearted woman, wrought for the
sanctuary after a heavenly pattern. Thus she writes of the
love of God—"Love something else! Why, there is nothing
else! It is all but a portion or reflection of Himself. . . .
All creatures are but faulty portraits with just one look, one
almost real look of Him we love supremely—caught ever and
anon by them that know His face, and so we love them too.
I know not what manner of vision pure spirits have of Him
in whose presence they abide; but I know, and am quite

sure, they see no beauty, and feel no love, and seek no happiness apart from Him : all creation would be a useless bauble if they saw not, and knew not their Creator in it. Other than His likeness could not please—other than Himself could never satisfy. He wrought the affections too pure for other tastes, He made them too large for any other feeling : and He formed them so that, without what would suit their affections and suffice them, it was impossible they could be happy. Then when He issued forth His great commandment, had it been a decree to be happy instead of to love, which is in truth His gracious meaning by it—it would have come to the same thing: there was no other way to be happy but by loving Himself supremely."

"Come, Lord Jesus, come quickly!" said the beloved John in his lonely Patmos. And how sweetly is this dying cadence of inspiration re-echoed in the last words of her whose heart made melody unto the Lord. "Thou blessed One, forgive our sad impatience. Thou wert not impatient, albeit heavy and exceeding sorrowful, while Thy love to us was tested to the utmost. Thou art not impatient now that Thy enduring faithfulness is tested still by the unwillingness, unfitness, and unreadiness of Thy promised ones which delay Thy coming. Oh! say in heaven Thy gracious prayer for us, that our faith fail not when our love desponds—trusting Thine when we cannot trust our own! . . . We 'seek a country;' we are far from home—we say so—we believe so —at times we feel so. . . . And now if Thou should come —if some kind calculator dates Thy day—and eager listeners hear, or think they hear, the distant movements of Thy bridal train—shouldst Thou find faith—dost Thou find love enough in Christian hearts, to wish it might be so?"

It may be that they who are patiently waiting for Christ will not have so very long to wait. Even now the earth seems to shake and tremble at the distant roll of His chariot-wheels. Say not ye—there are yet a thousand years, and then cometh the harvest. Is not the summer nigh at hand? The Jewish fig-tree shows signs of life — the Euphrates is drying up like a summer brook—"Men's hearts are failing them, for fear of those things that are coming on the earth, for the powers of heaven shall be shaken." "Wherefore I praised the dead which are already dead, more than the living which are yet alive"—for they are taken away from the evil to come. The beloved One hath been visiting His garden to gather His lilies, before the last storm of desolation. "Lo! thus He giveth His beloved sleep." Our friends sleep until the morning without clouds, when the Lord shall come to awake them out of sleep. Then again the second time Jesus will show Himself to His disciples. And on this wise He will show Himself. He will appear as King of kings, wearing many crowns, in that day of His espousals, and of the gladness of His heart. He will be manifested in the brightness of His glory, to dry up the tears of His people, as the "clear shining after rain." "For lo! the winter is past, the rain is over and gone—the time of singing is come. Arise and come away." Then the sleeping and living saints shall awake and arise and shine; and sing for joy to see their Lord, the King of Saints. He shall be glorified in His saints, and admired in all them that believe. They shall be to the praise of the glory of His grace, when the Lord of the Sabbath shall rest in His love, and joy over them with singing. Before them the prospect is a bright vista of ever-deepening bliss, and rivers of pleasure for evermore.

"The flowers shall appear" again "on the earth," and Paradise shall resound with songs of joy. Of the "increase of peace" there shall be no end, for the Holy Dove shall rest on the celestial Olivet, and flee away no more from the stormy winds and tempest. The Spirit of Love shall be grieved no more, and the Man of Sorrows shall weep no more, and the happy children of the resurrection shall sin no more, for ever. Blessed and holy are they that have part in the first resurrection. Blessed are they that do His commandments, that they may have right to the tree of life, in the midst of the garden. Our mother Eve disinherited herself and her children by disobedience; but the heirs of the second Adam shall inherit all things, and eat of the tree of life and live for evermore. The fiery sword that guarded "the sacrament and instrument of immortality" is quenched in the blood of the Lamb: and so the kingdom of heaven is opened to all believers. Therefore, "unto Him that loved us, and washed us from our sins in His own blood, unto Him be glory and dominion for ever and ever." Amen. E.

Isle of Man, 1847.

CHAPTER VII.

MANX NOTABLES.

WHILST Mrs. Elliott superintended the education of her children, and enjoyed, as only such a mother could, to watch the rapidly opening beauty of the character and mind of her eldest son, she herself perceptibly matured in holiness, and became increasingly rich in varied knowledge and experience of many kinds. Her house was the resort of all that was good and learned in Douglas and the island generally. Dr. Carpenter was a constant and beloved visitor there. He would come in with his beaming smile and warm words of greeting, and then enter into a conversation as racy and gracious as it was hallowed and elevating. He had a manner, it is said, of telling the most amusing stories, not only in such a way as to excite every one's risibility, but to end by doing every one good, and lifting them up into a higher region of principle and kindliness. His Irish humour was irresistible ; but he made it a rule, when telling his good stories, *never to mention names,* if by so doing he would be led to expose the weakness or folly of any one. It is recorded that on an occasion when retailing a capital story, and making all laugh as he dilated on the eccentricities of a certain individual, suddenly a person in the company exclaimed—"Oh! I know, Doctor, to whom you refer ; it is to Mr. ——."

The good Doctor's countenance fell—his lips closed—and not another word would he utter of his story.

Such was the loving nature of the man. His was the wit that edified, the charity that thinketh no evil, and

that threw the mantle of protection over the ridiculous
or frail fellow-creature.

To him might be justly applied the delightful saying of
Jean Paul Richter : "No one should laugh at men but he
who right heartily loves them."

The Rev. Benjamin Philpot, at this time Archdeacon of
Sodor and Man, was also one of Mrs. Elliott's frequent
guests. He had known her of course since her childhood,
having been from 1827 to 1832 incumbent of St. George's.
He was very dear to her ; and all her life she continued to
speak of him in the most affectionate terms. He and Dr.
Carpenter were her beau ideals of ministers of the Gospel.

Archdeacon Philpot shared with her in the wonderful
interest she took in the second coming of Christ. The
second advent was, it may be said, her favourite theme of
thought, and of conversation, when she came across any one
like-minded with herself on this glorious subject. It will
be seen how it imbued her thought in the preceding article
from her pen. She and Archdeacon Philpot never met but
what they communed together on that which was so precious
to the heart of each. Archdeacon Philpot had a family of
fifteen children, all of them with remarkable personal his-
tories, and all of them devout Christians.

Amongst Mrs. Elliott's literary friends two especially
may be mentioned, whose visits to her house were not few
or far between—these were Mr. G. H. Wood, a late lieutenant
in the army, and Mr. Wanton.

Lieutenant Wood was a most intense admirer of young
Willie Elliott and of his mother. He regarded Willie as
a precocious genius, and prophesied that one day his accomplished parent would indeed have cause to be regarded
as the most enviable of mothers.

"Lieutenant George Horsley Wood was son of General
Wood, and grandson of John Wood, Esq., the first Governor-
in-Chief of the Isle of Man, who was the direct descendant
of Sir Andrew Wood, the famous admiral immortalised by

James Grant in his graphic and historical romance of the 'Yellow Frigate.' The admiral received his coat-of-arms direct from James IV. of Scotland for his exploits on the sea."

In addition to his interesting ancestry, Mr. Wood was a poet, a musician, and an elocutionist; and in his own and in the opinion of many, he was above and beyond these a profound philosopher. He wrote sonnets and critiques on metaphysical subjects. The critiques were on articles by Reid and Brown, Berkeley, Collier, and others in the *Edinburgh Review*, *Blackwood's Magazine*, &c.

Most of his poems he published in a volume, a collection not unworthy of appreciation, and many of them very laudatory of the charms of beautiful Mona. Full of the eccentricities of erratic genius, Mr. Wood was nevertheless an undoubted scholar, and his range of reading had been very extensive.

The reason why he liked Mrs. Elliott so much was that he regarded her as a kindred spirit, but also because she allowed him to hold his own fantastical and equally dogmatic opinions on things generally, not thinking it sometimes worth her while to contradict him, holding that—

> " A man convinced against his will
> Is of the same opinion still."

As regards his other gifts, and his personality generally, we will allow the Rev. Thomas Brown * to speak, who knew him well, and whose graphic pen will do justice to a word portraiture of his old friend.

"Lieutenant Wood was grandson of Governor Wood, and was, I believe, a native of the island. He was educated at the Cathedral College, Hereford, why there I cannot imagine. He entered the army, and served for some time in India. Here it was that he became converted. I wish I

---

* Rev. T. Brown, alluded to before as author of Manx Ballads "Foc'sle Yarns," "Betsy Lee," &c.

could remember the name of the good man under whom
he experienced this change.   Mr. Wood was attached to
the force mounting guard on Napoleon at St. Helena.

"He settled in his native island about 1820, and married a
Miss Christian (if I mistake not) of London, belonging to
that branch of the Christian family settled in the metropolis,
and boasting amongst its members Archdeacon James
Christian Moore, and Mrs. Willian Moore of Cronkbourne.
He became a leading member of the Douglas religious circles,
and attended unceasingly most of the churches there.   My
father was at that time the minister of St. Matthew's, and I
think Mr. Wood was a great admirer of his.   But as years
rolled on, Mr. Wood developed the strong metaphysical
tendency for which he was so famed in the Isle of Man, and
gradually ceased to attend any place of worship.   He had
become devotedly attached to the opinions of Bishop Berkeley,
and thought he saw in those opinions the sound philosophical
basis for the evidences of Christianity.   The local clergy and
townspeople generally could not go with him in this conviction.   For a while I imagine he consorted with the Plymouth
Brethren.   They were probably terrified out of their senses
by the accession of a brother so eccentric and self-asserting.
At any rate his connection with them did not last long,
though Mrs. Wood (who, I ought to have said, was his second
wife) was a sister to the end.   Mr. Wood caught for a brief
space at a kind of rag held out by Mr. Dowe, a curate of
St. Barnabas.   It was the theory of the intermediate state,
which, supposing the souls of the departed to be wrapt in a
dreamless sleep until the judgment day, was conceived by
its champions to lend support to, or derive illustration from,
the Berkeleyan system.

"With him to believe, or even to see intensely a truth, was
to be possessed as if with some veritable demon of conviction,
assertion, propagandism.   However, for the pure, scientific
Berkeleyanism he found little sympathy in Douglas.   Most of
the worthy half-pay officers and their wives who constituted

the society of *literary* Douglas, were quite incapable of understanding even the terms used, and took refuge either in a gay gentlemanly indifference, or in the far-famed argument of Doctor Johnson—'Sir, I repel it *thus*,' mightily spurning the tombstone in Harwich churchyard. The tradespeople laughed and were rude, the clergy saved their reputation by a canny keeping out of the way.

"By dint of force and a dialectic method sufficiently unscrupulous, though by him regarded as perfectly honest, by the wildest gesticulation, by paradox, by terror, he would reduce an opponent to silence. Indeed if the amenities of civilised life were to be maintained, there was no alternative for the person who might unfortunately be drawn into a controversy with my dear old friend except silence, and that not so prompt as to be suspicious, but after a show of defence which left a colour of triumphal conviction. An immediate surrender, however good-natured, however carefully guarded against the merest *soupçon* of the ironic, would be resented with the profoundest disgust, with rage, in fact, and a bitterness too awful to describe or even to think of. Happy the interlocutor who would deferentially, intelligently, with a semblance of growing conviction, *subside* into the attitude of an interesting neophyte. Dear, grand old fellow! How I loved him, how *we* loved him! and yet how trying he was!

"He was a man of boundless sympathy, and proffered it as a sort of creed. *Proffered*—by the term I mean nothing unreal or pretended. Perhaps *confessed* would be better, if you take it in the sense which implies a *confessor* of a faith. It is rather a peculiar way to put it, but he really thought and spoke of himself as appointed to the function of sympathy, not as merely a follower of Christ, but in some sense His assessor or collaborator. Excuse must be made for the use of language so wanting perhaps in theological precision, and even reverence, in dealing with a character so singular and hardly to be described in terms of strict orthodoxy.

"Beside metaphysics, Mr. Wood had two other favourite

subjects of study, or rather pursuits—music and public reading, more particularly Shakespeare. At an early period of his life, during a short residence in London, he had taken lessons on the contra-basso from Dragonetti. He played this instrument very well, but also cultivated the violin. The contra-basso he used to call the 'cart-ropes.' His favourite composer was Corelli. Mr. Louis Garrett* played his accompaniments. Attempts were occasionally made to establish a Douglas orchestra : at any rate, *scratch* combinations would venture to solicit the services of Mr. Wood, and possibly regret having done so when the pupil of Dragonetti proved impracticable.

"I don't think Mr. Wood was a good reader. He read such pieces as the 'Bridge of Sighs' and 'The Ancient Mariner' with plenty of fire; but he suffered from what I can only call a trick of *snorting*, which grievously marred his efficiency, and, in the reading of Shakespeare, ought to have been considered as absolutely forbidding the attempt. The attempt, however, was repeatedly made, and Mr. Wood was laughed at and treated with much rudeness by the rising generation. At these insulting demonstrations one's blood boiled; but the only remedy was retirement. At last Mr. Wood saw this, and gave up appearing as a public reader.

"In 1867 I took my family to Falcon Cliff for the summer holidays. This was near Mr. Wood's residence. He would still play the violin, and we heard him with pleasure; he would bring it in for an evening. 'Hark! 'tis the Banshee's cry,' was especially remarkable for the weird grandeur of the performance. Here, too, for the entertainment of young people, he would exhibit his curious powers of facial expression, representing the character of a blind man, an idiot, and so forth. At such exhibitions our old friend demanded admiration, if need were, *extorted* it. We, however, needed no stimulus."

* Louis Garrett, Esq., an accomplished Douglas musician, and honorary organist of St. Thomas' Church.

This entertaining individual, accurately depicted by Mr Brown, was never weary of retailing, for the benefit of his privileged hearers, the account of his connection with the captivity and death of Napoleon Bonaparte, he having been stationed with his regiment at St. Helena during the latter days of the banishment of the fallen chieftain. His contemplation of the captive's appearance and life in exile is described by himself in a poem to the memory of the great Emperor. In this poem and in a preface to it he also draws a telling picture of the burial of the once mighty potentate, at which he (Lieut. Wood) was present. "The funeral," said he, "of the great but fallen and exiled chieftain was truly sublime and touching in its soldier-like simplicity. His coffin was borne to the spot he himself had chosen for his grave—over which a willow hung its weeping boughs—upon the shoulders of those who had once fought against him, but who now mourned over him with such heartfelt sorrow as the truly brave of every nation spontaneously pay to fallen greatness, and with such deep pity for his sad untimely fate, hastened as it doubtless was by the unnecessary rigour of his confinement, as could not have been drawn forth by the loftier claims of their own illustrious chief.* No gorgeous pomp and pageantry was there, but nature's wild and awful grandeur.

"The hallowed fane of his interment was the centre of a deep ravine, surrounded by rugged rocks and mournful trees; his requiem the fitful music of the moaning blast. The emotion felt by all was not produced by scenic effect, by martial strains, by sacred harmonies, the mighty organ's pealing tones, and full-voiced choir below ; it was from nature's source alone—genuine and spontaneous. They wept in very pity while beholding the humble obsequies of the man who, for a few brief years, had 'made the earth to tremble, and did shake the kingdoms.' They wept, in compassion, to think that compassion was all the tribute man could render,

* Wellington.

in this sad closing scene, to genius, bravery, and lofty aspiration. . . ."

In verse Mr. Wood adds :—

> "Oft have I gazed on this wondrous man,
>   But aye with strange emotions, undefined,
>   Akin to fearful dread and wonderment,
>   As if oppress'd by some mysterious power,
>   Like some poor bird beneath the serpent's gaze,
>   Spell-bound, and shivering with sudden fear ;
>   For, oh ! there was a magic in his eye,
>   That seem'd to penetrate the very soul,
>   And trace all secrets deeply buried there :
>   Thus could he read the thoughts of other men,
>   Himself—a sealed book—unread the while.

.   .   .   .

> But I did gaze upon that eye,—how changed !
>   When all its bright celestial fire had fled ;
>   Upon that pallid lip, where, e'en in death,
>   That smile still lingering play'd, that won all hearts ;
>   And I did hold that pale cold hand in mine,
>   Which once did grasp the sceptre of the world."

.   .   .   .

Lieut. Wood frequently recounted also how the Emperor, on his deathbed, asked for Dr. Archibald Arnott, the senior surgeon of the 20th Foot, who had "the honour and privilege of attending the illustrious captive and alleviating his sufferings;" and desiring that a valuable gold snuff-box might be brought to him, he with his dying hand and last effort of departing strength engraved upon its lid, with a penknife, the letter "N," and presented the memento to Dr. Arnott. "Dr. Arnott," said Lieut. Wood, "had served with the 20th Regiment, which so highly distinguished itself in the Peninsular War during the campaign of the Duke of Wellington against the French, and of this Napoleon was aware; therefore is this last act of friendship stamped with true magnanimity."

Twenty years after the interment of Bonaparte, it would appear that Lieut. Wood was again at St. Helena, and present when the potentate's coffin was opened, and the body displayed in perfect preservation.

> " What though lingering years had pass'd away,
>   That form remained untouch'd by fell decay ;
>
> .   .   .   .   .   '   .   .   .   .   .
>
> And some who ne'er had seen that face before,
>   Beheld, amazed, Napoleon slumbering there."

In the coffin, says Mr. Wood, had been placed Napoleon's well-known hat, and also a silver vase containing his heart, embalmed in spirits, which he, on his deathbed, had wished might be carried to Parma, and presented, as a token of undying affection, to his dear Marie Louise ; but even this last fond desire was not allowed to be fulfilled.

Another favourite theme of Lieut. Wood's at a later date in relation to the great Emperor was the fact that in 1852, on the occasion of his presentation to Napoleon III. at the Elysée Palace, he had had "the honour of presenting to the Emperor of the French an original portrait of his august uncle, the late Emperor Napoleon, as he lay in death (drawn by W. Rubidge, a talented artist at St. Helena, at the request of the French suite), and of receiving from His Imperial Majesty in return a very beautiful diamond and emerald ornament."

It is reported that on this memorable occasion Lieut. Wood also offered for the Emperor's acceptance a shaving-cloth blotched with Bonaparte's blood ; but that Napoleon, at the sight of the precious relic, exclaimed—extending his hands deprecatingly—" Non—non—je vous remercie, Monsieur ; gardez le je vous prie ! "

Another member of the great Bonaparte family known to Mr. Wood, and whom he regarded as a personal friend, was Prince Lucien Bonaparte. In all likelihood they met abroad. Prince Lucien, however, once visited the Isle of Man for the purpose of making a study of the etymology of the Manx language. He selected for his abode a little cottage in the mountains whose occupant was a simple Manxwoman, but who probably the Prince conceived would be of use to him in the object in view.

The Rev. William Drury, then Vicar of Braddan, being half a Manxman, knew Manx thoroughly, and the Prince not unfrequently visited at Braddan Vicarage. There on one occasion the writer's father had the honour of meeting him.

Lieut. Wood died in 1874, in his 81st year.

"What must he," remarks Mr. Brown, "have said in 1870 to Sedan, and the ruin of his *ci-devant* host of the Tuileries!"

And, adds the same friend—

"He lies in Kirk Onchan churchyard. As one stands on the grave it seems as if the world trembled. A quenched thunderbolt lies here, a man of noble intellectual endowments, of fiery energy."

Mr. Wanton, Mrs. Elliott's other habitual literary visitor, was also a most interesting but eccentric person. He was profoundly learned—his was truly a mind of varied and sound erudition, though his speciality in study was natural history. His habits were very much those of a recluse. His time of study was usually night. When every one slept, he waked; and when others waked, he often slept.

His admiration of Mrs. Elliott was certainly in no degree based on the fact that she tolerated his vanity, for he was not vain—the very reverse; he was, with all his peculiarities— and like Mr. Wood, argumentative propensities—a humble and devout Christian.

He valued his friend for her intellectual attainments, but more especially for the nobler qualities still of her generous heart. A favourite quotation of Mrs. Elliott's was—

> "Tis the heart and not the brain,
> That to the highest doth attain."

In this Mr. Wanton would have agreed with her. He had

one child, a hunchbacked daughter—a saintly creature with a brilliant intelligence—whom her father idolised and had educated for his companion. This daughter afterwards died in a most unexpected manner and time; and the shock of the sudden calamity acted so on her parent's feelings that he never fully recovered it.

Mrs. Elliott used to tell amusing stories as to how these two Manx celebrities, Mr. Wood and Mr. Wanton, would meet at her house, and engage in discussions that so inflamed them both that they would at last burst forth in personal invective like a volcanic eruption—hurling upon one another denunciations of implied stupidity and ignorance unequalled! "My blood," she would say, "would run hot and cold when I saw them meet and begin their controversies—many a time I have run out and given them up the room to themselves !"

CHAPTER VIII.

DR. CARPENTER LEAVES DOUGLAS.

It was now the year 1848. This was a time of unusual stir in Douglas. Dr. Carpenter had been the means of building St. Thomas' Church, and it was opened this year. The great Hugh M'Neil had vacated St. Jude's, Liverpool; and the offer to be his successor was made to Dr. Carpenter, whose fame as an earnest preacher and active successful minister had spread into many parts of England. When Douglas heard of the offer to the beloved pastor, a universal wail arose and spread throughout the community. The thought of parting with him could not be entertained for a moment. He had spent fifteen years in their midst of devoted loving service. Every good work in the island was associated with the dear Doctor. What would become of the schools without him? Only a short time previous he had preached two sermons on behalf of St. Barnabas schools, and the appeal had been so prevailing that £92 had been collected on the occasion.

But it was not one thing but everything in which a request from him met with hearty and spontaneous response! He moved all hearts, for in him every one had such perfect faith; and whatsoever he set about doing, men followed as sheep follow their shepherd.

Many were the attempts made to induce the Doctor not to go away. But it is said, and apparently on reliable authority, that from an unexpected source he was given the hint that his old flock, whatever they professed to the contrary, would really *at heart* be glad of a change. This information so staggered and benumbed his feelings that, as such warm impulsive natures as his often do, he resolved to act upon the word given him, and allow his precious flock to secure the fruits of what he had for so many years sown amongst them under a new shepherd. It need not be said that the tale whispered in the loving clergyman's ears was wholly false. His people loved him with a loyal unchanging love, and that it was so remained to be seen.

Dr. Carpenter accepted St. Jude's; and he left the island on March 15, 1848, to make arrangements for his new settlement. He returned to Douglas on the 24th. In 1832, when he came to Douglas, and preached for the first time, his text was Acts xx. 28; and now when he was preaching in the same church to his people for the last time, he chose the same text : "Take heed therefore unto yourselves, and to all the flock, over the which the Holy Ghost hath made you overseers, to feed the church of God, which he hath purchased with His own blood."

It was a memorable day in Douglas. St. Barnabas was packed with a devoted, saddened audience. Sobs could be heard all round, and streaming eyes were visible in nearly every pew. In that last sermon, in which the preacher so powerfully urged upon his audience abiding heart consecration to the God who had redeemed and sanctified their souls, he introduced an anecdote that seems to have laid hold of the hearts and memories of his hearers. "Sir Gilbert King," he said, "who was at Trinity College, Dublin, along with himself, was a very wild young fellow, and made it a practice to entertain young men to dinner in his rooms on Sunday. One Sunday he informed them that he meant to go to church first, but that on his return he invited them to visit him as usual, and he would enliven them with a pantomime of the preacher and his sermon. Accordingly the guests arrived, but no Sir Gilbert made his appearance. They again presented themselves the following Sunday; but the host, as on the former occasion, was not to be seen. Where was he? Sir Gilbert was on his knees, praying and supplicating God for forgiveness. He had been arrested in his wild career by the Gospel of Christ, and had become a new man in Christ Jesus !"

On Thursday, 20th, a meeting of gentlemen seat-holders was held at St. Barnabas to vote an address to the incumbent, when £180 were subscribed on the spot. This sum was afterwards augmented by the congregation and friends to £400. An evening was appointed, and the address and presentation were made. The spokesman was Sir R. Hagan. The reply by Dr. Carpenter, when acknowledging the speech and gift, has been preserved in Mrs. Weatherell's diary, as if to furnish additional proof that "the memory of the just is blessed," and "shall be in everlasting remembrance." We give it in full, as every recollection of this saintly man and beloved pastor must be still precious to the inhabitants of Manxland ; and his words to the present generation may be as a voice from the dead to quicken the living—an incentive to clergy and laity to follow in the footsteps of a predecessor who so diligently sought the temporal and eternal welfare of Mona's beautiful isle, and was permitted by God to reap with joy the fruits of his labour.

"Beloved members of my congregation and friends,—It is with self-abasement before God, and with heartfelt gratitude to you, that I have heard the words in which you have so kindly addressed me. If *your* feelings be such as they are at being separated from *one* whom you love, what must mine be when I am about to be separated from hundreds, nay thousands in all parts of this island, to whom I have long been bound by the strongest ties of friendship and affection.

"You have observed most justly that human praise is but a vapour, and that listening to a pastor is valuable only when it is the act of those who have learned to love the Lord ; so that I must remember that he alone is approved whom God commendeth, and you must try to love the Lord that you may be witnesses of my ministry known and read of all men; while we all ascribe not to poor worms, but to Him who calls sinners by His grace, and moves them by His Spirit to preach His Gospel, all the glory of whatever He has wrought through me, or through any man for the religious and moral improvement of His creatures.

"I have long since learned to believe that as a tree is known by its fruit, so is the dwelling of the Holy Ghost in the heart of a Christian made manifest by a desire to promote the temporal and eternal welfare of men, and I humbly bless God, not more for having led me to works of charity, than for having disposed your hearts to respond, as you have ever done, to the innumerable calls which have been made upon you.

"You know, I am persuaded, that 'it is more blessed to give than to receive,' and to your power I bear you record, that I found you ready to give, and glad to distribute; so that you must allow me to share with you a large portion of the privileges connected with the House of Industry, the Medical Dispensary, and the schools, all of which, with a sincere unconsciousness of your own co-operation, you have so generously and bountifully bestowed upon me. The same good hand of our God, which was upon me and others in commencing St. Thomas' Church, has been upon you in setting your affections to the House of your God, and leading you to build it, that He may be glorified. The Christian's highest honour is to be a minister of Christ; but they also are to be accounted very highly favoured who have the honour to promote and erect these temples to His glory, where His ministers may proclaim the glad tidings of His Gospel, and administer His sacraments, and where His people may offer in His presence their acceptable sacrifices of prayers and almsdeeds, and thanksgivings and praise. You cannot all be ministers of Christ and pastors of His flock, but you may all be builders of St. Thomas' Church, and of other churches, and this I pray you may be found ready to do. I am persuaded that the Church of Christ

should be a missionary Church, and that every minister of
the same should desire and pray and contribute of his substance to forward the *missionary* cause, and I have no doubt
but that in such a case blessings temporal and spiritual will
descend on individuals, on families, on churches, and on
kingdoms. For this cause have I laboured in conjunction
with my brethren in the ministry not to originate, but to
increase missionary operations in Douglas and throughout
the island; and while I thank God for all He has enabled
me to do, I also desire to acknowledge with unfeigned
gratitude the kindness, cordiality, hospitality, and zealous
co-operation of all the bishops under whom I have served,
of the clergy, and of the laity, through the length and
breadth of the land. I praise and bless the Holy Spirit
that His servants, the bishops and clergy of this diocese,
have been united in heart and hand in the missionary cause,
and I shall not cease to pray that He may lead them to
abound more and more in what is calculated to promote
'Glory to God in the highest, and on earth good will
towards men.' I have indeed endeavoured to teach you,
beloved, to give *yourselves* to the Lord Jesus, that of His
merits and death, and through faith in His blood, you may
obtain remission of your sins, and all the other benefits of
His passion, and then to offer yourselves, your souls, your
bodies, to be a reasonable, holy, and lively sacrifice to Him,
and may God in mercy grant that, through your having done
so, I may meet you at the day of judgment, wearing blood-
bought crowns, and reaping eternal rewards for even the cups
of cold water given for the sake of Him who gave Himself
for you. God did often enlarge my heart and opened my
mouth as I preached among you, that you might be saved,
for this I have to thank Him.

"And I have also to thank you because you gave me credit
for speaking the truth in love. You have been indeed my
hope, and joy, and crown of rejoicings in the presence of
our Lord Jesus Christ at His coming, and with my whole

soul I say Amen to your prayers that I may have abundant cause of rejoicing over you, for having testified with pleasure the Gospel of grace to save you. God knows I should mourn to testify against any of you that I had preached in vain. I am about to leave you, because I humbly believe that He who brought me hither, upwards of fifteen years ago, is now calling me away. He *can* easily and He *will* (in answer to many prayers) send you a far better and more useful pastor than I; but though I expect much, where can I ever hope to meet again with such forbearance in love, such attachment and kindness, as I have met with from you. But God will supply all our need according to His riches in glory by Christ Jesus. To Him, then, let us look and pray, and in Him let us trust. In a little while we shall separate, and in a little while we shall meet again—God grant it may be to part no more. Meanwhile let us be united in faith to one common Head, and to one another in spirit, sympathy, and love. I ask you to take care of the poor, and I promise that God will take care of you; and for myself, if anything be wanting to fill up the measure of your kindness, I ask the benefit of your constant prayers, that the fulness of the Spirit of God may be given to myself, my family, and the people about to be committed to my charge.

"And now, beloved, farewell! I wish that you may be in health and prosper, and that your souls may prosper. I wish that your dear children, whom I have loved and endeavoured to feed as the lambs of Christ, may grow up as His people and the sheep of His pasture. I pray that the God of all grace may protect and bless you and them, that He may justify you freely by His grace; teach, sanctify, strengthen and comfort you by His Spirit, guide you to the end by His counsels, and at last receive you to glory; and that Mona's Isle may flourish as a land of saints, and be exalted in righteousness till time shall be no more, is also the prayer of your grateful and attached friend and pastor,

"WILLIAM CARPENTER."

E

CHAPTER IX.

THE MANX CHURCH.

THE Elliotts did not leave St. Barnabas at the departure of
Dr. Carpenter, though they deeply deplored his loss; and it
seemed to them as if it never could in any measure be made
up to them.   It was in 1848 Mrs. Elliott in her letters first
makes mention of the name of the Rev. William Hawley, a
clergyman who was at this time paying his addresses to her
old schoolfellow, Miss Catherine Jefferson.   In 1849 Mr.
Hawley and this lady were married; and eventually he
became curate of St. George's, a church in which for something like six years as curate, and nineteen as incumbent,
Mr. Hawley lived the life of a true devoted servant of the
gospel of Christ.   Mrs. Elliott often refers to him in her
letters, and always in terms of esteem and affection.

St. George's was within three minutes' walk of the Elliotts'
house.   In later years they attended this church.   The incumbent in 1848 was the Rev. Edward Forbes.   He was
a great friend of Mrs. Elliott's.   Mr. Forbes was a most
estimable man and faithful preacher—one of the same school
of thought as Dr. Carpenter; and, like him, a most kind and
attentive pastor.   He was much esteemed by his people,
though at this date he had only been a year amongst them.
As time went on and he became better known, the attachment of his congregation increased, and he was deservedly
respected throughout the island.

It is refreshing to heart and mind to dwell upon the record
of the love and unanimity that existed in dear old Douglas
between pastors and people.   The people were what the

clergy made them. The latter were earnest men of God, and their congregations reflected their spirit. One common cause bound them together—devotion to Christ, and the extension of His kingdom at home and abroad, along with a loyal adherence to the principles of the Church of their fathers. No foreign element of usurped ecclesiastical teaching and practices had yet intruded to mar the concord and peace, and separate between brethren who were once *one* in the household of faith. The curates, it would appear, were like-minded with the incumbents—men of spiritual character and moral weight —influences for Christ and leaders of men. At St. Barnabas as curate, during the latter time of Dr. Carpenter's ministry, was the Rev. Philip Dowe. Mrs Elliott often spoke of this earnest young clergyman. She described him as a delightful person, combining fine intellectual attainments with a life devoted to the service of God and man. This Mr. Dowe was a frequent visitor at Mrs. Elliott's, and so was the Rev. John Flowers Serjeant, curate of St. George's. Mr. Serjeant was a little ugly man, but with a big loving soul. He laid hold of the people as if they were prey, pouncing upon them with the energy of a hawk, and retaining them in his grasp with the fascination of his strong individuality, and the warm good nature of his ever ready and ever true sympathy. His zeal in good works was unbounded, and his single-eyed efforts for the cause of God and good of man reaped the fruits of a responsive people's warm attachment and perfect trust.

Mr. Serjeant was born in Paris in 1815, and began his ministerial labours in 1842. He was afterwards well known in missionary circles as Suffragan Bishop to the Bishop of Madras. Subsequent to his curacy in Douglas, he spent many years in Paris, labouring amongst the poor especially of the gay city as he had done in Douglas. He never married—his bride was the Church of Christ. On one occasion some Douglas friends, when paying a visit to Paris, went to look him up. They knew the locality in which he lived, but his domicile they spent some hours in searching for. At last they discovered it, and could hardly believe their eyes—they described it as little better than an underground cellar! Right hospitably they were however entertained in this obscure dwelling; and once more enjoyed with the genial original little clergyman "the feast of reason and the flow of soul."

As an instance of the peculiarity of manner and appearance of this self-denying man, the writer can vouch for the truth of the following story :—

A certain school of young ladies who attended the Protestant Church in the Avenue Marbœuf, had not pleased the governess who had the charge of them in church, and she had reported their conduct to the head-mistress, who was French, and a Roman Catholic. Madame determined to make a new selection of pews, and she conceived that immediately beneath the pulpit, under the clergyman's eye, would be the fittest place. Consequently, one Sunday she said she would herself accompany her pupils to church, instead of the English governess, and see how the new pews would answer. It so happened that Mr. Gardiner, the incumbent, was absent that day, and Mr. Serjeant officiated instead. When the time arrived for the latter to ascend the pulpit and address his audience, his first necessity was to mount a stool; but lo! though this he did, his head and his head *only*, appeared above the level of the pulpit. His head was not small in dimensions—the very reverse; and his features were correspondingly striking and peculiar, his mouth almost extending from ear to ear. The sight of the strange individual excited the young ladies' risibility below as well as that of Madame herself; but this was nothing to when he delivered his oration. Stentorious and emphatic were his tones, and in his vehemence he threw his head from side to side, emitting drops of spittle that besprinkled the head decorations and dresses of Madame and her youthful family of pupils; especially was this the case when he ejaculated in tones, and with a manner never to be forgotten, the startling implication, "If you do not see this (the point of his argument) you must be as blind as veritable bats!"

"Oh, mes enfants!" exclaimed Madame on leaving the church, thrusting her fingers into both her ears, "shall I ever regain my hearing? *You shall keep your own seats.* My new dress is well-nigh ruined, and your feathers have suffered, I am sure?"

Of course the young ladies readily assented to the dictum on the preacher, but inwardly and to one another vowed a debt of gratitude to "the dear funny little clergyman," who had so unconsciously done them such a good turn, in securing for them the continuation of their well-liked and accustomed seats in the front gallery!

Mr. Serjeant died in 1889, much beloved and respected. Several articles at the time appeared in different religious periodicals on the subject of his singularly marked character, self-sacrificing and useful life. Previous to his being appointed Suffragan Bishop in 1877 to the Bishop of Madras, he was a student at the Church Missionary College at Islington; and then entered upon mission work at Tinnevelly, where he prepared young native pastors for the ministry, as he had a good knowledge of the Tamil language, the early part of his life having been spent at Madras and Palmacottah.

When in Douglas no one thought more of Mr. Serjeant than Mrs. Elliott. She admired the splendid vigour of his character, his genial humour, and simple, unostentatious mode of life. It will readily be assumed he formed one of the happy entertaining coterie that so frequently met at 31 Athol Street. Mr. Serjeant had a ready pen, and a keen relish for literature. The poems of Miss Barrett were at this time—though for years before the public—merely beginning to attract the notice of an occasional admirer; amongst the few in the little world of Douglas who would pronounce a decided opinion as to their merits were Mrs. Elliott and her following of literary friends.   With Lieut. Wood, Mr. Dowe, Mr. Serjeant, and others she would open up what she conceived to be the excellences of the powers of this budding poetess.   It seems almost incredible now to think that there was a time when the genius of Elizabeth Barrett Browning was doubted, or if not that, depreciated, and ˜by some even scouted as a thing of no existence.

In evidence of this it is peculiarly interesting to note that Eleanor Elliott penetrated at the outset the worth of Elizabeth Barrett, and pronounced upon it without hesitancy.   She delighted in the works that had appeared of the poetess; she studied them, and wherever she went amongst her literary acquaintances, discussed their beauties, interested her hearers, and induced many to follow her belief, and procure the works of Miss Barrett.

It was when filled with the conviction of a new-born genius on the literary horizon—and one whose theme was "Love Divine"—that our friend was determined to give forth her thoughts, and extend them as far as she could beyond her own immediate circle of acquaintances.   This she did in the very beautiful and interesting critique on Elizabeth Barrett's writings which will comprise the ensuing chapter, and which appeared in the *Christian Lady's Magazine* for 1850.   It will serve to show the critic's keen intellectual grasp and fine poetical perception; and more especially the deep well of heavenly love that bubbled up from her heart to her brain and instigated her pen.

In after years Mrs. Elliott's admiration for this poetess was much more qualified.   Her opinion was that after her marriage with Browning she fell off considerably in regard to the high religious tone and clear note of thought and aspiration which hitherto had so characterised her writings.

CHAPTER X.

THE "SERAPHIM" AND OTHER POEMS.

THIS was the first appearance of Miss Barrett's original poetry, her previous production being a translation from the Greek of Æschylus. She has since produced other poems; but we now confine our remarks to this one. She struck the poetic harp ten years ago, and yet the poetic world does not resound with her name. Perhaps the obscure grandeur of her style of expression, and the loftiness of her thoughts, have raised this original writer above the reach of popular appreciation.

It may be that she has "fit audience found, though few:" yet surely she deserves to be better known and more beloved by her Christian countrywomen, by those who love poetry when its theme is Love Divine; when it serves as a ministering spirit to religion, looking upward for guidance "as the eyes of a maiden unto the hand of her mistress."

They who delight in hallowed minstrelsy should be acquainted with Elizabeth Barrett. Some of her strains are like "an angel's song that makes the heavens be mute." An angel might pause in his celestial harpings to hear a sister spirit on earth sing so well.

What was said of Caroline Wilson may with equal justice be applied to this gifted lady. "She manifests in her writings the philosophic strength of 'spirits masculine,' combined with feminine grace and tenderness; a union of grace and strength which forms what we deem angelic excellence." In her melodious verse there is indeed both strength and tenderness, like honey in the stony rock. We agree with the opinion that "Mrs. Hemans was a poetess, but Elizabeth Barrett is a poet."

Her translation of the "Prometheus Bound" has won for her name a niche in the temple of classical learning. She is a scholar among scholars, and a poet among poets. Æschylus himself might smile complacently on the gentle English-woman who has so well interpreted his dead language in a living voice, and transfused the spirit of his Titanic thought into modern English verse. With her acquaintance with the old masters of the Grecian lyre, she acquired much of their statuesque grace of thought and style. Some of her compound words are fine specimens of the composite order of phrase distinguishing the language of ancient Greece. In that school of the Antique she has gained strength without sternness, and an impassioned power of speech without morbid sentimentalism of feeling. In mental constitution, our English minstrel is more a Greek than Sappho herself, the poetess of the Grecian isles. Sappho sang of earthly love, but Miss Barrett's favourite theme is Love Divine: this is the keynote of her sweetest music; it is the subject of her "Seraphim," worthy of the "Seraphim who love most." And so her enraptured strain soars far above the highest note of Sappho, "as the heaven is high above the earth;" as the effulgence of light ineffable outshines the phosphorescent halo of decay and death.

The purity of sculpture without its coldness, its dignity without its deadness, is the character of her noble mind. Like the statue of Memnon, with its musical response to the morning sunbeams, she seems to sing for joy, because the Sun of righteousness has illumined her inmost soul, and kindled all its harp-strings into a burst of praise.

"There is no greater fiction than that poetry is fiction," says this true poetess, who "wrote not because there is a public, but because these poems were *thought* and *felt*." Poetry is a form of truth with the loftiest aspect and the sweetest voice. The lark pouring out its minstrelsy at heaven's gate is as true to nature as the parrot repeating prose in a cage. Music or poetry, whether written or spoken or sung, is but an expression of some inner harmony; and the purest moral harmony is the combination of truth, justice, and mercy into a threefold chord of praise. Such is the deep harmony of scriptural poetry, as it resounds from the harp of Miriam or Moses, of David or Isaiah, of Hannah or Mary. Their voices are heard no more on the mountains of Israel; yet the Church is still vocal with those notes of praise, whose echo will never cease to vibrate through all eternity. The most ancient Ode on record is the joyous anthem of the Church triumphant, on the shores of the Red Sea. And again, in the solitude of Patmos (Rev. xv. 13), St. John heard with prophetic ear the prolonged chorus of that pealing hymn resounding from "numbers without number infinite, sweet as blest voices uttering joy."

The jubilant chant of Hannah is as a far-off prelude to the more enraptured strain of Mary, the most blessed Virgin mother. And that Magnificat is repeated every Sabbath day, and so it will endure until the dawn of a better rest, when the Lord of the Sabbath shall appear to complete the redemption of every one who is to Him as His mother, His sister or His brother; then He will rest in His love, and rejoice over them with singing.

We trust that Elizabeth Barrett will appear as a white-robed chorister in that choir of the true high Church whose foundations are on the holy hills. She seems now to belong to the free Church of spiritual worshippers, "whose temple is all space, whose altar—earth, sea, skies;" who find "sermons in stones, and good in everything." To such an illumined heart and mind all nature is revealed in a new aspect of light and life, as glowing with hues of love reflected from the Saviour's rainbow-girdled throne. Such a one will understand the quaint language of another Poet :—

> " . . . Each floral bell that swingeth,
> And tolls its perfume on the passing air,
> Makes Sabbath in the fields, and ever ringeth
>   A call to prayer.
>
> Not to the domes whose crumbling arch and column
> Attest the feebleness of mortal hand ;
> But to that fane, most Catholic and solemn,
>   Which God hath plann'd.
>
> To that cathedral, boundless as our wonder,
>   Whose quenchless lamps the sun and moon supply,
> Its choir the wind and waves,—its organ thunder,
>   Its dome the sky."

There is a healthy fresh air of piety in Miss Barrett's poetry : an undertone of hope in her saddest dirge ;—as there is a softening tendency in her gayest melody. After a dreamy excursion of thought, called the "Soul's Travelling," thus she returns to the safe resting-place :—

> " . . . Yea very vain
> The greatest speed of all these souls of man,
> Unless they travel upward to Thy throne,
> Where sittest Thou, the satisfying One,
> With blood for sins, and holy perfectings
> For all requirements."

And again, in "The Island," which is a piece of picturesque day-dreams, a sudden gleam from the excellent glory, seems to recall her roving mind from its wandering visions, as though the Lord looked upon her with "those deep pathetic eyes" of love, saying to her heart : "Wilt thou also go away ?" And this is the sweet response, in melodious verse :—

> " Shall I go backward to the world,
>   When Thou art very nigh ?
> And pay the price I promised her
>   For vision passed by.
> What time Thy covenant's control
> Would break all others from my soul.
>
> Nay, I endure ; but not because
>   The world imposeth woe ;

But rather that Thy hands perform
   The thing appointed so.
Those kindly wounding hands did brave,
Themselves, a deeper wound—to save."

Here is the principle of Christian resignation; not the erect pride of stoicism which scorns to feel, but chastened sorrow, weeping like Mary at the Saviour's feet—at the feet of Him who answered with sympathetic tears; who is still touched with the feeling of our infirmities; who can turn the shadow of death into a cloudless morning.

In the preface to this volume of poems the author discourses most eloquently in words of wisdom and of power. "Had Æschylus lived after the incarnation and crucifixion of our Lord Jesus Christ, he might have turned, if not in moral and intellectual, yet in poetic faith, from the solitude of Caucasus to the deeper desertness of that crowded Jerusalem where none had any pity; from the glorying of him who gloried that he could not die, to the sublime meekness of the Taster of death for every man. . . . He would have turned from the scenery of the Prometheus, to the rent rocks and darkened scene—rent and darkened by a sympathy thrilling through *nature*, but leaving *man's* heart untouched, to the multitudes whose victim was their Saviour—to the victim whose sustaining thought beneath an unexampled agony was not the Titanic 'I can revenge,' but the celestial 'I can forgive!' We know *love* in that He laid down His life for us. By this we know love—*love* in its intense meaning. Has not love a deeper mystery than wisdom, and a more ineffable lustre than power? I believe it has. I venture to believe those beautiful and often-quoted words, 'God is love,' to be even less an expression of condescension towards the finite than an assertion of essential dignity in Him who is infinite."

The subject of the "Seraphim" is the Crucifixion at Jerusalem, and the personages are some of the angelic host, gazing with dread amazement on that most awful sacrifice.

The intent of this sublime poem is thus explained in the preface. "My desire was to gather some vision of the supreme spectacle under a less usual aspect, to glance at it as dilated in seraphic eyes, and darkened and deepened by the near association with blessedness and heaven. Are we not too apt to measure the depth of the Saviour's humiliation from the common estate of man, instead of from His own peculiar and primæval one? To avoid which error I have endeavoured to count some steps of the ladder of Bethel, a very few steps, and as seen between the clouds." Let us pause on a step of this ethereal ladder to overhear some sad notes of angelic sorrow, of glorious sympathy with the setting Sun of Righteousness. It is a dialogue between Ador and Zerah, two of the celestial host :—

ZERAH.   "Thus! do I find Thee thus! My Lord, my Lord,

      .   .   .   .

      A man, and not a God,
      A worm, and not a man,
      Yea, no worm—but a curse?
      .   .   .   Thou
Grief-bearer for Thy work, with unhinged brow—
I have an angel-tongue—I know but *praise.*

ADOR.   Hereafter shall the blood-bought captives raise
      The passion-song of blood!

ZERAH.   And *we* extend
Our holy vacant hands towards the Throne,
Crying, 'We have no music!'

ADOR.   Rather blend
      Our musics into one!
The sanctities and sanctified above
Shall each to each, with lifted looks serene,
      Their shining faces lean,
      And mix the adoring breath,
And breathe the sweet thanksgiving!

ZERAH.   But the love—
      The love, mine Ador!

ADOR.   Do *we* love not?

ZERAH.   Yea!
But, *not as man shall:* not with life for death,
Now throbbing through the startled being! not
With strange astonished smiles, that ever may
Gush passionate-like tears, and fill their place!
Oh! not with this blood on us—and this face,—
Still, haply, pale with sorrow that it bore
In our behalf, and tender evermore
With nature all our own,—towards us gazing!—
Nor yet with those forgiving hands upraising
Their unreproachful wounds, alone to bless!
Alas, Creator! shall we love Thee less
Than mortals shall?

ADOR.   Amen! so let it be!
We love in our proportion—to the bound
Thine infinite, our finite set around,
And that is finitely,—Thou, infinite
And worthy infinite love! And our delight
Is watching the dear love poured out to Thee,
From every fuller chalice.   Blessed they,
Who love Thee more than we do! blessed we,
Beholding that out-loving lovingness,
And winning in the sight a double bliss,
For all so lost in love's supremacy!
The bliss is better! Love him more, O man,
            Than sinless seraphs can.

ZERAH.   Yea! love Him more.
    Voices of the angelic multitude.   Yea! more."

Here is the sweet burden of this seraphic song. Alas!
how heavily does it reverberate from the stony heart of
ungrateful man—"Love Him more!"

    "Teach us, Lord, to love Thee more."

The other poems in this volume abound with lovely
thoughts and pleasant words, "fresh as the morn, and varied
as the year;" and there are some beautiful hymns towards
the end, especially one to the "Weeping Saviour:"—

    "When Jesus' friend had ceased to be,
        Still Jesus' heart its friendship kept—

'Where have ye laid him?'—'Come and see!'
  But ere His eyes could see, they wept.

Lord! not in sepulchres alone,
  Corruption's worm is rank and free;
The shrouds of death our bosoms own—
  The shades of sorrow! Come and see!

Come, Lord! God's image cannot shine
  Where sin's funereal darkness lowers—
Come! turn these weeping eyes of Thine
  Upon these sinning souls of ours!

And let those eyes with shepherd care,
  Their moving watch above us keep;
Till love the strength of sorrow wear,
  And as Thou weepedst, *we* may weep!

For surely we may weep to know,
  So dark and deep our spirit's stain;
That had Thy blood refused to flow,
  Thy very tears had flowed in vain."

The stanzas on "Cowper's Grave" have the free flow of a
sighing and yet smiling stream, whose waters are overshadowed
by the tree of life, with its leaves of balm and blessedness.

"It is a place where poets crowned
  May feel the heart's decaying;
It is a place where happy saints
  May weep amid their praying.

Yet let the grief and humbleness,
  As low as silence languish;
Earth surely now may give her calm
  To whom she-gave her anguish.

O poets! from a maniac's tongue
  Was poured the deathless singing!
O Christians! at your cross of hope
  A hopeless hand was clinging

O men! this man, in brotherhood,
  Your weary paths beguiling,
Groaned inly while he taught you peace,
  And died while ye were smiling!

And now, what time ye all may read
   Through dimming tears his story,
How discord on the music fell,
   And darkness on the glory,—

And how, when one by one, sweet sounds
   And wandering lights departed,
He wore no less a loving face
   Because so broken-hearted.

He shall be strong to sanctify
   The poet's high vocation,
And bow the meekest Christian down
   In meeker adoration ;

Nor ever shall he be in praise,
   By wise or good forsaken ;
Named softly as the household name
   Of one whom God hath taken ! "

Is not this good poetry?—good for the head and heart?—
such as Christian women would do well to read ; with thank-
fulness to the giver of every good gift for His grace to this
gifted woman. He who teaches the birds to soar and sing
in the sunshine, has attuned her poetic soul to the harmonies
of heaven. Let us reiterate our aspiration, that, when all
earthly sounds have died away in eternity, her heart may
still make melody to the Lord, while her voice swells on
into a deeper tone of joy as it blends with the celestial choir,
who sing "Hallelujah, as the sound of seas." May our
glory also sing praise and not be silent, through all the long
ages of that undying day, that so—

   " We may all be poets there,
     Gazing on the chiefest Fair ! "

                               E. E.

CHAPTER XI.

CAPTAIN ALLEN GARDINER, R.N.

Who, alas! has not heard the story of the Patagonian Mission? It was in 1851 that Britain rang with the tale, and sorrow was felt and tears shed for the fate of the noble Captain Allen Gardiner, R.N., and his martyr band. Previous to the enterprise, Captain Gardiner had on a survey expedition been deeply moved at seeing the miserable state of the Patagonians—a people so low in human degradation that Darwin pronounced them incapable of being civilised. Captain Gardiner, however, resolved that he for one, by the grace of God, would make the attempt not only to civilise but Christianise this unhappy people. He returned to England, but on announcing his project met with little encouragement. Finally he came to the Isle of Man; and in Douglas, in Athol Street Schoolhouse, held his *first* missionary meeting before starting on his hazardous journey, the same building where St. George's Sunday-schools were and are held. At this meeting there were conspicuously present *two* who were heart and soul with Captain Gardiner in his enterprise—these were Mrs. Elliott and her son Willie.

We can only conjecture the nature of the speaker's appeal on that occasion, when bringing before his audience the burning need of helping those beings of their own flesh and blood, who were, nevertheless, in their persons and habits, little removed from the brute creation.

Willie Elliott sat intently listening—his great eyes open and flashing with the fire of an earnestness and sympathy that welled up in response to every word Captain Gardiner uttered, whilst his young heart beat loud and fast as the particulars of the intended expedition were unfolded by the zealous pioneer. He was himself, Captain Gardiner said, *ready to die*, if need be, in the attempt to start this Mission in the dark miserable region of Tierra del Fuego —the Land of Fire.

The meeting over, up rushed the youthful Willie to the speaker, panting with enthusiasm, and regardless of all observers. "I would like a card, Captain Gardiner, please, to collect for your Mission," he said, extending his little hand, trembling with emotion. Every heart was moved at the sight, and many a person present took a collecting-card who had no thought of so doing until impelled by the eager impetuosity and Christ-like example of the boy. Sweet child, what were thy mother's thoughts—what her intense feeling, when she saw thee—her heart's love—breaking through all restraint, and braving all eyes to win a golden opportunity of doing something in the name and for the love of the Redeemer of men! Eleanor Elliott had truly the reward that night, when she beheld her young son step on to the platform, anxiously tendering his request, of a mother's many prayers and sacred yearnings. Ah! dear mother, hadst thou known what so soon was to befall thee and thy darling, thou wouldst have clasped him to thy breast there and then with the convulsive energy of a last clasp of mortal love! But in mercy the future was veiled from thine eyes. *Willie Elliott's* was the *first* South American Missionary collecting-card given to any one by Captain Allen Gardiner.

The missionary party left England in September 1850, and what befell them afterwards is now a matter of history, familiar to many. It may not, however, be out of place to mention a few details of the tragic story, as the event and its results were of such painfully thrilling interest to the subject of this memoir; and as the South American

F

Missionary Society—the outcome of the fatal enterprise—was a Society for which she laboured as long as health and strength allowed her.

On the 5th December, Captain Gardiner and his party reached Picton Island. Here they had a disheartening encounter with the natives, who looked more inclined to murder them than to listen to their words of Divine mercy. They embarked on their ship again, and set sail for the opposite shore, on the south-west of Tierra del Fuego. Here they had no more success than formerly with the natives; also they lost one of their boats, which was run upon the rocks, the other they hauled on shore, and converted into a sort of dormitory. Soon scurvy broke out amongst the party. In April their provisions ran very short, and as sickness increased there was a great difficulty in getting more food. Everything in the shape of birds, fish, a fox, and even vermin that came in their way they ate. For months they lived on mussels, until the brave Captain Gardiner could eat them no longer, though he managed to drink mussel and limpet broth. One and another of the band were stricken down with illness, and yet in the midst of all this distress and semi-starvation the figures of Gardiner and his friend Maidment might have been seen by their dying comrades kneeling on the shore thanking God for His loving-kindness and mercy towards them. Finally, all were gone but Gardiner and Maidment, and of the two Gardiner was the weaker and apparently the nearer death. Maidment, however, died first, though he waited upon his fellow-sufferer almost as long as his own life lasted.

From Captain Gardiner's diary, written on that desolate shore as his life was wasting away, several most touching entries are given in the history of the Mission, circulated for the benefit of the South American Society. They all breathe a spirit of noble heroism and of most affecting Christian resignation under privations and sufferings of a most distressing kind.

Such was the pitiful end of those noble men who were left to their fate in the far-off region of Tierra del Fuego. Why the stores they expected never reached them it is useless now to inquire. They died as thousands of martyrs have died, their blood proving in the order of God the seed of the Church. They died, but the cause did not die. No, the heart of Christian England was stirred to sympathise in the work, and other devoted men were found to take up the mantle of the noble Gardiner, and start forth better equipped and better prepared in every way to prosecute the Patagonian Mission. Years of faithful service since then have redeemed the character of the Patagonians; and to his astonishment Darwin looked before he died upon specimens of that race so changed—physically, mentally, and spiritually—so humanised, in fact—that henceforth he not only pronounced his belief in the regeneration of the people, but became a subscriber to the South American Missionary Society during the remainder of his life.

1851 was not only a memorable year to Mrs. Elliott on account of the tragic conclusion of the life of the noble Captain Allen Gardiner, and the young Willie's early efforts on behalf of the Patagonian Mission, but this year also brought to a close the life of a great man who was very dear to her heart. It is not likely that she ever saw him; but he was a congenial spirit with whom she took sweet counsel in his many literary works, and whose life, as she had from time to time accounts of it, influenced in a great measure her own. This kindred soul was Neander Johann August Wilhelm—commonly called "Neander." Neander, it is well known, was by far the greatest of ecclesiastical historians. He was born in Göttingen in 1789 of Jewish parentage. In 1806 he renounced Judaism, and was baptized a Christian, taking the name of "Neander" (Gr. *neos*, new; *aner*, a man). His original name was David Mendel. His celebrity as a lecturer was almost world-wide, and students from the most distant Protestant countries flocked to his instruction. It is asserted that all great German preachers have in some form or other imbibed the influence of the teaching of Neander. What, however, above all so irresistibly appealed to the appreciation of Mrs. Elliott, and other of his numberless admirers, was his unbounded benevolence. All the proceeds of his numerous literary productions he bestowed in charity, or towards the extension of the knowledge of Christ. He was also a man of a most lovely and lovable disposition. Profoundly had Mrs. Elliott studied many of his theological works; his thoughts and noble aspirations possessed her mind, and became incorporated with her spirit as part of herself. Another reason, too, why he was so dear to her heart was that, to use her own words, he belonged to "princely Israel's hallowed race." "They shall prosper," she would say, "that love Jerusalem." When the announcement came of Neander's death, it was as if a familiar hand had been withdrawn from her own. With a weight of regret resting upon her, but at the same time with a holy joy of thanksgiving that one so meet for the mansions of everlasting day had been called to bask for evermore in the beams of ineffable love, she penned the following lines :—

ON THE DEATH OF JOHN NEANDER, an illustrious German scholar, formerly a Jew, named David Mendel, but afterwards baptized as John Neander on his conversion to Christianity, because the Gospel of St. John had been to him the word of life, and *Neander* means *new man.*

> "Let us make ready to go home,"
>   Neander said on his death day,
>   When the tired soul would flee away
> To rest, because the hour was come.
>
> To rest among the blessed dead
>   Until the dawn of morning light,—
>   "Now let us go to sleep,—good-night,"
> With dying voice Neander said.

And then his spirit passed away
  In sleep that deepened into death,
  Calm as a sleeping infant's breath,
Calm as the death of summer day.

An offspring he of Israel's line,
  Of princely Israel's hallowed race,
  But born again of heavenly grace,
And sealed with sacramental sign.

The dew of that baptismal wave
  Upon his spirit still abode,
  " He died to self, he lived to God," —
So spake they of him at his grave.

The loving heart is dead and chill,
  The hand that gave can give no more ;
  But still the mind of richest lore—
The noble mind, endureth still.

Engraved in many a shining word,
  His thoughts of wisdom yet endure,
  Of holy wisdom, high and pure,
Breathing the truth of Christ his Lord.

Calm was his spirit's parting breath,
  Serene his soul in days of strife ;
  A peaceful death, a lovely life,
Blest are such souls in life and death.

Little Willie fully entered into the feelings of his mother when she told him her friend Neander was no more. Nor was the dear boy slow either to state his approval of the verses his mother had written. He was himself a born poet, his soul was full of the fire of genius, and his large eye was like an orb where every impassioned and imaginative impulse of his being was mirrored in eloquent and serene beauty. In a word, Willie was his mother's second self, and each month, not to speak of each year, seemed to see him expanding in wisdom, knowledge, and grace. Most of his mother's favourite authors he dipped into, and sought to find something in them within the grasp of the appreciation of his young intelligence. They would sit for hours—

mother and son—conversing on the Word of God; they would walk together in the beautiful country lanes or beside the silver sea, discussing sweet themes of poetry; and the boy and his parent lived as in a holy dream. Their feet trod the earth, but their spirits dwelt in regions beyond the ken of ordinary beings. The two were a well-known and interesting picture to Douglas spectators. The very sight of them, with their chaste illumined countenances, did the beholders good; and profound was the love felt for both by many and many a sympathetic heart. Rich and poor inwardly blessed them as they passed by. That the mother entertained high hopes for her elder son no one doubted; but ah, how little did they know the *magnitude* of those hopes! With her idealising nature and glowing soul, she took in a sweep of vision of her son's future excellences impossible for any to imagine. Her whole being in its every pulsation was a perpetual theme of grateful adoration for the gift of this boy.

Little Philip was just as dear to the mother's heart, but he was a simple little fellow, not so far denoting any specially marked traits of character or signs of capacity.

CHAPTER XII.

GRIEF UNUTTERABLE.

IT was in 1851 Mrs. Elliot's brother, the Rev. Robert Weatherell, was appointed to the living of Elton, near Nottingham. This same year he was married to Miss Lydia Thorpe, whom he had met at Coddington, near Newark, where he had his first curacy.

During the first year of her brother's married life, Mrs. Elliott went to pay him and·his bride a visit. She was delighted with her new sister-in-law; and from this time they became life-long friends. Their correspondence is almost voluminous, and many of the letters edifying in the extreme. Everything almost seems to have been discussed amongst them but gossip—gossip has no place on these glowing pages; they breathe an atmosphere of pure and holy friendship and heart-satisfying peace and trust, and sweet heavenly joy illumined at times with sallies of mirth, and an imagination on Eleanor's part as of a flower spontaneously open to the brilliant and warm sunshine, and its petals reflecting the radiance above. The sight of Elton, when she first viewed it as the home and sphere of labour of her brother, charmed her poetical fancy. The fair Rectory looked to her as a nest of domestic comfort, and prophetic of a thousand innocent family joys; the garden as a paradise of quiet beauty; and the ancient ivy-clad church as a picture of interest retrospective and prospective. The old country churchyard, where the "forefathers of the hamlet sleep," provided a theme of contemplation ready to hand for the thoughtful spectator. Then the surroundings—they had their beauties and their interests that quite filled Eleanor's heart to overflowing; above all her eye dwelt with admiration on Belvoir

Castle, the not far distant beautiful and ancient seat of the
Dukes of Rutland. On the evening when she was first driven
to see this picturesque pile, it looked like a stately structure
in a dream—rising, as it seemed, out of a cloud of deep blue
vapour ; and the far extending umbrageous foliage that surrounded it, steeped in the prevailing ethereal hue.

This visit to Elton was most refreshing and enjoyable, and
when Mrs. Elliott returned to Douglas she had a picture to
sketch for her boy Willie his eyes were never tired of beholding. Willie was all eagerness and delight, too, to hear
about his kind uncle and new pretty aunt.

.   .   .   .   .   .

And now the scene must change. We have reached 1852
—a year in our friend's life which records a chapter that
blotted out for the time the glory of the material heavens,
and the radiance of a nature upon which her eyes had only
so recently feasted in joyous appreciation, and with a fancy
free from any cloud of foreboding gloom.

There are events and scenes in the lives of those the
biographer records that he would fain screen from view—
the curtain is drawn and he fears to lift it—trembling by
some untoward touch to mar the harmony of his narrative,
or by a profane hand to intrude on the sacred and hallowed
precincts of private feeling, and ruthlessly lay bare what
God alone and the nearest and dearest should look upon.
But alas ! these revelations must be made, even though the
attempt to limn them is difficult and well-nigh impossible,
except in mere outline or in dim shadow—a vague suggestion which the sympathetic and initiated must supply
with form and colouring and subtle interpretation.   A
crisis had come in the life of Eleanor Elliott—a crisis
which revolutionised her whole being ; her former life with
its joys and its aspirations and its calm radiant hopes was
swept away, and a great blank of darkness and blackness
indescribable left in its place.

It was May 1852 when in a room of 31 Athol Street a boy

lay dying—Willie, the beloved son of his mother. Oh ! what agony was there—hanging over the prostrate pining form, over the dim, once beautiful eye, fading, fading from the light of day. Oh ! who can enter into that mother's anguish ? Another mother, perhaps, who has lost her darling, her first-born. But this was a woman and a mother of feelings so intense, of yearnings so infinite in relation to that child, one who, yesterday, almost, had with her fine keen perceptions and heart's devotion, seen the laurel of triumph on his brow, the beauty of matured holiness expressed in his every feature, and the power of his manhood influencing all near and far away to a disposition and character kindred with his own ; and now, all this dream, these foreshadowed and sacred desires, dashed away, vanished, and darkness and despair usurping their place.

Willie had taken scarlet fever ; and in a short time it developed into a malignant form, beyond the power of earthly physician to check. His poor father, a skilful man in his profession, along with other leading doctors, had consulted together over the case, and used every known and available means to stay the progress of the disease. All in vain—recovery was pronounced impossible, and the mother received the sentence as one bereft of sensation and power of reasoning. She literally hung over her darling night and day, watching the young life ebbing faster and faster, each breath becoming more laboured, more faint, until at last all was quenched in the silence and gloom of death.

We feel we cannot dwell on this picture. The solemnity of it is overwhelming. The poor mother was turned to stone ; and in her own words, "the light of her eyes fled." Her darling was gone—gone ! In her hands was his collecting-card for the South American Mission, almost the last thing he had asked for. And to her own dying day, thirty years after, this card was a precious relic that bound her with a twofold claim to the interests of the South American Missionary Society, and with a fidelity and devotion known only to those who along with her were identified in the work.

In regard to this awful sorrow and its consequences, we can only quote what Miss Alice Weatherell, a niece of Mrs. Elliott's, penned when sending a packet of her aunt's letters: "These letters," she said, "will give you a great insight into the intense depth of her nature and feelings, though there is one thing to be said, which is, that to few people is given the power of expressing their feelings as it was to her. It has always been a mystery to me how her reason was preserved, for, I have been told, when Willie, her first-born and especial darling, was taken from her, her grief was so fearful that sleep departed from her eyes."

The sorrow of other near and dear relatives—and then the funeral—must be passed over; the only memento available of the close of that young life, whose "leaf had perished in the green," is the following sonnet written by Lieut. Wood, and inserted by him in the Manx *Sun*, a leading weekly newspaper.

On the Lamented Death of a Youthful Friend, Willie Elliott.

By nature gifted, and by grace refined—
A youth of virtue, pure and undefiled;
In mind a man, in innocence a child,
In whom were wisdom, goodness, truth, combined
With inborn genius, and with might of mind.

What though he sleeps in death's sepulchral gloom,
Soon shall he rise, arrayed in beauty's bloom,
In glory's bright immortal form enshrined:
Still we may mourn and shed a sacred tear—
Tears for the dead, what heart can e'er reprove?
'Tis nature's tribute paid to buried love.
The loved in life in death are doubly dear.
'Tis meet to mourn, for o'er that friend who slept
E'en but a while in death, we read that "Jesus wept."

G. H. WOOD.

Mr. Wood's sorrow for the noble youth, and his sympathy for the mother, were genuine; a true kind friend did he prove himself in this dark hour of human grief. Ah, universal was the sorrow felt and sympathy shown for that bereaved mother and dear friend; but nothing was of any avail to arouse her for long from her insensibility. And as in the words of Tennyson, it was said of her, "She must weep or she will die." Happily relief came, and the tears flowed; oh, what tears! And here again we must quote the words of the same niece: "After Willie's death she came to Elton, but the intense sadness of her countenance was such that every one remarked upon it; every morning in her bedroom there was a row of handkerchiefs completely drenched with her tears, just as if they had been rung out of water. A mother's heart, as she said herself, always dies at a child's death. Willie was her second self, highly poetic, imaginative, and deeply religious, so that of course they both were in perfect sympathy with each other. It seems mysterious her idol should, at the early age of fourteen, have been taken from her. Of course I do not remember the sad event, as I was not born; but I know that the day of Willie's death was as present to his mother thirty years after as if it had only just happened. The anniversaries of her children's births and deaths were spent mostly in prayer. I used to rather dread those days coming round, knowing what she suffered; though no one could really enter into her feelings, her mind being so far above that of ordinary people; as says Adolph Saphir in a dear little book called 'Weep Not': 'The loneliness of great minds is inevitable, they live in a lofty region, and therefore in solitude. As they are high above the generality of mankind, they must needs be alone; they are separated from their fellow-men by the comprehensive range of their thoughts and views, and by the elevated tone of their aspirations and feelings.'"

Elton, where the sorrowing mother went when finally she

was sufficiently restored to feeling and activity, her brother's beautiful Rectory, was in truth a peaceful spot : away from the turmoil of life, and surrounded by much that was exquisitely lovely in nature.

The boy died in May; and it was in the warm summertime his mother went to this fair country retreat, and amongst those who deeply sympathised with her in her overwhelming sorrow. Her brother was still her beloved companion as of yore : together they took sweet counsel, and she called him " Great-heart," because he entered so into her feelings and into those of others. Elton, during this visit, she found to be what she afterwards named in Manx phraseology, *Port-a-chee*—a haven of peace. Gradually the soft influence of the milk of human kindness and thoughtfulness, and the balmy and sweet country sights and sounds, along with the returning calm of the peace of God, restored somewhat to a more even balance and power of endurance that sorely tried heart. Willie she knew was before the Throne, encircled with the reward of the diadem of a rich young life dedicated to the service of the King. If she wept now, it was for herself, that she was bereft of the treasure of her son's dear companionship, and wealth of bright promises—

> " The fame is quench'd that I foresaw,
> 　The head hath miss'd an earthly wreath."

But she must bow; it was the sovereign Will, and "Shall not the Judge of all the earth do right ? "

Archdeacon Philpot had probably first instilled into his friend's mind the great interest in the second coming of Christ; but after Willie's death this interest became an absorbing *reality*. She truly waited and longed for the coming of Christ and the restitution of all things to the sway of the Redeemer King, with a daily, hourly yearning. Her whole life shaped itself afresh, and took a new colour; it was not now so much a heartfelt sympathy for and striving after all that was good and beautiful, and that tended to the coming of Christ, but it was a veritable identification with and incorporation into all that pertained to that glorious certainty. Every thought, every word, every deed had respect to the hastening of the Redeemer's kingdom. Her power from this time over the minds and lives of others resulted in a great and undefinably *constraining* and *thrusting* into importance the things of God. Her force in regard to initiation into spiritual realities was simply irresistible; the young, the old, the gay, the sad, all felt it; wherever she was, whatever she did, the outcome of her influence was, *Live for God;* it is the *one* thing needful: "Heaven and earth must pass, but My words shall not pass away." It was an indescribable power this that emanated from that matured saint of God, and yet it had not reached its climax. The Captain of our salvation was perfected through suffering, and those who follow in His steps have to undergo a like development—a like perfecting. And here we shall again quote from her niece's remarks: "The second advent of the Lord was a tremendous reality to her; no subject was more present to her mind, or had a greater interest for her, than the sudden return of the Master she loved so well and served so faithfully. She would say, 'Blessed and holy is he which shall have part in the *first* resurrection; on such the second death has no power, but they shall be priests of God and of Christ, and shall reign with him a thousand years.' 'Death,' she went on to say, 'is not the Christian's goal; no! not *death*, but *life*, when a perpetual youth shall be the portion of Christ's people. Death itself (though death to the believer is the beginning of life) is a horror, and the sting can never be taken out of the act of dying. The fulfilment of the verse in 1 Cor. xv., "O death, where is thy sting? O grave, where is thy victory?" will not be realised until *that* day. Then when the trumpet shall sound shall the saying be fulfilled, "O death, where is thy sting?" but not *until then.*'"

That day—the day of the Lord Jesus Christ's coming is
mentioned in every chapter in the Epistles to the Thessa-
lonians, two epistles of which she was particularly fond, and
always read with fresh interest.   She had a great dislike to
the hymn beginning—

> "That day of wrath, that dreadful day,
>   When heaven and earth shall pass away,
>   What power shall be the sinner's stay ?
>   How shall he meet that dreadful day ?"

It was in contradistinction to that hymn that she wrote
the following :—

> "That day of life, that day of light,
>   When Christ shall come again,
> As cometh morning after night,
>   As sunshine after rain.
>
> Then shall the silver trumpet ring
>   A pure reviving breath,
> Awake, beloved, arise and sing,
>   From Hades and from Death !
>
> The morning breathes o'er land and sea
>   A pure reviving breath,
> Awake, beloved, arise and flee
>   From Hades and from Death.
>
> The flowers appear upon the earth,
>   Fresh with baptismal dew,
> The dew of nature's second birth—
>   He maketh all things new."

Are not these lines beautiful, and do they not read like a
clear note from the silver trump of a life victorious over self
and the world—reaching forward with blest anticipation to
that time when the restitution shall be, and the increase
of His kingdom shall have no end—no end ?   "Wonderful
thought !" as she herself would say, "the government of
Christ shall go on for ever and ever *increasing ;* and this
world of ours shall be once more as before the Fall, the
abode of perfect peace."

CHAPTER XIII.

MONA'S CHOICE OF A BISHOP.

It was in December when Mrs. Elliott returned home from Elton—returned to the embrace of but *one* of her darling children. Little Philip was to fill, he alone, the awful blank that the special darling's death had occasioned in the mother's heart and life. She missed her lost one at every turn, and in every pursuit; for wherever she went, whatever she did, in it he had had a chief share. It is marvellous to conceive how *ever* we rise at all from some of the crushing blows of life; but He who created us, created us for Himself, and enables us to live our life with the breath of hope and renewed vigour that He alone can and does bestow.

In December of this year Gavazzi paid Douglas a visit, and on which occasion he delivered several lectures, attended by Mrs. Weatherell, and without doubt by her daughter Eleanor. At all events the principles inculcated by the great convert from Romanism were those firmly held and established in the heart and practice of the subject of this memoir.

These lectures, denunciatory of the Pope and Popery, were listened to with grave attention by the large audiences that crowded to hear the famous ex-priest and eloquent speaker. His descriptions of the horrors of the Inquisition were so graphic and minute in their details, that numbers of his hearers spent a sleepless night after listening to the freezing recital.

One of the chief points in his appeals was to beware of the Jesuits in the great Protestant Church of England—that there were at that time in England " more than one thousand of the subtle and baneful order, besides any number of female Jesuits."

Did Gavazzi speak as less than a prophet? Let the history of the advance of Roman Catholicism in Britain since then answer the question!

In 1854 an event occurred which conspired as much, or more than most things, to revive in our friend's heart and mind interest in what took place around her. It was the fact that the Bishopric of Man was now vacant; and a thing perhaps previously unheard of in Church annals, the people of the island were making a strenuous effort to secure a bishop of their own selection; and *who?* Dr. Carpenter! Yes, Dr. CARPENTER—who had been told four years before by the tongue of slander that his work was done in Douglas, that he was no longer needed in the island!

A regular canvass was made; and the excitement over this business was immense. In a very short time seven hundred signatures were obtained, representing the leading ecclesiastical and lay officials and principal Church people in the island. Even the Dissenters joined the chorus of voices that clamoured for the return of the beloved Doctor. The island appeared unanimous in its desire; and no greater tribute of appreciation, of love, and of respect could surely have been paid to faithfulness in the service of Christ.

The signatures obtained, a petition was drawn up, expressing public feeling in regard to Dr. Carpenter, and its opinion of his manifold labours in the diocese; and stating that in every sense he was the spiritual overseer and guide best suited to the religious views and needs of the Manx people. This petition was forwarded to the Crown, and with eager anticipation the answer was awaited. Alas! the solicitation was rejected; and the Hon. Rev. Horatio Powys, a High Churchman, was selected instead to fill the Manx see. The lamentation was bitter from one end of the island to the other; and it became a common saying that Bishop Powys, when he accepted the diocese of Sodor and Man, "entered upon a *sea* (see) of troubles." He was not the man for the Manx, who had too long imbibed the evangelical teaching of former bishops and become impregnated with the spiritual influence of Dr. Carpenter and his contemporary clergy, to tolerate the idea of a ritualistic overseer of the churches.

As an instance of how the feelings of the time have never been effaced from the memory of Manxmen, it will be interesting to quote the following paragraph from the *Isle of Man Times* as recent as January 30, 1892 :—

"Of the evil results of intruding a bishop with discordant views of Church doctrine and ceremonial upon a diocese like the Isle of Man, we have a striking example in Bishop Powys. A man of great personal energy, and full of love for his work and his people, his whole course as a Manx bishop was wrecked by his persistent attempts to force his High Church views upon the Manx people. Ultimately, defeated by their dogged resistance, he gave up the attempt; but so strong was the feeling against him, which had been excited by his proceedings, that he left the island, and spent the latter years of his life in the South of England, while the interests of the Manx Church suffered greatly in the conflict. The Manx Church, to this day, has not recovered from this disastrous struggle."

As we may not have occasion to mention Dr. Carpenter again, it may here be stated that he found it a difficult matter to succeed such a mighty and popular preacher as M'Neile. His ministry in Liverpool was not as successful as in the Isle of Man ; too much, in some respects, was demanded of him. He afterwards, however, found a congenial sphere at Penzance, where eventually he died, adored and lamented by his people.

In 1854 a learned acquaintance of Mrs. Elliott's passed away near Edinburgh, Professor Edward Forbes. His two sisters lived in Douglas; one was a maiden lady, the other, Mrs. Matthews, was a near neighbour of the Elliotts.

G

She will be remembered by some, who knew her otherwise less personally, for her often-to-be-seen large open carriage *under* which a great greyhound careered in keeping with the pace of the horses.

This year the Isle of Man shared in the national ferment created by the declaration of war against Russia. The 26th April was appointed to be kept as a day of humiliation and prayer to avert the calamities of this disastrous campaign. The Rev. William Hawley preached two remarkable sermons on the occasion, and gave token of the power which he subsequently exercised in the pulpit as an able and eloquent preacher.

It was soon after the events of this period that Tennyson published his "Charge of the Light Brigade," commemorative of the gallant feat of the brave six hundred at Balaclava. Few responded more heartily and appreciatively to the chorus of acclaim all over the land that greeted the production of this graphic and spirited poem than Eleanor Elliott; but a higher and far deeper appreciation of England's bard filled her heart, when alone she communed with that great and impassioned spirit that flooded its wealth of boundless and beautiful feeling on the pages of "In Memoriam." It was the record of a great love and a great sorrow such as she herself had known and that enveloped· her around with their undying memories.

As if to escape from the war-cries that filled the public ear, our friend and her boy went together to visit the English lakes about this time. It was there, especially at Grasmere, that possibly her love for Wordsworth's calm sweet poesy was intensified. And amid the silent, fairy-like scenery of that enchanting region, the mother sought to instil into her surviving son's mind something of that spirit which dwelt so richly in the heart and soul of the son who was gone. But young Philip had none or very little of his mother's and brother's imaginative temperament. He preferred to scamper about over hill and dale, exploring, and exercising his sinew and muscle.

Whilst dwelling on the pensive muse of her favourite lake poet, Mrs. Elliott also involuntarily conned and meditated upon the delicate feminine lays of Mrs. Hemans. She regarded Mrs. Hemans as a refined gentle spirit who translated the glowing emotions within her into an artistic composition of womanly grace and high-toned sentiment worthy of woman's warmest and purest approval. As she threaded the mazes of branching foliage by the sleeping waters of Grasmere's silvery lake, while all around the beauty and music of spring filled heart and ear—head aloft and eye mellowed with hallowed light and holy joy, she repeated half to herself and half to the silent beauteous world around the poetess's sweet lay, "The Voice of Spring:"—

> "I come, I come! ye have called me long.
> I come o'er the mountains with light and song!
> Ye may trace my step o'er the wakening earth,
> By the winds which tell of the violet's birth,
> By the primrose-stars in the shadowy grass,
> By the green leaves opening as I pass."

Mrs. Elliott's and Philip's return to Douglas was met with the news of an accident that had all but proved fatal to Frederick Grier, the former's nephew, and the son of Lieutenant-Colonel Grier. It happened in Ireland, at Tralee; he was bathing when cramp seized him and he sank. His cousin, William Dillon, had been bathing with him, and was dressing when a boy arrested his attention and pointed to the sea. William, though himself also suffering from cramp, unhesitatingly sprang into the water, and saved his cousin just as he was sinking for the last time. This brave William Dillon (we hope he is still living) was a nephew of Sir William Jeffcott, Chief Justice of Singapore, of the same family probably as the present Jeffcotts of Castletown, Isle of Man.

CHAPTER XIV.

ASTRONOMICAL STUDIES.

THE following year Mrs. Elliott and Philip again went from home, this time to Dublin. After their return the former, whilst she silently and unostentatiously went about her self-denying deeds of loving-kindness in Douglas amongst rich and poor, high and low (for she exercised herself perpetually in some shape or other for the good of all), she manifestly discharged with a double love and assiduity her maternal obligations on behalf of her son. She was pleased to see he gave evidence of a liking for music, and spent much of his time with Mr. Lewis Garrett in the organ-loft of St. Thomas' Church on practising and tuning evenings.

Mrs. Elliott's love for children was not confined to her own offspring. She loved children generally; but very especially those of her brother. It was as if the loss of her own darlings drew from her a wider and deeper concern in those of her nearest relatives and intimate friends.

It is so sweet in her letters to see how she always remembers the children, always something to say for them, or something to send them.

On one occasion, when enclosing some engravings for Mr. Weatherell's young sons, she adds in a letter to their father:—"I wish that they had been brightly coloured, and that the explanations were in simpler language. But you and Lydia can simplify it into a more childish dialect. You may remember how your favourite, Dr. Johnson, praised

Dr. Watts for bending his great mind down to the capacity of little children."

This interest never flagged, and was, if anything, accentuated as time went on. She, as it were, strove to bear a share in the education of these young people from a distance, feeding their minds with pure literature, and fostering their taste for the beautiful, with repeated contributions of bright and choice little productions of art.

Once more, in the year 1857, the tranquillities of home-life in the Isle of Man, as well as elsewhere, were rudely and terribly interrupted by the outburst of the fearful Indian Mutiny. A large public meeting was held in Douglas in October of this year for the Relief Fund in aid of the suffering soldiers, women, and children.

"The last intelligence from India," wrote Mrs. Elliott to her sister-in-law, "is considered somewhat more satisfactory; but it is a fearful state of things, adding a black page of fiendish wickedness to the history of human nature in its worst estate. It is an awful comment on the word of Scripture that 'the dark places of the earth are the habitations of cruelty.' The people are as vile as the gods of their idolatry, and grievous has been the result of England's unfaithfulness in withholding from them the Gospel of peace. It is to be hoped that after the dark night there may be the dawn of a better day for India and for the English there. The arrival of fugitives at Southampton must be an affecting scene. But now the great anxiety seems to be concentrated at Lucknow. General Neil, whose name is of such frequent occurrence, was in Douglas in the spring of this year, staying with Mrs. Wilson, Miss Gray's sister-in-law, in Athol Street."

The General Neil mentioned here was afterwards, as history too truly records, killed on the entry of the British troops into Lucknow; and "no better or braver soldier fell that year in India."

Miss Gray, whose sister had entertained the gallant officer

during his visit to Douglas, was a very great friend of Mrs.
Elliott's, and a most accomplished as well as agreeable companion.

In 1859 the Rev. Edward and Mrs. Forbes and their
family left Douglas for Paris, Mr. Forbes having been
appointed Chaplain to the British Embassy and Incumbent
of the Rue d'Aguesseau Church.

Since Dr. Carpenter left, no departure from amongst the
residents of Douglas caused more widespread and sincere
regret than that of Mr. afterwards Dr. Forbes.   Mrs. Elliott
and her household felt it very much ; and this kindly relationship with the Forbeses was one for life.

Amongst the books that seem to have attracted our friend's
special attention, and that she mentions in her letters about
this time, was Hugh Miller's "Schools and Schoolmasters,"
probably then recently published.   She appears to have been
intensely interested in the work as also in the author—"that
wonderful stone-mason," as she terms him.

Hugh Miller, however, was ever a favourite.   She alludes
to his sagacious knowledge in a letter to her sister-in-law,
Mrs. Robert Weatherell—a letter that must be quoted, as it
furnishes not only a sample of the edifying and interesting
correspondence that went on between these two well-balanced
understandings and intimate friends, but it will be seen in it
how jealous Mrs. Elliott was for the maintenance under all
circumstances of the truth of the inspired Word, and yet how
wholly free from that warped prejudice which so tyrannises
over the intelligences of some Christian people that they
cannot meet with an unorthodox or faithless objector without
railing at his blindness, and almost, if not altogether, brand-
ing the offender with personal dislike for his lack of Divine
perception, and for his, what they term, wilful profanity.
She, with that charity that suffers long, and in her mature
Christian experience, rather compassionated the erring one,
and craved above all things to smooth the path of his understanding, and remove from his feet all stumbling-blocks that

would further impede his progress and final attainment of spiritual intuition and knowledge. The following passage will perhaps illustrate her spirit and explain the drift of our meaning.

"I am glad that you and Robert have read Whewell's 'Plurality of Worlds.' The two pillars of its strength appear to be the geological and moral arguments. The moral argument especially is built up with much power and beauty; and the reasoning from geology is also admirable. A similar theory was published by the Rev. Robert Birks years ago, in a little treatise on astronomy, which I gave to Robert two years since. And if neither he nor you have read it, it is quite worthy of your perusal, for it abounds with noble thoughts and eloquence.

"In the preface to Whewell's last edition he refers to this work of Birks', and also to a kindred theory alluded to by Hugh Miller some years since. Recently this large-minded, extraordinary Hugh Miller has published a tract so excellent that I must send it to Robert. It is entitled 'Geology *versus* Astronomy,' and is a modification of Whewell and Brewster. Of course in the intellectual combat Whewell has the best of it; for his antagonist so far loses all self-possession as to overstep all bounds of reason and Scripture in the intimation that perhaps the atonement, the Divine Sacrifice, may be repeated again and again for the imaginary inhabitants of suns and imaginary planets surrounding them. This rash supposition is in the very face of revelation, 'Christ being raised from the dead, dieth no more' (Rom. vi. 9; Heb. ix. 25, 26; x. 12, 14). The idea of Brewster seems to be that all worlds are wasted and superfluous unless they are inhabited by rational accountable creatures. And yet during the long ages of geology this earth was unoccupied by man. Of course it might have been tenanted by spiritual creatures, such as Satan and his hosts; but that being merely a supposition of some thinkers cannot affect the argument one way or another. The earth was not wasted while untenanted by the human race, but it was passing through a process of preparation for man. And arguing from the known to the unknown, it is almost certain that our next neighbour the moon is a ghastly ruin untenanted by one living creature. But yet possibly in course of preparation for future inhabitants. And reasoning from *analogy*, if the nearest world outside is empty and bare, so may the others be *for the present*.

"And if the usual assertion that the other planets of our system are like the earth, and therefore contain rational inhabitants, is shown to be a groundless assumption, as the planets outside of Mars are quite unlike the earth in weight and structure and other conditions—then the argument from analogy fails at once; it breaks down at the first step. And, moreover, why imagine such unproved inhabitants when they are only in the way—a stumbling-block to some sceptical minds? It is true that Dr. Chalmers has beautifully answered that difficulty in his 'Astronomical Discourses,' applying the parable of the lost sheep to this sinful world, and the Divine tenderness of the Good Shepherd in bestowing such self-denying love and pity on the one wandering erring world. But the stronger ground seems to be the exclusion of such imaginary beings altogether from the discussion—to allow them no standing-room, seeing that infidelity is unable to prove their *present* existence. Hereafter it may be otherwise when other worlds may be colonised from this earth which would be quite another affair. Meanwhile, what harm is there in Whewell's supposition that if there is any life in Saturn it is of a low, pulpy, gelatinous nature?"

Of her love for astronomy, and especially in its relation to Biblical revelation and prophecy, further instances will be forthcoming in due course. The extract just quoted furnishes meantime an insight into that rare intelligence, enlightened and kindled by the live coal from off the altar of Divine Love and Truth, as well as enriched by diligent study and exceptional erudition.

CHAPTER XV.

PHILIP'S MARRIAGE.

Of late years, Philip having left school in Douglas, went to King William's College at Castletown; but in 1860 he appears to have vacated Castletown for Cambridge. It had been the boy's wish to enter the army, but his mother was completely against it, not considering, it is said, the military profession one that a Christian man should voluntarily choose. Accordingly Philip with reluctance gave up the idea of the army, and began his university studies with a view to the medical profession.

In 1862 he took his degree of B.A., which was a great relief to his parents' minds. He left Cambridge, and returned to Douglas. Whilst at Douglas at this time he became very constant in his visits at the house of Mr. and Mrs. Craigie. They had one daughter; she was several years older than Philip, but somehow or other he got drawn into a very marked intimacy with her, and eventually they became engaged. This engagement was not one of which Dr. and Mrs. Elliott approved. Mrs. Elliott would fain have sought the comfort, though too late for the advice, of her brother; but she almost feared to tell him of the projected marriage, feeling sure that he would deem the engagement premature and very ridiculous, Philip being so extremely young, to say nothing of the lady being so much older.

Whilst labouring under anxiety about Philip and his future, the mother insensibly dwelt, if possible, more than

ever on the memory of Willie. In a letter she writes at
this time she says :—

"This is the birthday of one who would be twenty-four
years of age, if he were here. But he is awaiting another
birthday into endless life, through the birth and death and
resurrection of our Redeeming Lord, who liveth and *was
dead*, and is alive for evermore.

"Every return of spring brings us nearer and nearer to the
coming spring-time of that new life. When Willie was a
young child he used to amuse himself with a childish play
which he called 'Dissolving Views.' One day when he was
going through it in his room, he took up a little anchor and
said, 'This represents Hope leaning on her anchor, and
waiting for the long land.' It reminds one of the voyagers
on a stormy sea who cast anchors out of the stern and
wished for the day."

She wished for the day—poor mother!—the bright resurrection morn when she should greet her darling again.
Though Willie was dead he was still in a sense ever living
to her. She, as it were, felt him about her, touched him
with her hand, spoke to him in that ever-recurring converse
of spirit with spirit. Philip, however, was now her all in
all in a more material sense. As the thought of his parting
from her by marriage overwhelmed her at times, she clung
to him with an intensity never before so apparent. Possibly,
as she regretted the step her boy had taken in regard to the
future, she remembered how she too had made her choice in
the matter of marriage irrespective of the odds against it;
and for this reason she must bear with the son who was just
after all following in her steps. Not probably that the
thought made the circumstance any easier to bear, rather the
reverse. What we sow that shall we also reap, was a sad
and painful reflection. Happily having at last confided her
doubts and her fears to her brother, he wrote her a most
kind and appeasing letter, which tended considerably to
lighten the cloud which had settled on her spirit ; and as it

was her nature to see most things *couleur de rose*, the rosy tint began to appear on the surface of the marriage engagement; and she set about making all due preparations of mind for the approaching celebration. She and Mrs. Craigie, her boy's mother-in-law elect, went frequently together to return calls and receive from acquaintances and friends their congratulations on the coming event. The marriage was settled to take place on June 15, 1864, Philip being twenty-one years of age. It was to be at St. Thomas's, the church the Craigies attended; and Mr. Weatherell had consented to come over and assist at the marriage service.

In keeping with the tastes of the Craigie family, the wedding was a very gay one indeed; and poor dear Mrs. Elliott joined in the festivities with all the apparent mirth and gladness of a happy parent on an auspicious occasion. And who shall say how much was real and how much assumed? Perhaps it was all real, she had such boundless faith in the love and compassion of a prayer-hearing God; and had she not confided to Him all her care? and would He not, if it was His holy will, make smooth the path of her child's feet, and bright and happy the wedded years before him?

The marriage over, and the return to a childless home, was doubtless a time of painful reaction; but this too was got over. She rose above self, and strove to realise that she had not lost but gained by the event; for she was now the mother of a daughter as well as of a dear son, and the son was the richer of a wife in addition to a fond father and mother.

The young people, of course, went on their honeymoon; and then on their return settled in Douglas until Philip had made arrangements for starting his medical career at Barrowden in Rutlandshire. Their departure did not take place until May 1866, two years after their marriage.

It was during the year 1866 the Rev. A. Hoskins was

assisting at St. George's.   He is now (1893) Vicar of St. James', Cheltenham.   Mr. Hoskins was even at that time a gifted divine, very devoted to the cause of his Master, and with a power peculiar to himself could arrest as well as inspire the hearts of his hearers to make Christ and His salvation their possession, and the things of God their great end and enjoyment of life.   A young girl of an exceptionally lively temperament, delighting in fun and amusement, was one day, while passing near St. George's Church, and when the bell was ringing for the week-day service, urged by a lady, her senior in years, to come in and attend the service.   The idea of spending the best part of a beautiful morning in church, when a ramble in the country or a sail in the sunny bay would have been much more to her fancy, was not welcomed very cordially.   The lady, however, pleaded, and young Miss —— was induced to enter. Mr. Hoskins preached that morning; and his address was one, as was usually the case with him, of original sentiment and of peculiar spiritual unction.   The young girl was affected—deeply and permanently; and all that was really spiritual in her nature was acted upon, quickened, and intensified, and it was soon made manifest, not only in her continuing to attend on all occasions the means of grace, but in a life devoted to the service of Christ.   That same young girl afterwards became one of the spiritual coterie that grouped itself round Mrs. Elliott; and together they often spoke of the indebtedness of Douglas to the services rendered by Mr. Hoskins on his visits at different periods to the Isle of Man.

Mrs. Elliott, in a letter written in February of 1866, says to her sister-in-law: "I find that Robert (her brother) is giving lectures on the Apocalypse, and I trust that the special blessing pronounced on the third verse may attend the word.   Sometimes I say to Mr. Hoskins, What a comfort it would be to my brother to be near you.   Robert and he would agree so well in heart and mind.   Some time ago he told us that he had been dreaming of Robert. He is a saintly person of deep piety and solid learning. He gives one the idea of a sort of Richard Hooker, whom he can repeat by heart."

Her frequent interviews and delightful conversations with Mr. Hoskins at this period contributed in no small degree to alleviate her pain at parting with Philip, and lessening the sense of loneliness and want she experienced in not seeing him about her. Mr. Hoskins and she were so much of one mind that the sympathy felt and manifested by him was very grateful and comforting to her.

This good clergymen at a later date, and when he was Vicar of St. Peter's, Cheltenham, a church in a poor district among poor people, was offered a good living in a suburb of Birmingham; but, not seeing his way then to leave the poor people amongst whom he was settled, he declined the eligible offer. This act raised him more than ever in the estimation of Mrs. Elliott and others of his numerous friends.

CHAPTER XVI.

A TELEGRAM.

" UNTO every one of us is given grace according to the measure of the gift of Christ. . . . And he gave some, apostles; and some, prophets; and some, evangelists; and some, pastors and teachers; for the perfecting of the saints, for the work of the ministry, for the edifying of the body of Christ." So says St. Paul, in words of mighty practical wisdom; and yet they seem so little realised in their import, or, at all events, acted upon in the Church and amongst Christian workers. How often it appears as if *one* individual should be and should do everything—combine all the gifts and qualities that God bestows *separately* upon *different* individuals set apart to labour in the extension of His cause. One would think, to judge of some earnest workers, that they regarded the Heavenly Overseer as a hard task-master, exacting from them the last drop of blood; whereas it is they, or if not they, it is the system under which they work that is so unreasonable. Individual talent is lost sight of in the vast sameness of the machinery and of the work turned out. All zealous they may be; all whole-hearted, true, earnest, gifted people; yet all undertaking the same task; and, in their eagerness of execution, running in each other's way and tripping one another up. Nay, should any individual worker have the hardihood to chalk out a way of his own, and engage in work of his own finding and selection, how often he is found fault with, as not doing his duty by his Church or by the community: he neglects, they say, this, that, and the other thing; and he takes up schemes of his own of a doubtful nature and of no manner of use. Why not do so-and-so? Why not follow the leading of so-and-so? Why be odd? Why, in a word, not do as they do?

Eleanor Elliott was one of the so-called "odd" workers. As before said, always about her Master's business, she yet made no mark in the religious world indicative of any great feat of labour. For a moment we will lift the curtain and lay bare some of the busy routine of that quiet, hidden, unremarkable, yet forcible Christian career. And, as we are about to do so, we are reminded of what might be conceived of an ideal explorer through dense forests and barren, trackless wastes. He goes forth, not to kill, but to tame, subdue, and save. Alone he sets out, alone he prosecutes his arduous and dangerous journey : there is no path before him, but what he makes for himself with persevering patience and risk. Wild beasts prowl around, and their cries fill his ears ; but his humane errand and the desire of discovery animate his heart and nerve his endeavour, and on he holds his way, and never relents, till by degrees he sees the fruits of his labour and the reward of all his toil. Another coming after him, with less of his skill, less of his courage and thirst of achievement, finds the path rough, it is true, but after all comparatively clear ; the wild creatures fewer in number, and not so fierce in character. They have learned to know the disposition of the adventurer—he is gentle and kind, he will not harm them ; and they will not harm him. Easy—comparatively easy for the second on the field. But who smoothed the path ? who subdued the ferocity of the wild denizen ? who opened up the way to tracts of unexpected beauty, verdure, and fruitfulness—who ! The succeeding traveller profits, but cannot tell to whom he is debtor ; perhaps he does not even ask himself. He only thinks of present minor difficulties, not of the greater that have been overcome by another !

Yes, our friend may be regarded as especially a Christian *pioneer*. No "odd" worker really, but in the truest sense most methodical; because "according to the measure of the gift of Christ" she duly fulfilled her calling in the Church and the community to which she belonged. She clashed with no one, but she smoothed the path of the feet of many who have followed after.

There are, or there *were*, dens of sin, filth, and misery in Douglas that no ordinary Christian worker ever put a foot into, not altogether from want of sympathy, but from positive dread—on the one hand of contagious disease, and on the other of foul language; and perhaps of personal attack and injury. There, however, Mrs. Elliott was as well known as were the uncouth wretched inhabitants to one another; there she walked and visited and taught and prayed for years of her holy self-denying life. Her practice was every morning to spend alone some hours in the study of the Word (which she studied on her knees), and in prayer. Then, her devotion over, she betook herself to the hovels of dirt and misery; and often until an advanced hour in the afternoon visited in the polluted slums of Douglas. On entering a house, no matter how sickeningly unclean, she would kneel down on the floor, join her hands fervently together, and with raised head and closed eyes, address the Father of all mercies on behalf of the inmates. As she knew the wants of each dwelling so well in all their particulars, she mentioned each need to the God of help; and above all prayed that the poor people might have their eyes opened to behold Jesus the Saviour of their souls, and their hearts made receptive for the truth by the visitation and indwelling of the Holy Spirit. Then she rose, sang a verse or so of a hymn, and then slowly and emphatically repeated a text of Scripture, never omitting the leading truths of salvation, such as "God so loved the world, that He gave His only-begotten Son, that whosoever believeth on Him should not perish, but have everlasting life;" and "The blood of Jesus Christ which cleanseth us from all sin;" and "Ye *must* be born again." After this repetition

A CORNER OF OLD DOUGLAS, AND ST. MATHEW'S CHAPEL,
BUILT BY BISHOP WILSON, 1708.

by herself, she then questioned her hearers as to what she
had said; and never did she leave their presence until they
were able to repeat the words correctly. This achieved,
she then asked them if they understood what they had
learned. Of course they rarely did, then began an explanation, and then another catechising. In some degree satisfied
with what had been taken in by her scholars—sometimes
very old pupils indeed—as also sometimes very young, she
questioned them about the needs of the body; and should
the case appear anything like a necessitous one, putting
her hand in her pocket, she gave to the only too eager
recipient what would assist the natural in addition to the
spiritual requirements, the former being always considered
by her conjointly with the latter. Quietly, and usually with
her head slightly bent, she sallied forth towards the door,
her step very slow and measured, as if she were in deep
thought, but in reality in deep communion with God, and
earnest in entreaty with the Divine Spirit on behalf of those
she had dealt with. Once more on the threshold, she knelt
down, prayed audibly—after which, another verse of a
hymn, and she was gone. This system of visiting she
practised in every house; and how much more of material
as well as of spiritual assistance she gave the Great Day
alone will declare. Her life was truly hid with Christ
in God.

And there were times when that pure and lofty spirit
entered houses where, it is safe to say, even the most
devoted clergyman never put, or could with any prudence
put his foot, let alone lift his voice in warning or entreaty.
Yes, into habitations of ill-fame—dens of foulest sin and
most terrible lawlessness she found her way. Many a time
she was positively refused an entrance; not by the men
who frequented these haunts of vice but by the women.
Calmly and determinedly she stood like a rock on these
occasions at the outer door of such houses, and implored of
the young men who were making their way in, not to go—

H

not—if only for their mother's sake! "I am a mother," she
would say, "and I implore you, as with a mother's love—
do not risk your souls in here!" Shamefacedly some turned
back; and when they did so the women within all but struck
that fair noble creature of their own sex, who stood like a wall
between the temptresses and the tempted. On other occasions she intruded her pure presence where oaths and drink
prevailed, and there raised up that voice of hers in holy
beseeching. Sometimes not in vain, sometimes at the very
risk of her life. The writer hardly knows now from what
source she chiefly obtained this knowledge of this devoted
life; for truly, in after years when she knew the subject of
this memoir almost as intimately as a daughter might have
done, she yet never heard her speak of her labours or of
what they were. She was ever the delightful companion,
tho' saintly influence that ennobled and raised to the higher
ntercourse of God and eternity; but conversation of self
there was none. Self was laid on the altar; Christ and
His cause were everything. Freely and enthusiastically, on
the other hand, she spoke of the good deeds of others;
indeed, the smallest effort on the part of any Christian
friend was commended and encouraged—praised beyond all
deserving. It was impossible to meet with such sympathy
and encouragement from any one as from her; and who
knew better how to give it? And strange, though so
conscious—she could not fail to be from the experience she
had—of the sin and worthlessness within the human heart,
and the deceitfulness of the human tongue, no being could
have been less suspecting, more utterly guileless than she
was. She saw beauty and she saw worth—and always *hope*
—where no other could. It was almost a vain task to get
her to believe evil of the most depraved at times. Her
heart was a centre of boundless love and pity.

One day—and here we tremble to proceed—that she had,
as her wont, been spending hours in the wretched region of
"Little Ireland," or Back Strand Street, she came home late

in the evening faint and weary and hungry—ah, she was often all these!—when a telegram was placed in her hands. It was addressed to her husband, but thinking probably it might be a call to some patient suddenly taken ill, she opened it—when, lo! these words met her gaze :—

"Snell to Philip Elliott, Esq.—Come at once. Philip has been vomiting blood and died suddenly this morning.

"BARROWDEN."

A cry—a piercing cry—a blank—a fall—and we know no more.

. . . .

No more! but what is contained in the following letter. It is from the Rev. Frederick Grier, eldest son of Colonel Grier, to his uncle, the Rev. Robert Weatherell, Elton. The Griers were now living in Douglas, and the writer of the letter was curate of St. George's.

"6 ALBERT TERRACE, DOUGLAS, ISLE OF MAN,
"*September* 20, 1866.

"MY DEAR UNCLE,—To-night a heavy blow has been struck in our family. A telegram arrived in Athol Street to the following import: 'Snell to Philip Elliott, Esq.—Come at once. Philip has been vomiting blood and died suddenly this morning.' Poor Uncle Elliott rushed over to this house with it at about nine o'clock, and mother and myself went over. Aunt Eleanor's grief is tearless, unrelieved by a tear—cold, deep, hard—a 'stony grief.' Mr. Elliott's is passionate, like a woman's. God help them this night.

"Mr. Elliott, accompanied by Mr. and Mrs. Craigie, starts to-morrow morning to bring home the mortal remains.

"*So* we go one after another, time leaves its marks and death makes its gaps, and we ask which of us is next to follow as we look round us on our family circle. Looking at him who has last been taken, I think of one whose prayer was, 'God be merciful to me a sinner,' rather 'to me *the* sinful one,' and I can but add, 'The Lord grant unto *him* that he may find mercy of the Lord on that day,' and teach us who survive, in this and other like daily spectacles of mortality, to see how frail and uncertain our condition is, and so to number *our* days that we may seriously apply our hearts unto that holy and heavenly wisdom whilst we live here, which may in the end bring us to life everlasting, through the merits of Jesus Christ.—Your very affectionate nephew,   FRED. GRIER."

After Philip and his wife left Douglas for their new home, and the former's new sphere of work at Barrowden, things had gone on apparently very well ; the young doctor was a favourite with his patients, and Barrowden generally was loud in his praise. All at once, seemingly with no specific cause, Philip was seized with a slight attack of bleeding from the lungs. On consultation it was deemed nothing of any moment. A short time went over, and, on the return of health, he was one day leading a horse out of the stable ; the animal kicked him in the region of the stomach. Philip bore the pain and said nothing. Some days after, however, bleeding began again, and soon became very excessive—progressing in quantity with terrible rapidity. Death was speedily the result.

So sudden had been the call, and so unaccountable, that for a time the event seemed clouded with mystery, both in Barrowden and in Douglas, when the intelligence was received and circulated. As to the widow, so paralysing had been the shock to her system, that for days she lay as dead. When Dr. Elliott and Mr. and Mrs. Craigie arrived at Barrowden, they found her in this sad condition. Mrs. Craigie remained with her daughter, and Dr. Elliott and Mr. Craigie returned to the Isle of Man, accompanying the body of the deceased.

What the return was to that home of woe in Athol St.

we never heard and have no means of ascertaining, excepting by what is inferred in a letter from the heart-broken mother. She, too, it was stated, lay paralysed, or literally turned to stone with speechless agony of grief. In a sense this sorrow was more powerful in its intense anguish than that she experienced when her first-born—Willie, the light and sunshine of her life—was taken. Philip was all she had left of the children God had given her; and what made his sudden death so bitter above all was the thought, was it well with her poor boy? Willie she knew was safe in the bosom of his Saviour; but Philip, poor Philip, he had given no evidence that he had passed from the condemnation of sin into life in Christ Jesus. He was a good-hearted, happy-go-lucky youth, who had never really seriously considered the great question of a personal salvation and reconciliation with a just and righteous God, through a loving and compassionate Saviour. He was not spiritually-minded, or at all events he had given no indication of being so, and this was the mother's bitterest and most crushing cause of grief. Could she have known that all was well with her beloved one, she would have borne up with less poignancy of woe and stubbornness of despair; but when the great comfort and rest for her stricken heart was wanting, she was overcome with a grief so uncontrollable, that many condemned it as nothing short of rebellion. Heedless the words fell upon her ears. Friends spoke but she heard not, or if she heard there came no response. An awful blackness—a night of utter inconsolable anguish rested upon her spirit, and even the voice of the Lord of life was, for the time being, dumb to her heart. Surely nothing is so terrible to bear to the true child of God as the sense of the withdrawal of the Divine presence and support. As the Saviour cried out on the cross, "Why hast Thou forsaken me?" so she now was, as it were, forsaken—alone with her woe— with a stretch of life before her, unrelieved for evermore on earth by the music of the voice, by the sunshine of the smile, by the warmth of the touch of any dear child of her own. All—all taken of those God had given, and that she had striven to rear for Him. A life lonely with loss was to be hers, and dark with irrevocable sorrow.

The funeral was a large one, as might be expected under the circumstances; and independent of the sympathy and respect that were so general for the bereaved parents and relatives, poor Philip had been a great favourite with his many associates and friends in Douglas. He was laid to rest in the family vault close to the entrance of the principal gate to St. George's churchyard.

Mrs. Weatherell recounts in her Diary how attentive and kind their dear friend and clergyman, Mr. Hawley,* was on the occasion. How he reasoned with her afflicted daughter so sensibly and lovingly that she seemed to be soothed, and in some measure comforted. Vain are almost all words—the kindest and best even—from the dearest on earth, when the hand of Death has been laid on what we prized above all. There is but this comfort, " Jesus wept." He shed the mortal tear; and He alone can wipe those tears He Himself has permitted to be shed.

* The Rev. William Hawley was now Incumbent of St. George's, having succeeded Rev. Edward Forbes in 1859.

CHAPTER XVII.

BLOW UPON BLOW.

THOSE of us acquainted with the sea, and who have watched its various movements, have no doubt observed how, when a storm has suddenly burst, the waves have arisen in unison and in wild commotion, and have reared their foaming crests on high; and how by degrees as they roll on the beach they gather volume, and as they recede and then fall forward again, how prolonged is each succeeding sweep, and how heavy and full in proportion the great emerald-lined billow before it at last unbends and breaks in tempestuous sound upon the strand, sucking into its momentary gaping and liquid lip the under-expanse of shingle and sand; —and how overhead the clouds gather in lurid gloom, the wind whistles with a shriller and more cutting blast; and all around the wild sea-birds, as well as the ships on the main, scud along as in keeping with the temper of Nature. Everything shares in the general upheaval; and the whole scene from an hour or so ago is changed, and may remain so for long: far away on the horizon blacker and blacker becomes the stretch of sky; and soon, very soon, every glimmer of remaining light disappears, and all becomes storm-cast and prophetic of a falling night of tempest and disaster. Well, such as we have seen on the fair face of Nature when her silver and her blue have given place to purple and deeper-hued dye, so does it often happen, if not in our own life, in that of some fellow-creature. Mrs. Elliott, a glorious being of intelligence and heavenly nobility

—a sunbeam and smile of God upon the earth, was called upon to pass through the gloom and horror of such a storm. It broke latterly in the death of her first-born, then in that of her Philip; and as one year and then another succeeded that last terrible night, it gathered in deeper and deeper density, till one bright light and another of human sympathy and love were wholly extinguished, and she was left in solitary darkness—a sad survivor to contemplate and inhabit the scene of wreckage and loss before her. But ere we dwell on the next result of that appalling visitation, we will linger awhile with our dear bereaved friend mourning over the death of her boy. Weeks went over, and how they passed was a matter between that sad soul and her merciful God.

Letters of condolence came in numbers, and the black-edged paper so additionally benumbed the receiver's heart and pained her eyes, that in after years she could not bear to get a letter in a mourning envelope. These letters received now almost all remained without an answer, so far as she was concerned.

The tears our poor friend shed at this time were so profuse and constant, and her long nights of sleeplessness so injurious to her system, that, though unconsciously to herself, her sight became affected. She no doubt attributed the blurred condition of her vision solely to outward causes; such as that the objects she looked at were not distinct in themselves. For instance, a book was brought to her at this period by a friend, "Notes on Exodus," by C. H. Mackintosh; and, at the earnest entreaty of the giver, she was induced to begin and read it. Soon finding its rich mine of biblical research and elucidation wonderfully comforting and uplifting to her heart, she went on with it, but often put it down from sheer inability to decipher with ease the print. The type of the said volume is certainly not very large, but there does not appear to be the smallest illegibility about it to one who can see well. In a letter which will follow to her sister-in-law, she complains of the want of distinctness as regards the type of this book. Already amid her other overwhelming trials, the Judge of all the earth, whose ways are other than our ways, and His thoughts than our thoughts, had permitted this calamity to alight upon His devoted child—the commencement of impaired sight. About this period she incidentally remarked to a friend: "Of all bodily afflictions the *loss of sight* seems to be one of the worst, but yet it is often mercifully accompanied with great peace and inward spiritual light. I know a blind man who is evidently taught by the Holy Spirit in a remarkable manner. He feels so deeply the great glory of the cross of Christ, 'the burning light that shines out from it—*there* you feel the breath of God,' so he expressed himself to me."

Seven weeks went over from the date of Philip's death ; and the first letter in all probability that the childless mother penned was the one, part of which we here insert, written to her constant and loving correspondent, Mrs. Robert Weatherell.

"DOUGLAS, ISLE OF MAN,
"*November* 20, 1866.

"Your letter of loving sympathy ought to be answered, and so ought Robert's very kind letter, written some weeks ago.

"Many letters of condolence have been received without a word of reply from the weary heart smitten down into the dust. Day after day goes by, and I count the days as one counts the hours in a dismal passage over a stormy sea.

"In this sad life we have had to mourn for our first-born, and now to weep bitter tears for an only son. My poor foolish darling Philip—how thankful I should have been to die for him ! But our Heavenly Father knows and orders what is best, and we ought to say to Him, 'Not my will, but Thine be done.' He gives and He takes away at the appointed times and seasons according to His purposes of

infinite love and mercy.   And surely we ought to trust the
loving wisdom of Him who has not spared His only Son,
but freely given Him up for us all.

"It was fully my intention to write to you on Saturday,
but a word hindered me from beginning in good time so as
to have finished a letter that night.   It was a word inad-
vertently spoken when we were at tea, and it made me
rush out of the room upstairs to my usual retreat in the
drawing-room, where I lie down on the floor weeping until
the carpet is wet with my tears.   The word, too sad for me
to repeat, is the usual term applied to the body when life is
departed ; but it smote me to the heart when applied to the
darling son whose return to this desolate house was so un-
speakably awful.

"The only relief from this agony was the memory of our
Redeemer, who said, 'This is *My body* which is given for
you.'

"From that body and that death on Golgotha springs all
our hope for the life to come—the endless life won back for
us by Him who liveth and *was dead* and is alive for evermore.   Very wise and good was your advice to take my
sorrow to the Man of Sorrows.   He has borne the heaviest
burden that ever was borne, the deadly weight of our hateful sins ; and when sorrow comes to us it brings our sins to
remembrance—as the widow of Sarepta cried out to Elijah,
1 Kings xvii. 18.   But the Saviour who came to make an
end of sin will yet make an end of sorrow and of death, for
death shall not always reign—there is another kingdom yet
to come when the will of God shall be done on earth as it is
in heaven.

"When Robert was here he gave me a beautiful meaning
of an expression in Luke xx. 31—'the Exodus' which
Christ should accomplish at Jerusalem.

"There is now in this house an excellent and delightful
book, 'Notes on Exodus,' which would be a feast of manna
to Robert.   As I go on reading, I think how he would

enjoy it but for one drawback, the print not being large
or clear.

.   .   .   .

"You very kindly ask me to visit you at Elton, dear
Lydia—and much I wished it at one time.   But now all is
changed; the summer of this earthly life is gone from me,
buried in the grave of my own Philip,—he used to be with
me at Elton.   And now there is but one spot on earth that
I wish to be borne to, and a change of air beyond this
world.

"It seems as though the Lord had testified against us,
that sin and rebellion have brought down desolation on this
ruined house, so silent now where young voices used to be.
Eight weeks to-day the last letter came from Philip to his
mother,—who is there now to speak that word to me?

"And when will it sound upon my weary heart again?

"Will He who pitied the mother at Nain, restore the
children in the morning, and give the young man back to
his mother?"

Can anything exceed the sublime pathos of this touching
letter?

If any weeping mother reads these pages, surely her heart
will answer to every pang and bitter tear expressed in the
foregoing.   But amidst all let us see that, dark as her
night of trial was, she still trusted in her Redeemer God,
and looked forward to the morning, the bright millennium
morning, of the coming of the Lord Christ; and the reunion
of loved ones now severed by the Jordan of Death.   This
reminds us that on one occasion, but at what period we cannot
say, she had a dream in which she saw her three children
that God had given and then taken away, once more restored
to her.   This dream was an immense comfort to her heart,
as she interpreted it as something like a Divine revelation
that her Philip (of whose portion in eternity she had been
so uncertain) was, as well as baby Henry and saintly Willie,

safe in the bosom of Christ, and awaiting with them the great day of the "coming of the Son of man."

It may be asked, what became of Philip's poor widow all this time? The storm deepens, and extends its spreading gloom. She, poor thing, instead of being able to take in some measure the place of her departed husband in his mother's heart and life, lay in a most critical state. Possibly she was not strong when she married; at all events, after Philip's death, she became a confirmed invalid. Time went over, until in the spring of the next year, she having returned to her parents in Douglas, was seriously ill, the victim of paralysis; and here we quote from another letter of Mrs. Elliott's. It gives a picture of a further account of woe.

"Douglas, Isle of Man,
"*June* 13, 1867.

"Your letter to me was full of kindness and so was Robert's. But my LAST visit to Elton was about eight years ago, when I believe my boy was with me. You liked him and he knew it, and he spoke of you accordingly. In his last letter to me he spoke warmly of his uncle Robert, whom he highly esteemed, with thorough respect for his character and talents. Three years to this day, June 13th, you and Robert came to this house to be present at the foolish marriage. And now the Craigies are in the depth of affliction, watching the sufferings of their only child, of whose recovery they have no hope. On Sunday night Dr. Nelson thought that she could scarcely live until the morning, and a messenger came to us towards midnight, so my husband went up and saw her; and an awful and heart-rending sight it is. He has seen her twice to-day, and I had a glimpse of her for a moment. Humanly speaking, there is no hope of recovery; if she were raised up from her present state of paralysis and exhaustion it would be by such a miracle of healing as in the revival of Jairus' daughter. And the same Hand of Mercy is still as strong to heal and bless and strengthen

them that have no might. He went down into the depth
of weakness and death for our redemption, and in His loving
wisdom and "exceeding largeness of heart" He, in His divine
providence, overrules every event for the highest ultimate
good. But He knows that no affliction for the present is
joyous, but grievous."

Only a little while after this letter was written the poor
sufferer passed away. So ended the sequel to the brilliant
marriage that took place amid festivity and rejoicing only
three years before !

The storm deepens, the waves swell as the wind rises and
blows its icy blast. Another is ill—the kind, long-suffering,
very patient Christian parent and bereaved grandparent, Mrs.
Weatherell. On May 3, 1868, just another year later, she
and Mrs. Elliott were as usual at St. George's Church,
when the evening service over, and every one taking their
departure, Mrs. Weatherell still remained seated. Her
daughter returned for her, and asked her why she did not
come. Mrs. Weatherell answered that she could not stand.
An icy hand was once more laid on poor Mrs. Elliott's heart
—a hand the warning feeling of which she knew too well.
A tremor ran through her frame, and she was conscious
that her mother had been overtaken by a seizure of something like paralysis. As well as her trembling limbs would
bear her she went into the vestry and told Mr. Hawley.
Mr. Hawley brought some of the sacramental wine and gave
it to Mrs. Weatherell. After drinking a little she revived
somewhat but was unable to walk, so she was carried, placed
in a conveyance, and taken home.

"After she came home," Mrs. Elliott writes to her brother,
"she rallied, and she now seems better, thank God. But
she was in a critical state ; and my husband's opinion is
unfavourable, though he says she may recover—and so she
may, for our lives are in the hand of God, who can give
strength to the weak to outlive the strong. Two years to
this day we took leave of our young Philip in this harbour

in this great cemetery of a sin-blighted world.   But the only Son of God died in this world and rose again and conquered death : and so in due season the last enemy shall be destroyed.

"It is a comfort that our mother can speak, and her senses are quite on the alert.   Her left side is affected by what seems to be a stroke of paralysis.   If it please God in His great mercy to spare her life, it would for a season turn away from my almost paralysed heart sorrow upon sorrow.   This house is to me as an awful grave in the valley of the shadow of death.   Yet the valley of Achor may be a door of hope to a home of life and love."

This letter from which the preceding account is taken is blotted with tears.   Mrs. Elliott's writing was generally beautifully legible and clear from any single erasure ; but this one is stained as if many a tear had been shed whilst writing it.   That ejaculation, "If it please God in His great mercy to spare her life, it would for a season turn away from my almost paralysed heart sorrow upon sorrow," is like a dumb cry to the Almighty Father to have mercy— mercy upon His poor child, and to spare her another re-opening of the tomb, and the obliteration of another life from her hearth and home.   It was not to be.   The decree had gone forth to the prince of the power of darkness : "Hast thou considered my servant, that there is none like her . . . a perfect and an upright *woman*, one that feareth God and escheweth evil ?—all that *she* hath is in thy power : only upon *herself* put not forth thy hand."   So the agent of death and of sorrow went forth from the presence of the Lord, free to smite the loved one, and crush deeper down into the dust that gentle bleeding heart so loyal to her God.   Once more was she to be refined as gold, even as fine gold, and made more meet than ever for the Master's use.

The hand of death was laid upon Mrs. Weatherell ; and No. 31 Athol Street was again the abode of unutterable grief—a paralysis of woe.   Mr. Weatherell came over to the funeral ; and the intercourse of this cherished brother was a source of great comfort and support to his sister.

Speaking of this last stroke in a letter to Mrs. Robert—now Mrs. Weatherell—our friend says : " You allude, dear Lydia, to the blank in this house—the sad bereavement which is to me another step downward into the valley of the shadow of death. But as this death is so terrible an enemy, the destruction of all earthly hope, let us be the more thankful to Him who has promised—' I will ransom them from the power of the grave, I will redeem them from destruction,'—the Faithful Promiser having Himself conquered death by dying, having ' fought with him that had the power of death, and this not without great loss of blood to himself,' as Christian says in the ' Pilgrim's Progress.'

"Do you know that beautiful hymn, ' The Pilgrims of the Night'? Robert would tell you that it was sung at this door by about 160 of the school children on that mournful Tuesday, because it was our dear mother's favourite hymn. She seemed to like it better than anything she had ever heard. She remarked to me once that the music seemed to say, ' Angels of Jesus, &c.' The children sang it sweetly as with one voice soaring up to heaven."

The sweet practice of Sunday scholars assembling, as many as possible, at the funeral of one of their schoolfellows, teachers, or any one very specially interested in their particular school, is very prevalent in the Isle of Man. They sometimes sing at the door of the deceased as the body is being placed in the hearse, and then again beside the grave. It is invariably a mark of respect and love ; and the fact that the practice was observed on the occasion of the death of Mrs. Weatherell, proves the young people regarded her as an esteemed and dear friend. Anything sweeter or more heart-stirring than this youthful vocal tribute of praise can scarcely be conceived.

Mrs. Elliott's house being midway between St. George's

School and St. George's Church, every Sunday she used to see the young people pass in the order of two and two, flanked with their teachers, on the way from school to church. It was a sight that peculiarly interested her, and one upon which she often dwelt in deep spiritual thought. Ever since she and her family had become identified with St. George's, she herself had taught in the schools belonging to this church, and she continued to teach there until not many years previous to the close of her devoted life. Inspired by the sight of the Sunday-school scholars' passage to and from school to church, she wrote these lines :—

"SUNDAY-SCHOOL CHILDREN GOING TO CHURCH.

" ' And wherefore is this sound ?' I said,
    Hearing the tread of many feet,
    Of children's footsteps in the street,
As to the House of prayer they speed.

They go from school to church, I know,
    Their way is to the church, said I,
    Because the Nazarene passed by
Our earthly pathways long ago.

A trail of light illumes the earth
    Along the path His footsteps trod ;
    He was our Brother and our God,
His coming was ' a glorious birth.'

A birth of hope, a glad day-break
    To guide the erring feet aright,
    His word was life, His touch was light,
The blind to bless, the dead to wake.

He drew young children to His breast,
    Willing that they His face should see ;
    Saying—'Let children come to Me :'
He blest them, and they shall be blest.

And all are blest who learn to tread
    The upward path to Him above,
    The Lord of life, the God of love,
The man that liveth and was dead.

Therefore it is that here below
    Their way is to the church, said I,
    Because the Nazarene passed by
Our earthly pathways long ago."

CHAPTER XVIII.

"ROB ROY" MACGREGOR.

It will have been inferred from what has gone before that Mrs. Elliott had been repeatedly urged by her relatives at Elton to go and pay them a visit; but over and over again she declined on the ground of her joyless heart, and that formerly when she went there it was in company with her loved son, now no more. Latterly, however, she wrote just after her mother's death, "You and Robert, dear Lydia, are most kind in your pressing invitations to me to visit you at Elton: and who knows what may happen some day?" Accordingly, in the autumn of 1868, she made up her mind to go to the sweet country retreat where, when Willie was taken from her, she had found calm and repose to her shattered heart. On the present occasion when she thought of going, she determined also to visit Barrowden, see Philip's last home, and some of those who valued his short stay and active work amongst them.

Finally in September she took her departure from Douglas. Dr. Elliott probably accompanied her as far as Elton, and then returned, his professional engagements preventing his remaining any time from home. The bright faces of her brother's young family as she entered the peaceful Rectory brought a feeling of rest and refreshment to her weary heart. She stretched out her arms to the sunny fair young creatures, and, pressing them to her bosom, let fall a tear that did not repel, but drew and bound them to her with additional sympathy and love. And then Robert and Lydia—those two dear and kindred souls—how comforting it was she could

find in their company what would only soothe and cheer.
Bravely she bore up, and sought to avoid being a check on
the merriment of youth, or a damper in her intercourse with
her brother and his gentle wife. But, alas! her efforts of
self-control, both before leaving Douglas, and now in company with the dear ones at Elton, proved too much for her
nervous system—combined above all with the resolve she
had made to go on to Barrowden. The latter thought
brought back her Philip's death and all its attendant circumstances so vividly that she seemed to live the sad
experience over again; and one beautiful Sunday evening,
when all was sunshine and joyous calm but her own heart,
her bodily strength failed her, and with an almost fruitless
effort she struggled to go upstairs to bed. She felt very ill,
and a cold shivering came on that warm bed clothing and
heating appliances could not drive away—sometimes shaking
with cold and alternately burning with fever. The doctor
was sent for, and he pronounced the attack to be gastric
fever. How tenderly and lovingly she was watched over
during this period by her relatives, and the children's faithful nurse Hannah, she herself records in more than one of
her letters afterwards. But for many weeks she lay so ill,
that finally her life was despaired of. Can it be wondered
at after the strain of grief she had passed through? The
marvel was that with her fine sensitive organisation she had
been able to bear up so long without a complete break down.
She longed for death during this period, if not at variance
with the will of her God; but it was denied her—she was
to live : He had work for her to do. She must glorify Him
with her brave endurance and firm unflinching trust that
though He afflicted, it was with a Father's hand in mercy,
and not in judgment.

She recovered. The joy manifested by those about her
—it was in itself a welcome back to life. The children
brought her flowers and sang to her; and the very little
ones played quietly at her feet. They loved their dear

Aunt Eleanor, and they must make her smile again! One of that youthful group, now a thoughtful woman, writes of that time as follows: "Grief was written upon her countenance, and impressed itself upon all who saw her; but when she was recovering Mr. Langstaffe used to come over and sing sweetly in English and French pathetic songs which soothed her, though they brought the tears to her eyes, reminding her of days gone by and those she loved and lost. She must have been ten weeks with us before she returned to her lonely desolate house. When she recovered she was not idle, but must be about her Master's business in visiting the few poor in this place, by whom she was welcomed."

Mr. Langstaffe mentioned above had once been a curate at St. George's, Douglas, and consequently was well known to Mrs. Elliott in former days. He was now Mr. Weatherell's nearest clerical neighbour, being vicar of the next adjoining parish. He was a very accomplished man—a linguist and a musician, as well as an able divine.

It was a great solace to our dear friend, when strong enough, to walk quietly from the Rectory to her brother's church close at hand. The calm stillness that pervaded the rural and ancient sanctuary, and the simple orderly service, were in keeping with her feelings, and acted pleasantly upon her tired spirit. It was ever a rest and a joy to listen to her brother reading the prayers, or preaching with his fine voice and thoughtful, earnest tone. Their views on most aspects of Christian teaching and life were in accord, or where one lacked the other supplied what was needed. The elder boys and girls of the Rector's family also sang in the choir, and sweet indeed to their aunt's ears sounded their fresh young voices; and when occasionally Robert, the eldest son, read the lessons, it was a satisfaction to her at the close of the service to encourage the stripling, and urge upon him to follow in his father's steps.

Finally, health being in a measure restored, she left charming Elton, and returned, as her niece expressed it, on her way to her "lonely desolate home," and as she expressed it herself, to that "ruined house, so silent now where young voices used to be."

Her journey was broken midway to Liverpool by spending the night with some relatives, from whom she met with great attention and kindness. They put her on board the *Snaefell* the following morning; and though in early winter, she had a very calm passage, and was able to remain on deck most of the time. The stewardess seeing her, started visibly, and exclaimed, "Why, Ma'am, I thought—thought——"

"That I was dead, stewardess?"

The stewardess's look was sufficient to notify that that was what she meant.

Later on, Mrs. Elliott heard a young sailor remark to some one she did not see at the moment, "Do you know that your old mistress is dead?" "No, she's not," answered a familiar voice, "she's getting well—and—there she is!" And hurrying forward came Jane, a former housemaid (now married), the young woman overcome with surprise and gladness.

In a letter which the traveller wrote on her return home, she says, speaking of the passage across: "Most of the time I spent on deck, sometimes watching the sea and the sky and the pathway of light over the waters towards the setting sun. And when it set behind a grey cloud, I thought of how it was setting behind the trees at Elton."

Four months went over and again we have a letter to Mr. Weatherell. This letter breathes a sweet air of restored calm if not of renewed buoyancy and life. Perhaps there was hardly ever any one who had passed through such deep waters of woe as Eleanor Elliott, and yet rose from them as if shaking from her garments the tear-drops of bitter grief, and standing erect a creature of serene beauty and life, with the smile of heavenly rest upon her face, and in her voice the tone of restored hope and joy and interest in all that

surrounded her.   She could gaze through her tears on the
beautiful world of Nature, and could admire and extol the
works of the artist that sought to portray the glories of that
nature's radiant and varying countenance.   She could speak
with enthusiasm of the great and the good amongst men, or
read with a burning interest the narratives of their noble
worth or of their heroic exploits.   Life with all its teeming
objects of attractiveness was no dead lost thing to her; she
rose with her Saviour victorious over the grave, and beheld
the world and all it contained as the scene of the Redeemer's
future kingdom, when all should bow before Him as King,
and be gathered together in Him as one both of things in
heaven and on earth.   It was His world—His beautiful
world, and one day to be renewed and made as fair again as
Eden before the Fall; and the creatures in it to be restored
to the heavenly image lost when Adam fell.   "For as in
Adam all die, even so in Christ shall all be made alive."
This was her creed, as this letter will show, and which kept
alive the light in her eye, the song in her voice, the life and
the hope in her breast, and the great love to God and man
and all His creatures in her large heart.

> "DOUGLAS, ISLE OF MAN,
> " *March* 16, 1869.

"MY DEAR LYDIA,—Your golden letter made me very
thankful yesterday, telling me that your cough is nearly
well, and that Robert's throat and voice are decidedly better.
It seems as though my poor mother's fears and anxieties
about Robert, at any unusual delay in his letters, were
transferred to me.   Of course these troubled thoughts are
unreasonable enough, for we ought rather to think of Him
whose heart of love and hand of power control all events,
and who has said, ' Why are ye so fearful? how is it that ye
have no faith?'

"What a delightful service for you last Sunday with

Robert and Robbie and Percy * in the pulpit and reading-desk (not that the boys were in the pulpit, though), and all your family in the choir except baby. You have reason to remember Heman the sweet singer in David's time, with his choral family of fourteen sons and three daughters. At the times of restitution perhaps this family will go on singing the songs of Zion which they learned long ago, with the Royal Psalmist Himself as master of the choir.

"In one of John Macgregor's † letters which you have seen, describing his canoe voyage to Damascus, he hopes that hereafter he may speak to Paul of Tarsus about that fair city.

"When I was at Jane's ‡ to-day we were speaking about John Macgregor, and my sister, who was well acquainted with the family (for she had stayed in their house near Dublin), mentioned some lines written by Hannah More § when he was a baby at Bristol after the loss of the *Kent*, and the Macgregors were then intimate with Hannah More. A copy of these lines was given to my sister by Elizabeth Macgregor, John's sister, and Alice ‖ wrote a copy for me this evening.

. . . .

"Last night at nearly midnight I read aloud to my husband your letter, and he was quite pleased to hear you liked the fish. A few days ago, when I repeated to Kelly ¶ Robert's complimentary remarks about the fish-curing and 'his varied

---

* The Rev. R. Weatherell's two eldest sons. "Robbie" (the present Rev. Robert Weatherell) succeeded his father in 1883 as Rector of Elton.

† Rob Roy—John Macgregor—the famous canoe voyager and interesting writer, son of General Sir Duncan Macgregor, K.C.B.

‡ Her sister, Mrs. Grier.

§ Author of "Practical Piety," "Caellis in Search of a Wife," &c.

‖ Miss Alice Grier, Mrs. Elliott's niece.

¶ Kelly, Dr. Elliott's faithful and very *sedate* servant.

and versatile talents, &c.,' a sort of grim smile came over Kelly's face.   He is a sort of Nestor who

"'Smiles in such a sort
As though he scorned to smile.'

"There is now in this room a lovely sunset picture of Loch Awe.   It has been sent up to me this evening, as I admired it so much that I could not help ordering it home.   And if you see it this summer you will admire it too.   You have not yet seen the real Loch Awe, but this picture may suggest some idea of its beauty glowing in the red sunset light.   'It's a far cry to Loch Awe,' as the Campbells say—and it's a far journey to reach it, other people may say who must content themselves with pictures of its fine scenery."

The reference in this letter to John Macgregor, the famous "Rob Roy," will be interesting to those who know his history, and have read his canoe voyages and wonderful exploits.   Mrs. Elliott was personally acquainted with this noted and excellent man.   Her brother-in-law, Colonel Grier, and General Sir Duncan Macgregor, K.C.B., 'Rob Roy's father, were at one time officers in the same regiment, the 93rd Highlanders; and the intimacy between the families had always been kept up.   It was probably at Colonel Grier's house Mrs. Elliott had first met the renowned canoeist.   The comparatively recent death of this remarkable man and unique character will without doubt have refreshed the memory of most as regards his history, and informed others who may not have known before of what he was in himself, and what he was enabled to do as a public and philanthropic worker, especially among the poor. Mrs. Elliott used to speak with beaming eye and glowing enthusiasm of her admiration for the noble "Rob Roy." Being a most fascinating companion and brilliant talker, he had no doubt enchanted her fancy as well as touched her heart with his recital of personal reminiscences and his numerous travels.

It will be remembered (the references to his life being so numerous on the occasion of his death) that his father was not only a most distinguished officer, but also a noble Christian, and that the son inherited these traits, which developed themselves in a way peculiar to his own character and intellectual endowments. When a baby he was with his father and his regiment on board the *Kent*, East Indiaman, when it took fire in the Bay of Biscay; and, to preserve his child's life, Sir Duncan wrapped him up in a blanket and threw him out of the burning ship into a boat, in simple faith that the God who had rescued the infant Moses would also rescue the infant John Macgregor.

It was after this incident that the celebrated Hannah More addressed the lines of which Mrs. Elliott writes, and sent them to the interesting child.

> "TO MASTER JOHN MACGREGOR,
> "*With a Pair of Shoes of my own Knitting.*
>
> "Sweet babe ! twice rescued from the yawning grave,
> The flames tremendous and the furious wave ;
> May a third better life thy spirit meet,
> E'en life eternal at thy Saviour's feet.
>
> "HANNAH MORE.
>
> "BARLEY WOOD, *May 25, 1825.*"

In one of her letters, Mrs. Elliott says : "By to-night's post I have received a letter, from what renowned person do you think?—from Rob Roy—that is, Mr. John Macgregor, and a prettily bound copy of the 'Loss of the *Kent*,' with his autograph at the beginning, in this way—

> "*From the first saved* (page 35).—ROB ROY."

The infant's wonderful preservation no doubt in after years affected and influenced the mind and heart of the mature man; and in return, John Macgregor voted the remainder of his days to the service of his Lord and Redeemer.

At the time that Mrs. Elliott knew him, he had made his first canoe voyage in Europe, the Levant and Holy Land; a voyage—as were all subsequent voyages—undertaken not purely as outlets for his adventurous disposition and love of exploit, but also because they would be the means of widening his range of general knowledge, and giving him an additional acquaintance with men and manners, so that he might the better work for their wellbeing and influence his surroundings *wherever he went* for the honour of his God and the further extension of the kingdom of Christ. Those who have read his works will have noticed how under a vein of humour he uttered the deepest truths, and with the smile on his lip and light in his eye touched the hearts of his hearers, and won their confidence not only in himself, but in the Lord whom he sought to exalt, and to engage all to know, love, and serve. Wherever he went he carried with him tracts of Divine wisdom and instruction to scatter around; and the distribution of these tracts not only left his personal impress on the receivers, but was as seed sown to spring up for the furtherance of the Master's cause in many lands, amongst divers people.

When in England he instituted notably the Shoeblack Brigade, having noticed how abroad persons had their shoes blacked in the streets by those employed for the purpose; and when the Great Exhibition of 1851 took place, Macgregor conceived it would be a grand idea to have a band of young waifs dressed up in scarlet uniform with their blacking brushes, to march through the Exhibition, and then station themselves at different posts, and offer their services to touch up the boots of those who might be inclined to have them so refreshed. The plan was a 'hit;" and now all know the widespread value of the

Shoeblack Brigade—how the poor boys employed often turn out useful and respectable members of the community. He it was, too, who inaugurated the Open-Air Mission; and himself used to hold open air discussions with atheists and atheistic orators, many of whom he silenced, and some of whom, by his arguments, but more perhaps by his philanthropy, he won from error, and brought into the knowledge of the Truth. Macgregor was also Hon. Secretary of the Protestant Alliance, and many other useful associations. A warm supporter of Lord Shaftesbury, he worked hand in hand with him in many of his lordship's noble endeavours.

To Mrs. Elliott his chief charm was that (in the words of one who has written well and truthfully of him) "his aim seemed ever to be to show that Christianity is meant to encourage and elevate the best feelings of our nature, by setting its stamp on every innocent and healthful recreation, with an ultimate view to our own best good and the glory of God." She was so thoroughly healthy herself in all her deep religious convictions, and in what she usually practised, that it was ever a delight and untold refreshment to her to meet with others, who, as children of God, walked truly as children of the Light—devoid of gloom and harshness and illiberality of creed and practice. Not that she was a broad Churchwoman, in the usual acceptation of that term. She was by no means a fellow-thinker and fellow-actor in much with those of the school of Kingsley and Stanley. She, whilst she avoided one extreme, did not fall into the other; her nature was as foreign to latitudinarism as it was to narrow bigotry and assertiveness. In a word, she was, or aspired to be—and to human eye succeeded in being—a wise, humble, transparent, loving follower of Him who was the Light of light and the Wisdom and the Power of God.

CHAPTER XIX.

FAVOURITE AUTHORS.

THAT our friend had a wholesome vein of humour and an ever ready fund of choice repartee, like those often displayed by her hero, Rob Roy Macgregor, is apparent by her apt classical reference when picturing in her letter to Mrs. Weatherell the condescending, half-grudging, yet gratified smile of her sedate man-servant, Kelly, on being complimented on his "varied and versatile talents."

This graceful liveliness in one who had grieved so much was like the outbreak of sunshine amid darkness and storm, all the more beautiful and welcome because unexpected, and by reason of contrasting light and shade, brilliancy and gloom.

These gleams and quiet sallies of fun were very frequent, but the writer in after years remembers on one occasion a ready retort, which especially fastened itself on her recollection. Mrs. Elliott was told of a certain gentleman who in ignorance spoke somewhat slightingly of a lady of her acquaintance, asking in a supercilious sort of way, "Pray *who* is Miss ——?" The lady in question being a person of undoubted consideration, and proud of her standing and antecedents, Mrs. Elliott, highly amused, replied, with a rare smile upon her lips, and suiting the action to the words exactly as Miss —— herself would have done in more mundane language, had she been confronted with the electrifying question :—

> "Know ye not *me!* Ye knew me once no mate
> For you, there *sitting* where ye durst not *soar :*
> *Not to know me argues yourself unknown.*"

And the manner and the tone in which she spoke the lines were inimitable, and as if taking in the whole position of the question with unerring accuracy and keen relish of comprehension.

Her range of literature was extraordinary, quotations from authors of strangely divers orders fell from her lips almost insensibly; and it was well nigh impossible to allude to any writer of note, sacred or profane, but what she was thoroughly up in his works, and able to expatiate on his style and general characteristics. To attain to this profuse as well as profound knowledge it was necessary for her to spend much of her sleeping hours, even into early morning, poring over books. Her thirst for reading, along with the bitter tears she had shed, tended to affect her sight very considerably, and often caused her husband to implore of her to desist from this unnatural practice of night-study; more especially now that her body was so weakened by sorrow and recent illness—not to speak of the hard usage it had to undergo from long abstinence from food when visiting among the poor, and often from voluntary fasting, for, without doubt, she fasted as a means of bringing her body in subjection to the spirit. Of this perhaps more anon.

In the meantime we must regard her as evidencing by the grace of God a marvellous mastery over personal afflic-tion, and resolving to give herself up if possible more un-reservedly than ever to the service of the King, glorying in her trials if by them she could honour Him the more.

Amongst the books she carefully read and considered about the period that she was, so to speak, recovering from her repeated blows of grief, was Newman's "Apologia Pro Vitâ Suâ."

Writing to Mrs. Weatherell she says:—"This morning in reading some pages of Newman's *curious* Apologia, I felt inclined to read aloud to Robert (as when he was here) some passages, but no speaking-trumpet could convey the words so far over sea and land."

Curious indeed must this work have appeared to her whose theological views were so distinct and well formulated in their clear utterance and expression of Truth. She could not have regarded it as anything else than a display of misguided intelligence and erratic imagination. Yet that she could admire the genius of the author, at the same time that she sadly smiled at his audacious whimsicality of sentiment and declaration, is without doubt. Prone rather to pity than censure, many a prayer would she offer during the perusal of the volume for the genius that was too evidently doomed to singe its wings and destroy its true spiritual usefulness in the idolatrous flame of its own kindling.

Her knowledge of Scripture was so profound and extensive that she may be almost said to have known it, chapter and verse throughout, by heart; and did she hear a sermon faulty in doctrine or in spiritual tendency, she was miserable, and could not rest until she had pointed out the error to the preacher, however painful the effort to do so might be. It was laid upon her conscience, and she must speak. Life or death might depend upon the utterance. The Rev. A. Hoskins, Vicar of St. James's, Cheltenham, her old friend of bygone days, writes: "She was a woman of unusual intellectual power, of much reading, of clearest theological views and those well established, and above all of sincere and exalted piety; and though not censorious, yet as a candid friend, would deal with the erring one."

Writing of her remarkable acquaintance with Scripture, one is also reminded of her equally accurate knowledge of the "Pilgrim's Progress" and "Holy War": the first of these she could recollect almost word for word. A biography amongst a multitude of others, of which in later years she used to speak a great deal, was the "Life of James Hinton," in which altruism is the prevailing theme. The following extract from this work she would repeat, as if it were burnt into her heart as well as stamped upon her memory. "We see that if He sends us sorrows and difficulties, He only sends them because they are the true blessings, the things that are truly good, what He Himself took when He too was a man amongst us. He would have us like Himself with a happiness like His own, nothing below it, and so, as His own happiness is in sorrow and infirmity, and ever assisting and giving, and sacrificing Himself, He gives us sorrows too, which are not the ills we should think them, but are what we should be most happy in, if we were perfect, and had knowledge like Him. So there is a use and service in all which we bear in all we do, which we do not know but which He knows, and which in Christ He shows to us."

"In Memoriam," since she had passed through yet deeper waters of sorrow, was more than ever a text-book of her heart's most sacred feelings. How tenderly she would repeat those lines descriptive of Mary, the sister of Lazarus, in the presence of Jesus, after His raising of her brother from the dead :—

> " Her eyes were homes of silent prayer,
>   Nor other thought her mind admits
>   But, he was dead, and there he sits,
> And he that brought him back is there.
>
> Then one deep love doth supersede
>   All other, when her ardent gaze
>   Roves from the loving brother's face,
> And rests upon the Life indeed.
>
> All subtle thought, all curious fears,
>   Borne down by gladness so complete,
>   She bows, she bathes the Saviour's feet
> With costly spikenard and with tears.
>
> Thrice blest whose lives are faithful prayers,
>   Whose loves in higher love endure ;
>   What souls possess themselves so pure,
> Or is their blessedness like theirs ? "

We think we see her as, in after years, she used to murmur these lines half to herself and half to her hearer, her gaze meanwhile penetrating, as it were, a far off and holy region of thought and sight only discernible by herself.

Of missionary records, the lives of the heroes of the Gospel in distant uncivilised lands, the Life of Moffat held a foremost place in her estimation. Her love and admiration for him were unbounded; and were intensified from the fact that he was personally acquainted with Mrs. Deeping, an aunt of Mrs. Robert Weatherell's; and from Mrs. Deeping she heard reminiscences of his life related by himself that drew him the closer to her heart.

Mrs. Deeping was a most holy woman, and an intimate friend of Mrs. Elliott's. She was a true missionary in spirit, and delighted in nothing more than opening her house and purse to the requirements of the soldiers of the cross. Moffat once stayed with her; and it was for her album he composed, and with his own hand inscribed in it, the lines so often quoted since in missionary journals :—

> " My Album is the savage breast
> Where darkness broods and tempests rest
> Without one ray of light.
> To write the name of Jesus there,
> And point to worlds both bright and fair,
> And see the savage bow in prayer,
> Is my supreme delight."

The verses so delighted Mrs. Elliott that she never forgot them, and often referred to them.

When talking about her hero Moffat to her young nephews and nieces and others, she used to say : " The young, grand man—God's gentleman—when only nineteen, left his post as gardener, and went forth to endure dreadful hardships among the Bechuanas for *fifty* years ! "

And then, in her own graphic way, she would describe how he often had to tie a belt round his body to quell the pangs of hunger ; and how the Bechuanas would roll upon the ground shrieking with laughter when he told them that

God was love; their idea of love or anything nice being *diseased meat.*

Travel interested her intensely, and when reading the extraordinary adventures of Charles Waterton, she did not share the common belief that his accounts ·were for the most part over-coloured or altogether fabrications; and that she was right, after confirmation of the narrator's statements very fully proved.

Prophecy, and conjointly with it astronomy, she studied largely, and conversed upon with her brother whenever they met.

Amongst prophetical works, she studied very closely, and with great delight, Elliott's "Horæ Apocalypticæ." It was no doubt additionally attractive to her, being the production of one who was uncle to Sir Charles Elliott, the present Governor of Bengal, who married Louisa, one of the beautiful daughters of the late George William Dumbell, Esq. of Belmont, Douglas—a family in whom Mrs. Elliott was always interested, on account of the affection she had had for their mother.

Amongst purely religious writings of the evangelical school, in addition to those of Neander and others already mentioned, our friend valued very highly the works of Pascal, M'Cheyne, Guthrie, Simeon of Cambridge, Chalmers, Monod, Adolphe Saphir, Punshon, Spurgeon, &c.

Amongst religious mystics, with whom she had a strong affinity, she delighted in Fénélon, Madame Guyon, and others of the great Jansenist leaders and reformers of Roman Catholicism.

We remember with what intense interest she read the "History of Port Royal," by Mrs. Schimmelpenninck, in which the character of the Mère Angélique is so ably depicted—the young and beautiful abbess who, in her teens, set about the reformation of the great convent over which she presided, and brought all her family, the distinguished Arnaulds, under her powerful and regenerating influence.

K

Of philosophical writers she may have had her favourites, but of those who were *not* was Carlyle, to whom, or perhaps more particularly to his style, she had an unmeasured dislike.

"His style," said she, "is execrable ; it reminds one of *a heavy cart rumbling over a newly macadamised road !*"

Style had an immense deal to do with her likes and dislikes of authors. It was no doubt the exquisite perfection of rhythm and polished refinement of diction generally that charmed her as much as anything in Tennyson. Any approach to incorrectness or uncouthness in speech or composition discomfited her almost visibly. Whereas a cultivated tone, harmony of thought, and ease and grace of expression, as visibly enchanted her ear, put her at her ease, and met a response in her beaming countenance. In evidence of this, the Rev. E. W. Kissack, Rector of Ballaugh, Isle of Man, writes : "Mrs. Elliott was at Oxford during the great Oxford movement, and she has told me how she still remembered at St. Mary's the wonderful reading of the Scriptures by John Henry Newman, then Fellow of Oriel. She never, she said, could forget the power of his reading, and how it seemed to open out the Scriptures to her in a new light. The man's face and manner lingered in her memory like the effect of some great picture by a great master. He was a master of English, and knew how to render it ; and in his own memory the echoes of the English Bible lingered like the sound of sweet bells of childhood to the end of his days."

The very soul of poetry herself, her knowledge of poets and their writings was such, that to measure it would be a puzzle as to where to begin and where to end.

Not to speak of Chaucer, Spenser, &c., of the remote English period she was perfectly familiar with the less noted celebrities of the Elizabethan age, Raleigh and others.

Then the great songsters of Latin and Greek antiquity,

she had a mind to appreciate, reading them of course in translations. Whereas with England's Shakespeare, Herbert, Milton, and others that followed them down to modern times, she was unreservedly at home; and in each, at least with few exceptions, there were points at which mutual intelligence, fancy, or sentiment touched and were at one.

Herbert's quaint muse she loved; Moore's hymns, too, she was very fond of, especially the one beginning—

> "Thou art, O God, the life and light
> Of all this wondrous world we see;
> Its glow by day, its smile by night
> Are but reflections caught from Thee.
> Where'er we turn Thy glories shine,
> And all things fair and bright are Thine."

Keble was at her fingers' ends; Scott was a joy and a day-dream to her; Byron she met on the descriptive ground, regarding his word-painting of Nature as grand and true, and his Hebrew melodies in keeping with the sacred sublimity of his subject. Wordsworth, Elizabeth Barrett, and Felicia Hemans have already been noticed as especial favourites.

And as for the mighty geniuses who stand foremost on the poetical list of different climes, she trod with them the beauteous paths of fancy, and on the Olympian heights, feasted with them on the nectar of their glorious imagery, philosophic discernment, and exquisite diction; but wherein any failed in chastity of thought, truth, and reverence of feeling, she turned sorrowfully away, and could not participate in their glowing page. Not for her was the sweetest or noblest strain shorn of moral and spiritual significance and grace.

Though this omnivorous reader included amongst her literary bill of fare varied forms of fiction and secular products of many kinds, she had a habit both touching and beautiful, which she especially observed in the presence of

the young.   It was to read, or cause to be read, a portion of
the Divine Word before ever opening a secular volume—
emphasising by this practice the Scriptures, "The entrance
of Thy word giveth light," and "Seek ye first the kingdom
of God, and His righteousness; and all these things shall be
added unto you."

CHAPTER XX.

CORRESPONDENCE.

In keeping with her versatility of reading was also her versatility of writing. Her delightful letters to her young relatives furnish a sample of this. To the weak became she as weak, that she might gain the weak—all things to all—for the Gospel's sake ; that she might by all means woo and win love and devotion, not for herself, but for Jesus her Lord. Her mission was to extend the kingdom of Christ in every possible way and wherever possible.

The following from a letter to little Alice Weatherell is a specimen of her attractive power of unbending to the level of the understanding and attainment of her correspondent :—

"You do not remember my face, because when I was at Elton last you were a very little child, not much more than a baby, going about on the grass after your mamma, like a little lamb. I remember the look of your fair hair in that pretty garden in the summer time. Now you are so much grown up that you can read and write, and nurse the baby Maude, the sweet little sister who was sent to you last year. You can learn from the New Testament how the Lord Jesus, the Good Shepherd, loves His little lambs. And as He is so very kind and gentle, you should say to Him, 'Lord Jesus, teach me to love Thee.' The more you love Him the happier you will be now and always. And though you do not see His lovely face now, yet He sees you and takes care of you every minute. And He has given you a happy home with your kind papa and mamma and brothers and sisters."

A picture of grave beauty introduced into a letter of like

adaptability to the age and appreciation of her nieces when older is this :—

"Yesterday I was not out all day, but your uncle went a long way on a journey of kindness. He went to Kentraugh, beyond Castletown, to Mr. Gawne's, in quest of ice to lay on the head of the young hospital doctor, dangerously ill with typhus fever. No ice could be had in Douglas, and there was none at Kentraugh, though they have ice-houses there. To-night it is not required, for the young head is cold enough, and the warm young heart ceased to beat this morning. On Saturday night he seemed better, and better yesterday. In October this young Englishman * came to Douglas, and bravely and kindly he has done his work in the hospital, and from house to house visiting the poor of this town—over much work—for in one day it is said that he visited ninety persons or houses. He caught a violent fever from an outdoor patient; and to-day, when your uncle Elliott was in the room with him and his mother and brother, the kind young man breathed his last, and the broken-hearted mother sank fainting on the floor.

"May the blessed Saviour who has passed through death speak peace to her heart, and may His Spirit sustain and comfort her ! This sad event has been very grievous to me to-day, though I was but slightly acquainted with the young man, having only spoken to him twice; but I heard so much of his kindness. And such brave warm human hearts are not very common in this selfish world."

Of another stamp altogether we have the correspondent's acknowledgment of Christmas gifts from her nieces — a sprightly little bit of descriptive painting of the same order as that so usual in her conversation :—

"Many thanks for the beautiful and comfortable presents which you have so kindly made and sent to me. When the postman's knock was heard at the door on Saturday it was

* Fothergill was the name of the young doctor.

answered by Eleanor Grier, who came back into the room with her hands well filled with letters from her Elton cousins, and also with the large parcel, which was opened and its handsome contents unfolded before the admiring gaze of the company in this room, namely, Eleanor, her mamma,* Mrs. Louis Howard, and your old aunt Eleanor, who thanks you heartily for your warm and seasonable benefactions. Some hours elapsed before the letters from Eleanor and Alice were read. And then your uncle had the pleasure of hearing that the soft and pretty grey muffatees were for him. He is greatly obliged to Alice and he will put them on for her sake, and he hopes to write to her soon. But at present it is almost as impossible for him to do such a thing as it would be for a bird on the wing to write a letter.

"So Marian and Alice will understand that though he does not write it is not because he does not think of them.

"It is said that 'fine feathers make fine birds,' therefore I ought to be a very fine old bird with all the finery that is upon me at this moment—the rich purple shawl on my shoulders, and the bright scarlet slippers on my feet. But with all this grandeur I must try not to be quite as proud as a peacock—though my shawl and slippers are so extremely pretty and so very well made.

"With love to your papa and mamma and to Alice, Herbert, and darling little Maud, and to the shawlmaker and shoemaker, believe me, my dear girls, your affectionate aunt,   ELEANOR ELLIOTT."

And here follows a picture of truly exquisite feeling and touching beauty—an incentive to solemnise and instruct the hearts of her young friends :—

"Last week," she writes, "I sent a *Herald* to your papa in which was a poem containing ever so many Manx names, and narrating an old battle of the days of long ago, when the

* Sister of George William Dumbell, Esq. of Belmont.

fierce old sea-kings from Norway and Denmark used to
ravage the Manx coast and other coasts. They were very
bad old times, and we may be thankful that our Lord
Christ has spoken peace to the heathen, and that a day
will come when there shall be an end of war and strife and
sin. For the kingdom of the Lamb will surely come.

"A very dear and gentle child * who belongs to that
kingdom died on Friday evening, peacefully and happily.
His face was lovely, beaming with sweetness and intelligence,
and in his heart was the love of Jesus. He endured great
pain with patience, saying, 'What is it to the pain of Jesus?'
But now the pain is all over; it came to an end on Friday
evening, when it seemed that a heavenly light came to light
him home. He lay on a couch in the kitchen, for he was
too ill to be carried upstairs, and his mother and aunt were
with him. There was no gas-light or candle-light in the
kitchen, and the fire was low and dim. 'Mother,' said he,
'what light is that?' 'Willie,' said she, 'it is night.' 'I
know that, mother,' he said, 'I see a light you cannot see,'
and he laid down his head and died.

"He was eleven years of age, this dear child of light—of
such is the kingdom of heaven—and very lovely it is to see
such fruits of the Spirit, such patience, meekness, and love."

A friend writes, "Mrs. Elliott was a believer in dreams."
And we may say with truth that *exceptional* dreams under
exceptional circumstances were frequently considered by her
of prophetic import and divinely sent. We have seen what
comfort she herself derived from a dream that presented to
her the re-union with herself of her three sons. And on one
occasion, after dreaming about seeing her mother, she wrote
to her brother: "It seems to me a great comfort to be allowed
to see our friends in visions of the night; to meet them in
dreamland, as in a spiritual world, which for the time is as
real as this waking world. How thankful I should be to

* A child of humble parentage whom Mrs. Elliott used to visit.

spend every night with William, Henry, and Philip. But they will come again from the land of the evening, because of the birth and death and resurrection of the Prince of Life. We look for the resurrection and the life."

And no doubt dreams of warning as well as of assurance were often weighed by our friend in her own case, as in that of others, with grave interest and significant inquiry.

The correspondent whose remark we quoted writes :—

"One bright day in spring, the spring of 1864, I remember meeting Mrs. Elliott. I was with my sister Maggie. She stopped us and said to Maggie (who was then in *perfect health*), 'Oh, Maggie, I dreamt of you last night—you were dressed all in white;' and I said, 'Maggie, you are going to be a spirit in heaven!' Strange to say, a few months later my sister was *a spirit in heaven*, having died in August. When I mentioned the circumstance afterwards to Mrs. Elliott, and told her how her dream affected me when Maggie began to be ill, she said, 'Oh yes, I knew when I heard of her illness she would not recover—that dream warned me not to expect it.'"

Though we mention the subject of Mrs. Elliott's belief in dreams, it is with reserve, as she herself, perhaps, would have done. Nothing she feared more than by any ideas or sentiments of her own, not essentially matter of divine and necessary credence, to mystify or mislead the faith of any one.

With the same reserve we would allude to her habit of *fasting* at special seasons and under special circumstances. She never spoke of her practice to any one herself; and it was only those who were in close intimacy with her perceived how in every point she sought to follow in the steps of the Master. He fasted and prayed; she did so too. He suffered hunger and cold, and spent nights in heavenly communion and prayer; she humbly and falteringly followed where He led, identifying herself with His holy sufferings that she might the closer enter into His great heart of love and spirit of divine self-sacrifice. Her life was one of absolute communion with her Saviour and unceasing prayer. Prayer was the habitual breath of her soul rising on behalf of all with whom she came in contact. Did she meet with any one in every respect companionable and pleasant, yet an alien from the kingdom of grace, she never took them to task, and thrust the pearl of salvation by faith into their unwilling acceptance. No, she prayed, prayed continuously, that the Spirit *Himself* would deal with the poor erring heedless soul, ready to perish for the lack of the truth as it is in Christ Jesus. And praying, she watched, watched for that precious soul; and we believe in most cases it was permitted to her to lead the benighted wanderer into the fold of the true Shepherd. The Rev. Wm. Hawley, who, knew her so well, and fathomed the secret and power of her holy devoted life, writes :—"Two traits were very conspicuous in her. First, while so spiritually minded and holy, she was so perfectly free from all shibboleth, twaddle, or cant; which is so offensive to persons of taste, especially if not decidedly godly. Again, she was so full of sympathy, she always entered really into your feelings if you had anything to tell; she listened not merely for the sake of being polite, but she made the matter personal to herself, because *she loved her neighbour as herself.* Most self-denying as regarded self-indulgence of any kind, she was 'firm as an oak' when she had made up her mind."

Truly, her beautiful tact and fulness of sympathy, as noted by Mr. Hawley, enhanced the power of every word that fell from her lips, and rendered even her silence eloquent. May we like her cry, "Lord, deliver us from *ourselves !*—humble *self*—keep me low at Thy cross, that Thou mayest be all in me; and I myself but a voice—a movement—a sign for Thee !"

CHAPTER XXI.

FRANCO-PRUSSIAN WAR.

IT was the year 1870, a memorable year in the annals of Europe, as well as in those of the friend whose individual history we strive in some degree to commemorate in these pages.

It was the year of the outbreak of the Franco-Prussian war, when Europe shook with the noise of that conflict which brought such disaster to the aggressive power; and such gain and ascendency to the power invaded and recklessly defied. It was in April of this year our friend, startled and saddened by the agitations of the times, had another reason for fear and great misgiving. And as we are about to name it, we are insensibly reminded of the saying of the much tried and patient Job, "The thing which I greatly feared is come upon me, and that which I was afraid of is come unto me."

Gradually her precious sight had been more and more waning; and the volumes that she loved so dearly were becoming less and less decipherable; and the heart that had been so desolated was once again to be, in course of time, the abode of a dreaded and yet greater isolation and desolation.

Those of us who have in full preservation our faculty of sight, how little can we realise what it must be to have it withdrawn: and especially terrible was it, we may well believe, in the case of one whose vision was, humanly speaking, now her chief source of gratification and almost only solace. Without it—how—how sad! No more intercourse with the great and the good of bygone ages, or of living but remote ideal acquaintances. No more feeding on the wealth of their intelligence, and the sweetness and the beauty of their kindred spirits! And sadder, more crushing still, no more gazing on that beauteous world of nature—that theme of perpetual rapture—that mirror of the face of an all-glorious and beneficent Creator!

In her distress she sought advice; and the result of it was that she must go away and consult some eminent oculist. Finally the one recommended was Dr. Meurer, a famous German eye-surgeon. He was this year in London, and the opportunity to see him was favourable.

In April of 1870 she took her departure, and on the way visited once again the dear ones at Elton. From them she received all the hope and encouragement they could bestow as to her final recovery from the affliction that was threatening to cast its dark pall upon and envelop in gloom the remaining years of her chastened existence.

Dr. Meurer was seen. He pronounced the disease to be cataract, but said nothing could be done for the present. He would in the meantime prescribe for an application, but in a year or two he must see her again.

In September she returned to Douglas, and it was this month that the writer first became positively acquainted with her. It was at a picnic given by our vicar, Mr. Hawley, and Mrs. Hawley.

The picnic was at Glen Meay, and the writer, being the only juvenile of the party, kept a good deal in the rear, taking refuge, for the most part, under the wing of Mrs. Hawley.

Concealment, however, was not to be permitted for long. Mrs. Elliott had followed the recluse with her sympathetic eye, and very soon induced her to emerge from her hiding; and instinctively the young girl felt she had gained a friend in the gentle quakeress-looking lady, of whom she had often heard, but of whom personally she knew little.

In the evening, on our return from the picnic, we all assembled at Mrs. Moffat's, at 20 Finch Road. It is only necessary to name that name to recall to many insular minds a family of noted courtesy and Christian benevolence. Miss Elizabeth Moffat, who is very musical, played beautifully the evening in question, and Mr. Hawley, so beloved by us all and so accomplished in mind, delighted us with many a graceful poetical reference and quotation. A stranger, a learned divine, interested us with a flow of ready converse on many themes, heightened by a brilliant imagination and ready humour; whilst Mrs. Elliott, in whose presence it was impossible for any one to be dull, kept the ball rolling with perpetual variety of suggestion and charming approval. How calmly bright—how benign was her countenance, and how elevated and elevating every word that fell from her lips; how kindly and graceful her deferential regard and consideration for others; how ready she was to say the pleasing word, to *look* the affectionate thought! The writer, though young and far from sedate, succumbed to the influence of this ennobling nature, and henceforth bowed before a power she felt, and which, though only in a degree, she could analyse and explain.

And here we will endeavour to present the appearance, as when first we knew her, of this friend whose life was like that of a silent stream, permeating alike with its elevating holy influence the haunts of the poor and debased, and the homes of the wealthy and refined.

She was at this time about fifty-seven years of age. Her stature was somewhat diminutive and slight rather than the reverse; her head evenly balanced and very compact in its development; the form of her face a full oval, her skin very fair and smooth—almost no wrinkles; her brow clear and expansive, her eyes a quiet brown, her nose large and aquiline but well formed, indicating by its size and certain marked lines at the corner of each nostril a character of vigour and great determination; her mouth gentle and clearly cut, but also emphasised at the corners with grave decided lines. Her chin had a like pronounced contour; on her brow rested smooth silky grey hair, which contrasted harmoniously with the clear complexion and grave sweet look of the general expression of the face.

It was a face of strangely calm endurance, utter *guilelessness*, and yet of a passionless strength; strong and sweet were the features, and very restful the bearing of the whole figure even to the matter of dress, which was invariably black, relieved about the throat and hands with white lace or muslin. Looking at her one would say, that is a nature which can no longer be moved by the blandishments or agitated by the fears of a vain uncertain world; the waves of sorrow and disappointment and care may have beat upon it with all their force, but the storm has been weathered—the anchor is fixed, the sails are set as of a vessel waiting the tide to enter its harbour of rest.

Between September of 1870 and April of 1871 public sympathy in Douglas had been largely called out on behalf of the sufferers of the Paris siege. Amongst those still exposed to the dangers of the times in France were the Rev. Edward * and Mrs. Forbes and their family. This was the same Mr. Forbes who, before the appointment of Mr. Hawley, was Incumbent of St. George's, Douglas. From Douglas he went, it will be remembered, to Paris to the Church of the Rue d'Aguesseau, having been appointed chaplain to the British Embassy.

The reign of anarchy, however, had begun in France, and it needed no additional cause to make it the painful subject of many minds, and the general theme of conversation amongst persons interested in their fellow-creatures, and the events of contemporary history.

Mrs. Elliott writes on September 5, 1870, in her usual graphic way: "The air is pure and pleasant now after the

---

* Afterwards the Rev. E. Forbes, D.D., Vicar of St. Olives, Old Jewry, London.

storms at the beginning of this month. When September comes it seems that summer is gone—the very name has an autumnal sound; and the wind and rain sobbing and sighing last week seemed to bewail the departing summer. Within the space of two months the war storm in Europe has swept an Emperor from his throne; and now the Republic in France takes up the war-cry."

April 4, 1871, she writes: "A few minutes since the Manx volunteers marched through this street in the moon-light, the band playing a lively tune. It is to be hoped that they will never be required to play the part of National Guards. Paris is in an awful plight with the red flag of Terror waving over the grand palaces of the Louvre and Tuileries.

"In to-day's paper there is an account of a battle between the Government army and the insurgents, 'the National Black-guards,' as they have been well described. What a mournful Christmas Paris has passed through, and now what an Easter is approaching! These wild Communists in one of their proclamations speak of the 'redemption,' and the 'regeneration' which the country requires; but they expect it from their idol, 'the Republic,' and not from the true Redeemer, who died on Calvary to redeem and regenerate the slaves of sin. These Communists, it is said, have ordered all ministers of religion to leave Paris."

Sometime during the early period of the war (the date in her letter is not given), she, writing to her nieces, says: "If you were here now, your young eyes and voices would be often employed in reading aloud the newspapers. In this horrible, hateful war there are two objects of personal interest to me—one Prussian, the other French—the kind and clever German oculist, Dr. Meurer—who, I trust, with all his household, may escape uninjured; and the pale gentle boy, the Prince Imperial, the young lad of fourteen, who ought to have been kept away from the horrors of this

wicked war. Certainly the course of events in France is
like a comment on the Scripture word, 'Scatter thou the
people that delight in war.' The French, with their false
notions of glory, are learning a terrible lesson. It is to be
hoped that a timely peace may save Paris from ruin."

In the summer of 1871 Dr. and Mrs. Elliott visited
Coniston, and on their return to Douglas found some of
the young people from Elton, and Hannah their nurse, at
their house in readiness to welcome them back. This was
about the beginning of a long series of visits that the young
Weatherells afterwards annually paid to their uncle and
aunt. At the close of their present visit, Dr. and Mrs.
Elliott themselves prepared to leave Douglas again—this
time for Germany, as Mrs. Elliott had made up her mind
to visit Dr. Meurer once more, and ascertain from him the
expediency of operating now upon her eyes.

The following delightful little note was written by her
to her brother when she and Dr. Elliott had just crossed
by the steamer from Douglas to Liverpool—written *on the
wing;* and yet how fair and sweet it is—breathing, as
always, the native air of her poetical and loving soul!

"Lime St. Station, Liverpool, 7 min. to 3 p.m.,
"*August* 4, 1871.

"John Bunyan describes the River of Life as 'curiously
beautiful with lilies.' Our house has been beautiful with
very fair lilies for a few summer days, and now they are
transplanted again to their own peaceful garden at Elton.
. . . We are gratified to find that the dear girls were so
pleased with their visit, and content to remain with us.
Their uncle again and again said, 'We miss the children.'
You may tell their mamma that they were pleasant, affectionate, and obliging, and it was a pleasure of hope to
expect them and Hannah, and it is a pleasure of memory
to think that they have been with us so lately.

"We have had a fine passage to-day, thank God. We came in five hours. The sea and the sky were beautiful and blue and quiet. We are waiting for the 4 o'clock train for London."

After apparently a month of travel and sojourn in different places, the travellers finally arrived at Coblenz, whence the following was penned :—

"HOTEL DE GÉANT, COBLENZ,
"*September* 12, 1871.

"Through the good hand of our Heavenly Father we have been brought safely to this beautiful place to-day. Our room overlooks the Rhine (Wacht am Rhein), and at the opposite side of the river is the grand fortress of Ehrenbreitstein (the broad stone of honour), almost as strong as Metz, as a soldier told me this evening. We left Cologne this morning, at a quarter to nine, and had a charming sail up the Rhine in a fine American steamer, passing on our way the 'castle crags of Drachenfels,' and arrived here about three in the afternoon. We soon set out in quest of Dr. Meurer. It was rather a long walk, as his house is some way out of the town. But the kindness of two German young ladies was something extraordinary — one came out from her hall door and walked a little way with us, and another went on patiently walking beside us for nearly a quarter of a mile until she could point out the very house. A handsome house it is, in a pretty country situation; and after we had sat waiting some time on the balcony outside the drawing-room, Mrs. Meurer, who had been out driving, I believe, returned, and then the doctor appeared on horseback. He was very kind and courteous, and carefully examined my eyes with an ophthalmoscope, and said that the disease had made no progress; and he slightly altered the prescription, ordering something else, something stronger, instead of spirits of lavender, to be mixed with the iodide of potash. I have reason to be thankful for the opinion thus expressed; it is a great mercy from the Author and Giver of light. And the Saviour, who blessed the clay and the waters of Siloam, is still the Good Physician.

On our return from Dr. Meurer's house we came back to this quay, and walked across the bridge of boats to the other side of the Rhine to visit the mineral spring of Ehrenbreitstein. Marian and Alice will remember the cup which Mrs. Harris * gave to their uncle that he might drink of this spring, which she had found invigorating. And he did drink of it, and drank her health there, and so did I. It is strong iron water. Two soldiers escorted us to this place with much civility, as it was not easy to find the way. We may probably (D.V.) leave here to-morrow."

Our next news of the travellers is contained in the following:—

"DOUGLAS, ISLE OF MAN,
"*Sept.* 30, 1871.

"Through the continued care of our Heavenly Guardian we have been brought home in safety this evening. On Thursday, on arriving at Boulogne from Paris, we found that a telegram had been sent to prevent the boat from sailing to Folkestone that day, as the equinoctial tempest was so wild. And yet the next day (yesterday) the sea was so subdued by Him who ruleth the waves thereof, that we passed over quickly and calmly in an hour and three-quarters to Folkestone. Thence by train to London, and last night to Liverpool; and this morning, or rather at 1 P.M., we passed over a glittering sea, bright with sunshine and quite calm. It was a pleasant passage of

* Wife of Samuel Harris, Esq., now Vicar-General of the Isle of Man.

five hours and three minutes. In this we have reason to be thankful.

"On our return from the Coniston excursion in summer we were greeted at the door by the fair young faces of Marian and Alice—a pleasant and a cheerful sight. When this journey of earthly life is ended, may we all be welcomed by the gracious Redeemer, who is the light of the heavenly home!

"On Sunday last, at the Chapelle Evangélique in the Avenue de la Grande Armée, what a wonderful sermon was preached by Eugène Bersier on Rom. viii. 15! What a word of reconciliation, sweet and winning as the voice of an angel! He is considered the best preacher in France, and he is greatly respected and beloved. In the morning and evening we attended the English services in the Rue d'Aguesseau, where Mr. Forbes preached well and faithfully. And on Monday morning we breakfasted with Mr. Forbes."

CHAPTER XXII.

THE LINK OF FRIENDSHIP.

EUGÈNE BERSIER mentioned in the last letter was the golden link that first bound the heart of Mrs. Elliott to that of her young friend, the memorialist. It came about in this way. The latter was lent a volume of Eugène Bersier's sermons in the original French; and she was so struck with their freshness, beauty, and extraordinary philosophical and analytical power, that she could not rest until she had found one who would appreciate them along with her; and such she conceived of all people would be Mrs. Elliott. Accordingly one Sunday, as both were leaving the Sunday-school, the memorialist ventured to address her ideal acquaintance, and ask her if she was familiar with the name of Bersier, and with any of his works; and if not, might she be allowed to borrow from a friend for her a volume of his sermons that she had just read herself? "No," was the answer, "I do not know the name at all; and I think I'll not mind reading the sermons. One sees so many sermons!"

Memorialist was sorely disappointed, and went her way with a feeling of intense regret at her heart. Happily the following Sunday, Mrs. Elliott had been led to change her mind, and going up to the young lady, she said, "Will you after all be so kind as to borrow for me the volume you mentioned of Bersier's sermons? I have made inquiry about him, and I am told he is one of the greatest of French pulpit orators, and in every respect a most interesting man."

Delight was depicted on our countenance in return for the confirmation of our good opinion of the preacher, and for being permitted to have the privilege of getting the book in question for one whose further acquaintance we longed so much to have, and whose sympathy with Bersier's productions we humbly felt would coincide with our own. And so it proved. And then began an intimacy between that noble soul and the writer, which every interview was to deepen and render more precious and permanent. In a very short time, one evening every week was set apart by Mrs. Elliott for us to meet and read together Bersier and other kindred authors. Delightful evenings they were—unique and outstanding in a lifetime! In her presence one felt in another and higher region, and as if breathing an atmosphere purified and sanctified by all that was lovely and ennobling.

Bersier's brave conduct during the Communistic insurrection in Paris was told by our friend the first evening we took tea together. She mentioned how she had heard that he publicly denounced the murder of the Archbishop of Paris; and that his daring reflection on the cruel public wrongs enacted at that time had brought down upon him the displeasure of the incensed masses, and in retaliation they had committed him to prison and condemned him to death. But subsequently, the tide of public affairs having changed, he was released and restored to his privileges as a minister of the Gospel and a loyal and devoted French patriot. But, added Mrs. Elliott, the terrible privations he suffered during the siege, and the agony of suspense regarding the issue of his imprisonment and the well-being of his fugitive family had told so upon his constitution that after his release he was stricken with an illness from which recovery for a while was pronounced doubtful. His church during the siege he had turned into an hospital, and with his own hands he ministered to the wounded and dying; and spared not his life, if need were, in his care of others. On the return of peace, this valiant and good man was rewarded by the presentation to him of the Red Ribbon of the Legion of Honour.

As we write, the memoirs of this noble and highly gifted Bersier have been probably published, though we have not had the privilege of hearing whether it is so; and consequently a full and correct representation of those times that he passed through will no doubt have been given, or should they not have appeared they will in all likelihood be forthcoming in course of time.   For when, a few years ago, Bersier was called to his eternal reward when still at his post, a loyal servant of his Master, he died, if not altogether full of days, full of earnest and memorable labour, and of honour in the service of God and man.   Mrs. Elliott's further admiration of him was expressed in another letter to her brother, where she says : "Last night Mrs. Hawley came to see me, and brought with her a copy of the *Daily Telegraph*, containing some eulogiums of the unparalleled French preacher Eugène Bersier, whose voice I so often wish to hear again.   It was Miss Skottowe who first told me of this wonderful preacher, and borrowed a volume of his sermons for me.   When we were abroad I heard of him again and again.   On our way to Basle, as we were waiting for a train, an Alsatian lady spoke of him with ecstasy of praise.   When I said to her, 'There is a preacher in Paris whom I wish to hear,' she replied at once : 'I know! Bersier!' and then she went off into notes of admiration—not exaggerated.   How thankful I was afterwards to be allowed to hear him in Paris.   Last Sunday my husband was not at church, and I read (or rather translated) to him a sermon of Bersier's on John the Baptist, ' Le Prédicateur de Cour ' ; and my hearer did consider it something superlatively excellent."

The Alsatian lady, Mlle. Dietsch, mentioned in this paragraph, became a constant correspondent of Mrs. Elliott's. This intimacy with a fellow-traveller was in keeping with many another she formed in a similar way.   Wherever she went she chained people to her, and the chain once forged continued strong and durable.

1871 was the year when the heir to the throne, His Royal Highness the Prince of Wales, was dangerously ill of typhus fever, and the prayers of the nation were requested on his behalf; in answer to which that life, that apparently just hung in the balance, was miraculously given back. Very beautifully in a letter Mrs. Elliott alludes to the occasion: "'There,' says she, 'shall be signs in the sun and in the moon and in the stars.' On Sunday morning the telegraph wires were flashing out with lightning speed under the sea and over the land of Britain a solemn fervent prayer for one young life, the heir of the throne. Was such a thing ever known before since the world began? . The prayer arrived here before the morning service, and it was prayed in the churches. May it please the Hearer of prayers to vouchsafe a gracious answer."

How painful anything was to her that was unreal and misleading in its spiritual tendency, the following will show. She *could* be angry, and when she was her words were severe and uncompromising.

Several years after this date, one of England's foremost ecclesiastics and renowned preachers visited the Isle of Man, and preached in Douglas; and his morning sermon at St. Thomas' so offended Mrs. Elliott that she alluded to it in a letter to one of her nieces in the following terms: "This afternoon Miss Skottowe kindly came to read aloud to me the report in the *Herald* of ——'s sermon of last Sunday morning at St. Thomas' Church. You may remember, dear Marian, that one Sunday morning, at the beginning of last year, you and I went to that church and heard an excellent sermon of pure Gospel truth from Mr. Washington * on the text, 'To me to live is Christ.' It was good and profitable to hear and remember such a discourse. But this highflown piece of empty magniloquence is very different,

* Rev. Marmaduke Washington, M.A. At that time Vicar of St. Thomas', Douglas.

as you will find if you read the report in the *Herald*. You will see that this flashy oration is a vainglorious display of artificial flowers lit up with fizzing sky rockets. But it was a charming satisfaction to . . . who nodded and winked at each other, after their manner. But one thing is certain, that if St. Paul had preached in that style to the Corinthians, no one would have fallen prostrate on his face under an overwhelming conviction of sin. 1 Cor. xiv. 24, 25. The discourse at night at St. Barnabas' was much better, more practical and profitable, a fine florid moral sermon, but of course without the three R. R. R.'s of Rowland Hill's wholesome prescription."

Dean Stanley also preached at St. Thomas' a very brief period before his death, and our friend pronounced his oration " A thing of naught."

She did not at all approve of Stanley on the ground of his latitudinarian principles, and very especially of their outcome as regards the lax observance of the Lord's Day. For the same reason she objected to the otherwise amiable and charming Charles Kingsley.

Though in 1872, when we were in close intimacy with the subject of this memoir, many years had elapsed since her last son died, yet she never alluded to him or to any of the great sorrows she had passed through. That they were, however, always uppermost in her mind and stationary in her heart, frequent references to the past and the dear ones who were gone in her letters to her brother or his wife sadly testify :

> " Her deep relations were the same,
> But with long use her tears were dry."

In January of this year she writes to Mr. Weatherell : " Sunday the 14th was my Philip's birthday, though he was born on a Saturday and baptized on the 22nd January, the anniversary of little Henry's burial. The shadow of death falling so often and heavily turns this world into a great cemetery.   Death has reigned a long time.   But grace reigns and will reign *through righteousness* unto eternal life through Jesus Christ our Lord."

This year Mrs. Bluett, the widow of the late High Bailiff (Chief Magistrate) of Douglas, died.   She was a friend of Mrs. Elliott's, and writing of her death, she says : " Yesterday morning at four o'clock one of the best of Christian women passed away from this region of storms into the peaceful rest of Paradise.   Mrs. Bluett—Mary Bluett (who may be numbered with the Lord's Marys)—departed this life to be with Christ, which is far better.

> " ' Fear no more the heat o' the sun,
>   Nor the furious winter's rages ;
>   Thou thy worldly task hast done,
>   Home art gone and ta'en thy wages.'

" This is Shakespeare's Dirge of Cymbeline.   But no dirge need be sung over Mary Bluett.   The angels would welcome her with songs of joy.   For she was like a quiet angel here below in her ministrations of mercy and charity, and her beneficent care for the poor, the fallen, and the lost. . . . At Christmas she was thought to be dying, but she rallied for a while, until last Friday, when she became much worse. And now she is well for ever.   Her children are to be pitied but she is blessed.   She was a meek and lovely Christian character, diffusing a gentle light, not flashy, but softly luminous, like the Milky Way."

This is fair word-painting and touching heart-testimony ; and those who survive of Mrs. Bluett's relations will read with pleasure this tribute to the life and memory of her they loved.

It was a comfort to our dear friend that her sight did not at present perceptibly grow very much worse.   She still read and wrote a great deal, but with the aid of powerful glasses.   And on every occasion, when at all possible, she engaged her visitors to read to her.   Her young friend, whose place in her heart was daily expanding, was very useful in reading aloud to her the many subjects they had in common; and occasionally acting as amanuensis in the way of letter-writing. She had many pet names for her girl friend (whose name is Katherine), such as Mignonette, Chérie, Carine, Carina, but more frequently Karine; and for the future, to facilitate our mode of designation when speaking of this favoured individual, we will call her *Karine*.

Most charming were the little notes that dear Mrs. Elliott used to write to the latter; her weekly invitations to tea, to come and read, to accompany her here or there, &c. They were almost always in French (Karine having been educated in France), and sometimes in French verse, usually of a most playful, airy description; and when the two met, it was always as if the mutual encounter were one irradiated with light and pleasant mirth. *Never* did she sadden the girl's heart with recitals of woe or depress with anticipations of a time "when the keepers of the house shall tremble, and the strong men shall bow themselves. . . . Or the silver cord be loosed, or the golden bowl be broken." Sufficient for the day was the evil thereof. A similar remark is made by the Honourable Theodosia Wright, who for the first time visited Douglas about this year (1872), or perhaps a little later.

"How great," says Mrs. Wright, "must have been her sorrows in losing all her children! and yet, so far from murmuring, she never once alluded to them during all the months I knew her. Once, in a letter long afterwards, when speaking of her failure of sight, I think she said it was caused by weeping for her children."

The Honourable Mrs. Wright, daughter of Lord Denman, "the fearless and upright judge," who defended Queen Caroline, was an acquaintance Mrs. Elliott was very delighted to make; and on the occasion of her first visit to Mrs. Wright she took with her an extract from some periodical which related to Lord Denman when a little boy, mentioning amongst other interesting incidents the fact that he had been put under the care, when he was three years old, of the celebrated educationalist and authoress, Mrs. Barbauld.

Mrs. Wright was greatly pleased with Mrs. Elliott's graceful tact in bringing this little notice as a sort of declaration that she was already interested in the new visitant to Mona, and that it was a special pleasure to make her acquaintance.

" I thought it very kind of Mrs. Elliott," said Mrs. Wright, "to welcome a stranger to the island in so friendly a manner; and she proved indeed a most delightful and improving friend."

Charles Ichabod Wright, Mrs. Wright's late husband, was the well-known translator of Dante. And one day she and Mrs. Elliott specially enjoyed a rare intellectual interchange of thought on men and things, as well as high and more blessed communion on the Lord whom they both served. On this occasion, at the request of Lady Loch, they visited her at Government House, and there discussed at will the distinguished minds in whom all three were interested — Mr. Wright and his elegant and poetical gifts; Lord Denman and his illustrious career and exalted character; the Honourable Edward Robert Bulwer Lytton, the poet, Lady Loch's brother-in-law, known in the world of letters as Owen Meredith, and as the son of Lord Lytton, the famous novelist, poet, orator, and statesman. And in connection with these personal relatives and noted men, a whole host of interesting personages who had left their mark, or were leaving their mark, on the pages of time, formed the theme of a racy, delightful conversation between these souls of mutual sweetness, intelligence, and cordial sympathy.

Mrs. Wright spoke of that day in Mrs. Elliott's company as one of the most congenial in her whole life.

Elizabeth Loch, daughter of the Hon. Edward Villiers, and grand-daughter of Earl Villiers, when she married

Henry Brougham Loch, G.C.B., Lieutenant-Governor of the Isle of Man (afterwards Governor of Victoria, and at present Governor of Natal), was very young, being only nineteen when she came with her husband to the Isle of Man in 1863. Exceedingly beautiful in person as also in character, and with extraordinary tact combined with affable dignity, she from the very first so ingratiated herself into the hearts and lives of the insular people that it has been said, "Never was there even the shadow of an adverse opinion pronounced on Lady Loch."

Her household exercised in a minor degree the same wholesome and elevating influence; for as regards her dependants she was a protectress and ensample, and "in her tongue was the law of kindness," which regulated everything under her roof.

A warm supporter of all that tended to foster the welfare and elevate the tastes of the community, she took in after years, when it was started, an active and influential part in the Young Women's Christian Association, addressing the young women herself, when so requested by the leading spirit of the movement, the honorary secretary, Miss E. Willson. And in 1881 she and the Governor inaugurated the Isle of Man School of Art, a branch of South Kensington Art department, Lady Loch enrolling herself for a while, for example's sake, as a student in the school.

In 1882, when Sir Henry and Lady Loch left the Isle of Man for Victoria, no persons in their special and high position were ever more honoured and more regretted on their departure from the insular shores than were they.

CHAPTER XXIII.

ANTIQUARIAN LORE.

WITH the vision of a hawk our student watched for every discovery from the lands of Biblical history that would throw additional light on the authenticity of the page of Holy Writ. In February of 1872 she was especially excited about the reported unearthing of a second Moabite stone ; and writing to her brother she asks, " Has Mrs. Deeping heard of this second stone ?"—the Mrs. Deeping mentioned elsewhere, whose tastes and pursuits coincided with those of her friend.

It would appear, however, that this alleged discovery was altogether a mistake, only *one* Moabite stone remaining so far to testify to the inaccuracy of the report—the stone discovered in Moab in 1869 by Dr. Klein, a German missionary, the announcement of which intensely interested Mrs. Elliott at the time. It was to her like the crying out of a divine voice from the ages gone by—a direct and further confirmation of the truth of scriptural history, and establishing irrefutably the record of the sacred page.

It will be remembered that this remarkable erection of black basalt, discovered by Dr. Klein, was afterwards purchased by M. Clermont Ganneau, a member of the French consulate at Jerusalem, and placed in the Museum of the Louvre at Paris.

This stone, with its interesting inscription, is truly a startling reiteration of Biblical history recorded in 2 Kings iii., and reads like a chapter of Old Testament Scripture. It is the record of Mesha, King of Moab, who, after the death of Ahab, rebelled against the King of Israel, and was victorious in his rebellion. In the inscription he describes the revenge he took upon the Israelites for their former oppression of his country. The characters used are Phœnician, and differ very little from those in vogue on the western side of the Jordan; showing that the language of Moab was almost similar to that of the Hebrew settler on the eastern side of the river. These venerable characters to be seen on the Moabitish stone present to us the exact mode of writing practised by the earlier prophets of the Old Testament. At another time an inscription in the Himyaritic character called forth our friend's interest. It was reported to her as having been seen and copied near Cabul by the Rev. Charles Swinnerton, a Manxman, and brother to the distinguished sculptor and to the equally distinguished painter of that name. Mr. Swinnerton's copy appeared in the *Graphic* of February 14, 1880.*

The characters seemed to bear a resemblance, in the estimation of one of Mrs. Elliott's sagacious informants, to a curious inscription seen by Mrs. (afterwards Lady) Brassey in Easter Island, the southernmost island in the South Pacific. Another inscription of a like character is to be seen in the Ladrones in the North-West Pacific. "So," writes Mrs. Elliott, "those Himyaritic people must have been a very widespread race in early days."

In keeping with her interest in Biblical inscriptions, she hailed with untold satisfaction the arrival in 1873 of the Shah of Persia in England.

Writing to a relative she says: "The arrival of the Shah yesterday would be a great sensation with terrific thunder of

---

* Mr. Swinnerton here stated, "The inscription probably belongs to an age anterior to the Christian era. So few inscriptions were left by the destroying Mahomedans in 1050 that the one or two known to exist are of intense interest. This one has never been copied by a European, and probably never seen by one before."

guns and uproar of shouting. There is a clever cartoon of him in *Punch* as the Persian 'chat' between the British Lion and the Russian Bear. However, there is a peculiar interest about this Eastern monarch as a representative of an empire founded by Cyrus the Great, whose name is emblazoned on the page of prophecy. And it is something new for an oriental king of so old an empire to visit our shores."

Even the politics of the subject of this memoir were deeply coloured with scriptural, as well as hereditary bias. Gladstone she regarded as a most dangerous man, and could in no respects tolerate him or his policy. Her thoughts of him were those of John Arthur Roebuck, who remarked: "It may be that Mr. Gladstone, the Prime Minister of this country, may not be inclined to (R.) Catholicism. I do not say yea or nay as to that, but I do say this, that if he were inclined to Catholicism, he would do exactly the thing he is now doing."

But Beaconsfield she admired and supported. Much, no doubt, on account of his brilliant parts as a statesman, but chiefly from the fact that he was a Jew, a descendant of "princely Israel's hallowed line," and an opponent to the innovation of Jesuitical principles and Popish practices into Britain. She did not forget his startling declaration: "What is the power beneath whose sirocco breath the fame of England is fast withering? Were it the dominion of another conqueror—another bold Bastard with his belted sword—we might gnaw the fetters which we could not burst. Were it the genius of Napoleon with which we are again struggling, we might trust the issue to the God of Battles, with a sainted confidence in our good cause and our national energies. But we are sinking beneath a power before which the proudest conquerors have grown pale, and by which the nations most devoted to freedom have become enslaved—the power of a foreign priesthood. . . . *Your empire and your liberties* are more in danger at this mo-

ment than when the Army of Invasion was encamped at
Boulogne."

The great statesman's *coup-de-main* in buying up the
Egyptian shares of the Suez Canal she regarded with
peculiar interest, and as an act of more than human foresight and astuteness; and the cutting of the Suez Canal—
the tongue of the Egyptian sea—a direct fulfilment of
prophecy: "And I will make all my mountains a way, and
my highways shall be exalted. Behold, these shall come
from far; and, lo, these from the north and from the west;
and these from the land of Sinim" (Isa. xlix. 11). And
again, "Prepare ye the way of the Lord, make straight in
the desert a highway for our God" (Is. xl. 3).

A grand phenomenon in the heavens of Eastern Europe,
also gave wings to our friend's fancy, and subject for contemplation and speculation in 1872. It was the appearance,
after an elapse of twenty years, of the so-called comet,
"Biela."

"By this post," she writes to her brother, "I send you
a *Herald* with a startling paragraph about a new comet.
You can tell me if you have seen it noticed elsewhere, and
what other astronomers think of it. Though it seems that
no other astronomer, except this one at Geneva, has noticed
this fiery flying comet, which may come as a flaming fire-
brand to set fire to this earth. If this news be true (and
something like it will happen sooner or later), it turns all
earthly news to ashes."

Ancient monumental stones and hieroglyphics were not
the only testimonies of bygone ages that appealed to Mrs.
Elliott's interest. She revelled also in legendary lore, quaint
ballads, a number of which she knew by heart, and ancient
customs generally.

The Bacons of Seafield, near Douglas, were related to her
sister's family, and Miss Marian Bacon, Major Bacon's
second daughter, was a special favourite of Mrs. Elliott's.
One day she and Karine went together to lunch at Seafield,

Mrs. Elliott describing to her companion on the way a wonderful glass goblet which she said she must be sure to ask Miss Marion Bacon to show her, as Karine had never seen or heard of it before.

On arriving at Seafield, in due course the goblet was produced by Miss Bacon and its history unfolded, which was to the following effect :—

"The 'Luck,' or Fairy Cup of Ballafletcher, came into the possession of the Fletcher family along with the estate of Kirby, in the sixteenth century—the Kirby * estate being held on the tenure of providing for the entertainment of the Bishops of Sodor and Man when going to and from the island. The Fletchers were a distinguished Lancashire family who held important official positions in Man under the Earls of Derby. Previous to their ownership of the precious relic it had belonged, so tradition affirmed, to Magnus, King of Norway, and Lord of Man and the Isles, who took it from the shrine of St. Olaf; and perhaps as expiation for his crime of sacrilege, returned it to the Church, or the Church's representative, the bishop, who on his visits to the island and residence at Kirby used it as his peculiar privilege.

"The last of the Fletchers, the custodians of the cup, died in 1778, and the relic then passed into the possession of the Bacon family, which, in the female line, was related to the family of Fletcher; retaining with it, however, a serious responsibility, for it possessed a *Lhiannan-shee*, or 'Spirit-of peace,' its guardian spirit, who, according to an ancient tradition, would keep its owner in peace and plenty as long as the cup was preserved unbroken, but who, if it were broken, would haunt the unfortunate person who broke it, and cause the peace and plenty to depart."

* Kirby, near Douglas, now the property and residence of Deemster Sir William Drinkwater, was in ancient days situated close to the sea, as Port-a-chee, the adjoining land, by its name testifies. Since then the sea has receded nearly a distance of two miles.

M

"It reminds one," said Mrs. Elliott, her eye glistening with interest and animation as Miss Bacon recounted the legend, "of Longfellow's 'Luck of Edenhall!'" And as she held the dainty goblet almost with sacred awe in her fingers, and waved it lightly, she repeated the lines :—

> "'This glass of flashing crystal tall
> Gave to my sires the Fountain-Sprite ;
> She wrote in it : *If this glass doth fall,*
> *Farewell, then, O Luck of Edenhall !*
>
> . . . . . .
>
> Glass is this earth's Luck and Pride ;
> In atoms shall fall this earthly ball
> One day like the Luck of Edenhall.'"

The cup, Miss Bacon informed us, was never used except on Christmas and Easter days, when it was filled with wine, and quaffed by her father, as head of the house, to the health of the *Lhiannan-shee.*

Whether she added that it was also used on those annual occasions when, on June 18th, Major Bacon had been wont to celebrate the victory of Waterloo, we do not remember. But the venerable host of Seafield was one of the few surviving heroes of that memorable fight ; and up to the time of the death of the Duke of Wellington, he always commemorated the event by giving a dinner-party, to which were invited other distinguished veterans and near relatives.

As regards ancient customs, Mrs. Elliott, on June 1, 1872, writes to her brother an amusing account of the last night's and early morning's proceedings of the Qualtagh. How the unseemly rat-a-tat-tats on the brass knocker at midnight, and in the small hours of the morning, had disturbed the slumbers of the household, and excited their temporary provocation. Between the lines, however, one can see she was in no way displeased by the boisterous display of a custom of wont and usage, and which bore upon its venerable face the approbation and sanction of time immemorial.

The Qualtagh may be explained as follows :—

" On New Year's Eve the occupants of farmhouses and cottages smooth the ashes on the floor, in the hope of finding on the next morning the impression of a fairy foot. The direction of the foot is supposed to predict, if *towards* the threshold, a death, if *from* the threshold, an increase in the family during the year. As soon as the New Year dawns a number of young men go from house to house, singing a verse expressive of good wishes for the family, after which they are hospitably entertained. It is considered important, however, that a dark person should first enter the house. The rhyme is as follows :—

> " Again we assemble, a merry New Year
> To wish to each one of the family here,
> Whether man or woman, girl or boy,
> That long life and happiness all may enjoy.
> May they have potatoes and herrings in plenty,
> With butter and cheese, and each other dainty ;
> And may their sleep never by night or by day
> Disturbed be by even the tooth of a flea,
> Until at the Qualtagh again we appear
> To wish you as now all a Happy New Year."

CHAPTER XXIV.

CHRISTIAN GIVING.

AFTER Karine had become very intimate with Mrs. Elliott, her visits to gloomy Athol Street were much more frequent than they were ever previously. One Monday morning, on her way to her friend's house, she saw a great crowd gathered around the hall door, and asking an acquaintance who was passing the meaning of the gathering, she was answered :—

"Oh, do you not know this is Monday morning; and your friend Mrs. Elliott, from nine to ten o'clock, makes it the occasion of bringing together all the vagrants of the town, and by distributing pennies to them, encourages them in idleness and drink !"

This was one view of the matter, the other was that there was no poor-law in the island, and that the needs of the poor weighed on that loving heart, and rather than pass over an indigent case, she incurred the risk of doing *some* harm, but she trusted *more* good. She was not a tactician in matters of charity and the dispensing of favours generally. She gave where love or where pity impelled her, and she left the results with Him who sees not as man sees, and weighs the thoughts and intents of the heart according to the decision of His all-righteous judgment. Every Saturday the faithful servant Kelly was despatched over the town of Douglas to change silver or gold as the case might be, and return the amount to his mistress in pence to distribute on Monday morning. And truly it was a sight to see men, women, and children in various degrees of rags and dirt and misery depicted on their faces, waiting in a crowd at that door until the hour had arrived to open it. And then the benefactress herself appeared ; and taking each poor creature in his or her turn, she distributed an alms, and gave a solemn admonition to keep pure, not to drink, not to lie, not to steal; and to be able to follow out this good intention, to pray unceasingly for the gift and power of the Holy Spirit to make them strong in the hour of temptation, and to preserve them always from the Evil One, who seeks to entrap and destroy the careless and prayerless.

Some, on the other hand, were taken, one at a time, into an inner room, where what passed between the soul of the pure and the impure, the heart of the wise and the heart of the ignorant and foolish, the life of the holy and the life of the unholy, God alone knows, who took count of each word uttered, of each prayer prayed in the secret of that mysterious chamber.

"Finally," said a niece of this saintly woman, " the morning's work was done, the last single knock answered, the last word spoken, and she was free to retire for communion with her Master before going out into the lanes and highways to teach the poor of Douglas."

In summer the scene at the door of No. 31 was also remarkable. At that time of the year the streets of the town swarm with itinerant musicians of different nationalities. Soon they discover their friends ; and Mrs. Elliott's house was literally besieged by them. Words were spoken, texts from Scripture quoted in their mother tongue, tracts, Testaments, helpful little books, &c.—all in their own language— distributed, and contributions in pence for music played, or songs sung, or smiles smiled through brilliant lips with shining teeth, and eyes black and lustrous with Southern glow. Romance tinctured even our friend's acts of charity as well as the deep spring of divine love which filled to overflowing her great warm heart.

She was a subscriber for years to the Religious Tract Society, and always had a supply of religious literature at hand either to give or lend to people waiting for the doctor. Did she hear any one in the surgery, off she trotted with willing feet to drop "a word in season"—"here a little, there a little."

Dr. Cathcart, one of the deputations from the Religious Tract Society, reports what an interest it was to pay her his annual visit; she had always something new to tell him of the work the Society was doing. Instead of his being called upon to inform her, she more frequently forestalled his acquaintance of fresh facts, by giving him a full and glowing account of the latest tidings she had heard or read of.

With equal ardour she received year by year Mr. Weyland of the London City Mission; and her conversations with this good and energetic secretary were brimful of interest. She was fond of quoting one of Lord Shaftesbury's sayings, "Were it not for the work of this noble Society, London would not be safe for a night; but a mighty hand keeps the lawless in check."

Her young nieces in the summer-time, when they came to visit her, would contemplate their aunt's doings, and listen to her words with wonder and admiration. She was to them, as to Karine, a marvel of holiness and wisdom. They had every opportunity to study her inner life and its outcome in the home; and their youthful keen observation resulted but in one verdict—that she was a *saint indeed*—holy in thought, word, and action; and gifted as few are gifted with knowledge and a brilliant and powerful intellect.

Among those who bear a like testimony is Miss Fannin of Burleigh. Writing of her friend she says:—

"Hers was indeed the life of a *saint;* and do you not think its keynote was *love?* I remember being frequently struck with this feature in her character—love to the most unworthy. How we did reverence her with that enthusiasm which is pleasant now to recall!"

There was one of her nieces for whom she had—we do not call it a preference—but a very special regard and sympathy;

it was Marian, Mr. Weatherell's second daughter. Marian in very much resembled her aunt. She was a sweet gentle Christian girl, with a fair face and fair golden hair like her sisters, but with a manner so subdued and winning one felt inclined to say and think of her, " Truly an ideal clergyman's daughter, and apparently one who knows well what it is to be in the company of Jesus."

And so it was. Marian was a friend of Jesus, she walked in His footsteps, and lived continually by faith in the Son of God. She had a missionary spirit, and a gift for English composition which greatly interested her aunt. On one occasion she went to a missionary meeting at Bottesford, near her home, and heard a missionary of the name of Duncan, who then worked in connection with the Church Missionary Society and did a remarkable work in British Columbia, evangelising the savage Indians and bringing them under the amenity of the Gospel. The lecture he gave at Bottesford so interested young Marian Weatherell that she took notes of it, and afterwards produced an account so able and fascinating that her aunt had it published as a tract.

Writing to Mr. Weatherell she says :—

"How can I thank Marian enough for the delightful narrative which she has so kindly sent to me. . . . It is well expressed and well done, a highly creditable production of the young reporter. It has been read aloud to me by two blooming young ladies, with blue eyes and soft sweet voices, something like Marian herself. Two hours after the MS. arrived two ladies called for my subscription to the Church Missionary Society. The younger one was a Miss Roskill (a daughter of Mr. Joe Roskill), and she read to me more than four pages of the manuscript. She was much interested, and it will probably have a good effect in deepening her interest in the work. So Marian's labour is not in vain. And yesterday Miss —— called to see me, and read aloud the whole narrative from beginning to end with lively interest. Certainly the brave young Duncan was called to

his work by the same Holy Spirit who separated Barnabas
and Saul for their missionary work. And being so called
and sent, the Word of Life has been confirmed by signs
following in a manner quite supernatural and astonishing.
These converted Indians will be a crown of rejoicing to
their good evangelist in the good morning that is drawing
nigh. Who knows how near it may be?"

During the summer of 1872 Marian, accompanied by the
nurse Hannah, came on a visit to Dr. and Mrs. Elliott; and
such a joy and refreshment was it to her aunt to have the
young girl with her that she sadly missed her when, at last,
she was obliged to leave for home.

"How dull and empty this house looked when you were
gone," she wrote; "and what a long time it seems since you
went away! If Elton seems quiet to you after Douglas, so is
this house since you left. The weather changed after your
departure, and it seemed for a few days as if the summer
warmth and sunshine had come and gone with the halcyon
birds from Elton."

Mrs. Elliott again left alone, Karine visited her very often,
almost daily. One Sunday in August the Rev. William
Lefroy of Liverpool, now the distinguished Dean of Norwich,
was to preach at St. Barnabas, and the two friends went
together to hear him. His sermons were for the benefit of
the St. Barnabas schools. The occasion was one of interest
to Mrs. Elliott, and a red-letter day in the case of Karine—
marking an eventful epoch in the history of her theology
and of her life. They both agreed that they had listened
to a ninteenth century reformer.

That their insight and foresight were not far wrong after
events seem to prove. For truly Dean Lefroy's unceasing
effort and great powers of oratory all point to the fact that
his aim is to reform manners and customs in the Church
and in society for the honour of God and good of men.

One of his texts that day at St. Barnabas was, "Also in
thy skirts is found the blood of the poor innocents" (Jer.

ii. 34). And with most extraordinary unction, pathos, and power he pictured "the crime" of Judah in her day, and in reference to it the crime of England in hers. Moloch was the god of retrograde idolatrous Judah in the wicked King Manasseh's generation and reign; and to the rapacious deity was sacrificed the blood of youth and innocence. Gold! gold! the preacher declared, was equally the god of England in the generation and reign of Queen Victoria; and to this cruel and all-tyrannous idol was sacrificed the blood of the land in its young and innocent children!

And with dramatic effect and startling application, he recited a lengthy quotation from Barrett Browning's "Cry of the Children."

So inspired were the two kindred souls and entranced listeners—Mrs. Elliott and her girl friend—and impregnated with the Luther-like spirit that breathed from the preacher's denunciatory appeal, that D'Aubigne's Reformation, the writings of Luther, Erasmus, Melanchthon, and other of the great Reformation fathers of Christian Europe, became for a long time afterwards the theme of their conversation, study, and reading. And this was especially so when, in a short time, Mr. Lefroy's powerful orations were followed up by an equally graphic and stirring lecture on the subject of Erasmus.

Writing to her niece Marian, after the Sunday's sermons, Mrs. Elliott says: "Last Sunday was the St. Barnabas Anniversary; and Miss Skottowe and I went there morning and evening. The highly gifted Mr. Lefroy prayed, read, and preached on both occasions. The collections amounted to £41, the largest Anniversary collection since the time of Mr. Alcock at St. Barnabas." Good as the collection was considered, it fell far short of the £92 cheerfully contributed for the same object in the days of Dr. Carpenter.

About this time, Karine, who was in delicate health, left Douglas to visit the English lakes with a French cousin of hers, Mademoiselle Léonide Mailly, and whilst at Keswick, Mrs. Elliott writes to her young friend a pretty letter in French :—

"Mignonette," she begins, "bien des remerciements de votre lettre si fraîche respirant l'air du lac et de la montagne. Il me semble que vous et Windermere sont en rapport, et comme le lac est le miroir limpide du ciel et de la terre, ainsi, votre lettre en est le réflet de la belle nature qui vous entoure. Vous dites en vérité que c'est un paradis. On peut bien croire que quand la mer ne sera plus dans la nouvelle terre, il y aura des lacs pour réfléchir ses paysages d'une beauté immortelle.

"Nous avons sur cette vieille terre le lac de Galilée avec les saints souvenirs de Celui qui l'a traversé une fois à pied, et souvent dans la barque des pêcheurs. Il y a quelque chose de grand et paisible être au milieu de telles scénes.

. . . .

"Qu'elle doit être grande sorcière mademoiselle, votre cousine, de vous avoir transformée en 'lionne'—la lionne qui mange! Quelle métamorphose! Peut on trouver un nouveau La Fontaine pour écrire la nouvelle fable de Léonide et sa lionne !"

The above facetious allusion to "la lionne qui mange !" and the new fable with Léonide and her lion as the subject, was a play on a remark probably made by Karine, that she had become strong under her cousin's care, and ravenous as a lion !

Karine's next journey was to London, in the company of Miss Marian Bacon ; and Mrs. Elliott again writes to her, but this time in English :—

"MY DEAR UNREASONABLE KATIE,—In your former letter you advised me (with kind consideration for my infirmity) not to send an answer. And now in your second you pretend to be angry that my answer to you was not as long as it was to Miss Bacon. The wonder was that either of the *deux amies aux yeux bleus* got any answer at all from the stupid old creature who is neither blue-eyed nor clairvoyante.

"Your papa, I heard, said you were not coming home for two or three weeks, as you said something about your going to see Mrs. Wright.* If you should visit our dear friend, will you ask her whether I am still to hold her good little book as a hostage of her return some fine day. If she goes on postponing her return I may be dead before she comes, and then she might not so easily regain her book!

"Did I ever repeat to you an anecdote related by Mrs. Hemans of a French nobleman of the old régime who wrote thus to a friend : 'Par respect je vous écris de ma propre main, mais pour faciliter la lecture, je vous en envoie une copie !' Eh bien ! ma chérie, qu'en pensez-vous. Does the saying apply in either your case or mine ?"

The latter sentence referred to something she had received in Karine's handwriting which she had not been able to decipher ; and her own writing she took for granted was somewhat illegible owing to her failing sight. But at this time her writing, though not as regular and extremely delicate as formerly, was perfectly distinct, and such a thing as an erasure never occurred.

* The Hon. Theodosia Wright.

CHAPTER XXV.

THE OLD FRENCH MISER.

APART from her eyes, which troubled her very much, Mrs. Elliott was not at all well in 1874 and 1875. She was also frequently depressed. One has a hint just here and there from her letters that this was so; but in conversation and appearance she gave no sign of the load of pain and sorrow that often weighed her down. In the spring of 1874 she was especially saddened; and, on being pressed to go to Elton, wrote:—

"You are rejoicing in the song of nightingales in this month of May, the month of lilies and of fresh life and beauty. But to me it is darkened with the shadow of death—a season of sad memories. On the 19th of May our Willie was called away; on the 2nd of May, Philip walked down these steps for the last time; on the 2nd of May, Colonel Grier died; and on the 3rd of May our mother was stricken down in St. George's Church."

(And could she have foreseen, it was in a future month of May she too was to be called away.)

"But," continues she, "what is this whole earth but a great cemetery now while death reigns? But it will not be always so, for the empire of death has been shaken by the death and resurrection of Him who liveth and was dead. And at His return, when He shall call to the heavens above and to the earth beneath, the earth will cast out her dead. Then they shall return from the land of the enemy."

In the autumn of 1874, Mr. Weatherell, anxious about his sister's health, crossed over to the island to see her.

His visit was a joyful surprise, and writing about it afterwards she says : " How can I ever thank you enough for your recent pilgrimage of brotherly love to visit your poor weak sister ? It was a blessing and refreshment at the time, bringing with it the air of a better country, even a heavenly—and it is a comfort to one's heart to think of it now."

Summer returning, she again revived, buoyed up with the expectation of having her young nieces to stay with her for a while. Alas ! the visit had to be deferred, and she was sorely disappointed.

" I said to my husband at breakfast," she writes, " that it would seem a strange summer without the fair-haired girls. They remind me of the famous pun of Gregory the Great, when he saw the fair-haired Angli in Rome, that if they were Angli they ought to be Angeli. Not, however, that there is any scriptural reason to suppose that the human race will ever be transformed into the angelic. But the children of the first resurrection being thus made 'equal to the angels,' will have good cause to adore the Redeeming Love which has thus delivered them from the bondage of corruption into the liberty of the glory of the children of God."

One day about this time, when our friend was feeling very weak and unable to do much of her wonted work of visiting, &c., Karine went to see her, and she said to her :—

" Karine, I am going to ask you to make a journey to the Union Mills * for me. I want you to go and see a very remarkable friend of mine, a French gentleman of—I will not say a prepossessing appearance and elegant entourage, but an individual of otherwise distinguished parts ; seeing he has been, according to his own version, a government official of vast importance, and is the possessor at present, though you would not think it, of a considerable fortune ! "

* Village about three miles from Douglas.

Karine was all alive with interest. *She* had never heard of this person before. "Had he just come to the island?"

"No, he has been here for years. But listen and I will begin and tell you in sober language how I came to make his acquaintance.

"One day not very long ago I was passing the hotel in this street, and I saw as I thought a poor beggar man sitting on the door-steps. I accosted him with a few remarks and then offered him a penny. He thanked me with an air of extra-ordinary courtesy, and said he had quite sufficient of this world's goods; but he should be extremely grateful to me if I would pay him a visit, as he should like to converse with me on some important subjects, and make certain proposals, in the decision of which I might be of some use. Accordingly I went to see him in his den over the archway on the South Quay. A more strange and dreadful place you can hardly imagine. It was one pile of dirt and confusion. Books in quantities, and to judge from their smell, moulder-ing in dust; grimy bits of furniture, heaps of chopped wood, and on view to the few and favoured, a bed of a construction perfectly unique, and made entirely according to the owner's prescribed and carefully drawn-out plans. It consists of what looks like an oblong box raised a little from the ground, and heated when required, he informed me, with paraffin lamps, prevented from doing mischief by a sort of shelf above made of sheet iron; and this again placed beneath the mattress, or what serves as such, viz., a heap of shavings. The space which encloses the lamps is glazed all round, and can be opened by means of sliding panes, so as to enable the interesting denizen to regulate his heating apparatus. Protruding also from this wonderful bed, he pointed out to me a shelf, which served partly as a table, and partly as a receptacle for his very toothsome provisions, their appetising and pleasant flavour, however, being open to a difference of opinion! His Norwegian cooking-boxes he also exhibited and explained their utility. They are padded with thick material, so as to prevent the escape of heat, in the manner of a tea-cosy; and into these he pops his pan of soup, or whatever it may be, that he has previously brought to a boil over a lamp, and in process of time his meal cooks itself to perfection.

"In further conversation this astonishing individual informed me he had been employed by the late King of Naples in transacting certain important matters of state. As regards his social proclivities—religion *I* am afraid he has none—he professes to be a follower of Robert Owen; and his desire is, he says, to carry out the teaching of this, as he termed him, great philanthropist. For this end he denies himself with the view of benefiting his fellow-creatures. Much of his library, he said, was composed of Owen's works and those of Jacob Holyoak, another admirable type of humanity. But what he had especially in view in regard to benefiting the Isle of Man, was to erect a building after his own design as an improved substitute for the present Industrial Home. I told him I was acquainted with a young lady who frequently visited this Institution, and I should like him to have a talk with her, as she would no doubt be interested in what he had to say, and able perhaps to advise better than I should. After paying this extraordinary visit, and reflecting on my hero, I bethought me to ask the High Bailiff if he knew anything really about him (again and again he spoke of the High Bailiff as a personal friend). Mr. Harris replied that he did indeed, and that he is actually a *very rich man;* also that it is pretty evident he was once employed in some lucrative, perhaps, but doubtful official capacity under the French or Italian Government."

"You astonish me!" said Karine. "What is this extraordinary being's name?"

"Baume—Monsieur Baume. And for the benefit of country air—having been rather unwell lately—he is at present located in a poor woman's cottage at the Union Mills. You will easily find it—it is just at the bottom of the hill—almost at the summit of which is the spot which commands that surpassingly lovely view you know so well, of mountain and vale, which furnished Martin * with the idea and subject of his Plains of Heaven. I must, however, give you my card, as he made me promise that I would give it you, so that he should have no doubt in receiving you that you are my *bonâ fide* friend and coadjutor ! "

Karine was delighted with the mission assigned her. She was quite anxious to see this oddity. Accordingly the young lady was not long about prosecuting her visit to the Union Mills, and when there soon discovered the whereabouts of Monsieur Baume. His landlady informed her, when she asked for her lodger, that he could be seen—that he was in bed in her kitchen. Whereupon she ushered the visitor into the said apartment.

Seated up in bed was a very dirty old man ; on his head a greasy battered old slouched hat, covering a considerable portion of his features, and almost touching the tip of his elongated nose ; and this in its turn almost meeting his curbed and pointed chin—both features combining to form as they encountered a veritable nut-cracker nose and chin ; and his half hidden, small, black, keenly-piercing eyes presented a first impression of extreme cunning and arch hypocrisy.

" Monsieur," said Karine, advancing towards the bed, presenting her card as directed, and speaking in French, " I hope I find you well. I have come to see you on behalf of our mutual acquaintance, Mrs. Elliott."

" Ah, Mademoiselle," said the old gentleman, eyeing the card closely, and then raising his hat with the air of a courtier, " quel plaisir inattendu ! Pray be seated, and do take that seat furthest from me, where I can view the fair face that I am sure is the just accompaniment of that kind sweet voice."

* Martin, the celebrated painter, lived at Harold Tower, Douglas, and is buried at Kirk Braddan Cemetery.

Karine obeyed, and seated herself in full view of the hideous old Frenchman, where he could watch her, and where she could equally watch him.

"Now, Mademoiselle," said he, "before we begin to speak on the very important business I have in my mind, and in which I am informed you may be able to assist me in bringing it to a practical issue, I wish to tell you that I am no mendicant. You see my outward man is well cared for"—pointing to his coat and hat—"and I can assure you my inner man is also well sustained. Do you see, Mademoiselle, these jars by my side?"—he pointed to some tall earthenware vessels on his bed and resting against the wall—"well, I will show you their contents—most wholesome and palatable food, I can assure you."

"Why, what have you in them?" asked Karine artlessly.

"If Mademoiselle will rise, I will uncover and she shall see."

Mademoiselle rose accordingly, and Monsieur lifted the brown paper which served as cover to the jars, and she looked in as she was bid, and there beheld a green and brown mixture that she did not think looked as inviting for an article of food as Monsieur would have her believe.

"It does not look very nice, Monsieur," she said; "what can it be?"

"Ah, in this country, Mademoiselle, you are not as ingenious as we foreigners nor nearly as frugal. My mixture is composed of chopped snails which I gathered myself, and fresh green cabbage, or it was so a few weeks ago when I compounded my wholesome diet."

Poor Karine tried to look composed and politely appreciative.

"Well, Mademoiselle, you are satisfied—you have come to see me as an honoured acquaintance on equal terms, though I am of course your debtor as regards the trouble you have put yourself to, in taking so long a journey to call upon one whose only claim upon your courtesy is, that

N

I have I believe been so fortunate as to excite in some degree the interest and regard of the good and kind Mrs. Elliott, whom I have no doubt you value as I do as a delightful and most intelligent acquaintance?"

Karine assented, and Monsieur proceeded.

"Well, Mademoiselle, I have a plan. This is a beautiful world, is it not? and this is a sweet island! I came here, I can assure you, because I believed God had a special favour to the lovely spot. Well, here I have lived quietly —though I hope with considerable profit to others as well as myself, for some twenty-five years, and here I mean to die. Before I die, however, I want to carry out a scheme I have been long maturing. It is this, to erect a beautiful building entirely covered with glass for the accommodation of the poor children who are the inmates of what is termed the Isle of Man Industrial Home."

"Do you think, Monsieur, that is a good idea to have it all covered with glass?"

"*Certainly*, Mademoiselle, the reason for which is, that God's blessed sunshine may penetrate the abode and fall upon the young heads, and cause the dear creatures to flourish and bloom like lovely flowers! I wish boys and girls to be together, a happy family growing up with feelings of mutual love and consideration; and then in due course my best idea would be realised—the young things would intermarry. And that is what it should be, and what would render this island, as regards the offspring of the otherwise neglected poor, a veritable paradise!"

Karine thought to herself it is best (wiser and less trouble) merely to listen to this random reasoner. At last, after a further parley, the drift of which she could barely follow, she rose, thanking Monsieur for taking her into his confidence, and saying she would communicate his benevolent purposes to those she knew interested in the Institution he proposed to benefit. At this he pricked up his ears, and was very anxious she should promise to get together a com-

pany of ladies as a committee to wait upon him from time
to time, and hear and discuss with him his long-fostered and
well-prepared plans of operation.

Mrs. Elliott's deputy was too wide awake to be entrapped;
it was very clear to her they were dealing with a visionary,
and she replied she did not think a ladies' committee would
answer at all, much better that he should gain the co-operation of the High Bailiff and other such persons of experience
and influence in such an enterprise. Finally contriving,
amid a disconnected effusion of compliments and thanks, to
make her escape, the visitor was followed to the door of the
cottage by the landlady, who in a very confidential tone
informed Karine that Baume was a dreadful man, and such
a miser! "When my back is turned," she said, "he calls
to my little boy and says, 'Johnny, get up on that chair
and get me that little bit of butter you see there!' And
when the disgraceful creature," she said, with a look of
disgust, "hears a herring cart go round, he calls to me and
asks me to go out and buy him a halfpennyworth of herrings
—isn't it dreadful, miss? When he was in Douglas I am
told he lived on the offal of the market, in fact he picked
up what was thrown out to the dogs, or would buy up
stale fish or any nastiness he could get cheap!"

Karine, highly entertained by her day's experience, returned to Douglas to report to Mrs. Elliott how she had
fared with the extraordinary M. Baume.

This was not the only visit the young lady paid to the
miser. She went another time, but took a friend with her.
On this occasion the cottager had had her lodger removed to
a small room upstairs. And up a narrow staircase to this
uninviting chamber the laughing pair ascended. The object
of this visit was pure amusement. Monsieur, as before, was
in bed, and very unwell, he informed his visitors, and on
a small table beside him was a plate containing some undis-
tinguishable and horrible-looking confection. Karine did
not do more than venture to glance at it, and asked no

question. Monsieur begged her to approach nearer that he might see her to better advantage ; he had thought much of her since her visit, and felt sure she could help him in his scheme. Also he would like to see her father ; he thought, as he was an old gentleman, they might both go together to Buxton for the benefit of their health. This was more than Karine and her friend could stand, and they had difficulty in controlling their sense of the ridiculous. Monsieur again began to wander over a string of notions that had been careering through his brain ; but Karine, perceiving that nothing was to be arrived at, and that they had had their fun, did her best to withdraw. Her friend, meaning to be very gracious, extended her hand to Monsieur ; but suddenly he, as it were, recoiled, shuddered, and said, " No, no ! I long ago made it a rule never to touch the fingers of a woman ! " Then, as if trying to partly undo what he said, he added : " Excepting in some very rare case. For instance, for the dear Mrs. Elliott's sake, I beg to shake hands with Mademoiselle Skottowe, if mademoiselle will permit ? " Karine was only too glad to arrive at a definite point in their interview, and placing her hand in Monsieur Baume's, he just touched it, and she, as hastily as she could, bade the cavalier adieu.

Some time went over, and Baume not recovering in health, he was moved to Douglas, and was lodging for some time in Duke St., but was finally conveyed to Castle Mona Lawn by some persons who held themselves responsible, and there placed in comfortable apartments, and provided with every care and attention. It was probably at this time that one day Mrs. Elliott received a note from the High Bailiff, with a request on behalf of M. Baume that she should again go to see him. Alluding to the visit in a letter to Mrs. Weatherell, she says :—

"The enclosed note came to me yesterday from the High Bailiff, and you can show it to Robert and the girls, who have seen this extraordinary M. Baume. In compliance with the note, I called this morning on M. Baume; and you can tell Robert he was shining with cleanliness, and that he looks now like a *clean* French nobleman; and that he is meditating a noble act of munificence, to give away nearly all his money for charitable purposes, and to live himself as a pauper on a few shillings a week. Let us hope that his good resolutions may be carried into effect. He said to me to-day, 'I am going to do something that will startle you.' Should the surprise be an agreeable one, so much the better. It is said that he possesses about sixty thousand pounds in money and property, and if this were well bestowed, it might be of great benefit to many persons."

The poor miser did not live long after this last removal, and his death revealed what he had stated to be true, and what Mrs. Elliott repeats, viz. "That he was a rich man, the possessor of property, real and personal, amounting to something like sixty or seventy thousand pounds."

This immense sum, for the disposal of which for years the owner had from time to time drawn up settlements that were never completed, owing to the English law of mortmain, could not at the last moment of the testator's life be bequeathed, as he wished, for educational and charitable purposes. Consequently, he was obliged, when at last induced to make a decided settlement, to bequeath it absolutely to trustees, as their personal property, with simply the moral proviso to use it as the testator would have willed had he had on his deathbed the legal power to direct. These trustees were seven in number, and consisted of some of the chief Government officials of the island.

The Industrial Home, and it only, benefited immediately by the demise of the testator, receiving a gratuity of £3000, which handsome sum enabled the Home committee to purchase the present fine building on the height of Burnt Mill Hill.

The remainder of the Baume estate apparently, though

after an elapse of nearly twenty years, is still in abeyance in the possession of the trustees, and entirely at their disposal, either to be given or not to be given, for the purpose and use for which the original proprietor had, according to his own statement, for a long succession of years, accumulated and hoarded it.

Visitors to Douglas entering St. George's churchyard will view, on the right hand of the path leading direct to the church, the costly Aberdeen granite monument which records the burial-place and munificent benefactions of Pierre Jean Joseph Henri Baume.

Truly this pyramid rises as if in mockery of him who lies below. For, sad to tell, the deathbed of poor Baume was, as recounted to Mrs. Elliott by an eyewitness, one truly appalling. He breathed, so report alleged, his last uttering words of dreadful sound, and testifying in his departing moments that he had lived a life darkened with crime, and rendered miserable by remorse and despair. His intended benefactions were probably meant as an expiation for a life of sin, weighing like lead upon an unenlightened conscience. Truly, "What shall it profit a man, if he gain the whole world, and lose his own soul? Or what shall a man give in exchange for his soul?"

The poor creature, it was said, desired to see one loving Christian in his sickness unto death, and that was Mrs. Elliott. And once or more she saw him. But even Karine could not extract from her what passed between the miserable sufferer and his visitant of mercy. She would only shudder when his name was mentioned; and finally she asked that it should not be mentioned at all.

CHAPTER XXVI.

SEEING "COULEUR DE ROSE."

THERE was scarcely a religious meeting of any kind, or special Church service, but what was attended by Mrs. Elliott and Karine in company. The former may truly be said to have kept missionary interest alive in Douglas by the intense interest she herself displayed in its operations at home and abroad, and giving her countenance, as before stated, in every possible way to the work and the workers. Agents, lay and clerical, from England and elsewhere, whenever they visited the island, were often her guests for the time.

Her interest was, however, very specially manifested on behalf of the South American Missionary Society (Patagonian Mission) that her dear Willie, when only fourteen, established by his youthful efforts in the island, and as honorary local secretary for which he had devoted the remainder of his short life. The Society's deputation invariably stayed at 31 Athol Street when they paid their yearly visits. And in 1875, on the occasion of one of these visits, Mrs. Elliott made a strenuous effort to renew the claims of the Society, and wrote an admirable appeal in one of the newspapers which had its due effect in reviving the zeal of those that had become lukewarm and careless, and in stirring many hearts that would otherwise have remained callous and dead to the need of supporting a god-like and humane enterprise.

It was about this time when the Rev. Alfred Millard William Christopher visited Douglas, possibly for the first

time, and preached at St. Barnabas'.   His name was without
doubt familiar to Mrs. Elliott through his excellent publica-
tions, for, hearing of his advent and his intention to preach,
she sent a request to Karine to accompany her to hear him.

Writing of the occasion she says :—

"Last Sunday evening (September 28, 1875) Miss Skottowe
and her father accompanied me to St. Barnabas' Church
where Mr. Christopher preached. 'Christopher' is an excellent name for a clergyman, and this man's evangelical
doctrine quite agrees with his name.   He is serving his
Master faithfully at Oxford.   He is Rector of St. Aldate's,
and every Saturday evening he has a prayer-meeting at his
Rectory, attended by about 120 undergraduates.   On Sunday
evening he preached on the text, 'We love Him because He
first loved us.'   It was a written sermon, followed by an
extempore address.   In the address he spoke of the good
work now going on at Oxford and Cambridge ; and said that
at Cambridge open air services are held in the marketplace,
sanctioned by the Provosts and Chancellor.   A great con-
trast to the state of things a hundred years ago, when six
men were expelled from *St. Edmund's Hall*, Oxford, for
extempore prayer.   'I have lately,' said Mr. Christopher,
'been reading the indignant remonstrance of George Whit-
field addressed to the Chancellor.   These six men were pronounced by Dr. Dixon, the Head (or Master) of St. Edmund's
Hall, to be the six best men.   "And if," said George Whit-
field, "six men are expelled for extempore prayer, it is time
to expel more for extempore swearing !"'"

Mr. Christopher frequently after this visited the island,
and in every likelihood continues his visits, as his son and
his wife and family have been for long residents at Douglas,
and are now at Castletown.

It may not be out of place to mention here a little incident connected with this good Oxford clergyman and the
same lively young lady who was so much influenced by the
preaching of Mr. Hoskins.   Miss —— was at a picnic, at

which Mr. Christopher was also present; and during a part of the day, as the weather was not very propitious, it was proposed to have a dance in a large room of an old empty house. Miss —— danced along with the rest, but in one of the pauses in a quadrille, when she was standing absently apart, Mr. Christopher, who was watching the young people, quietly went up to her, and in his gentle voice said—

"You look a little thoughtful. Will you take this from me?"

And he put into her hand a leaflet, one of his golden messages, fulfilling the divine precept to sow the precious seed of living Truth "beside all waters"—"in season and out of season."

Karine, we have said, was the close companion of Mrs. Elliott on most occasions, public and private; the young lady had scarcely a thought or a feeling apart from her gifted and gracious friend. She preferred the latter's society to almost all other, and found in it subject even for merriment as well as instruction and spiritual edification, as much and often more than in the gayest circles of mere worldly amusement. Many a good laugh they had (or one of them had) when conversing together, or when perusing the volumes they both delighted in, and the younger read to the elder. It was after one of these lively occasions Mrs. Elliott wrote to her niece Eleanor the following graphic account of her and Karine's display of sentiment in respect to the subject of one of their readings :—

"When your uncle was writing to you last night he said that Miss Skottowe and I were screaming with laughter over a French book that we were reading. This was true so far as she was concerned. But as for me, many a year has passed since I screamed with laughter at anything. When your Aunt Jane and I were very young we used sometimes to laugh until we could scarcely stand. But this was long, long ago. Last night Karine was reading to me in French an oration of Bossuet on Marie Thérèse, wife of Louis XIV.

And the excessive flattery lavished by the bishop on Louis le Grand—the Great (sinner)—was so preposterous that as Karine read the inflated phrases and looked at the same time at the contrary look in my old face, she was so amused that she kept going off into *éclats de rire.* Enclosed you will find a specimen of this magniloquence. Such incense of adulation was enough to intoxicate any French head.

"As we read the history of that reign of Louis XIV. in the light of these days we see that the ' whirligig of time brings its revenges'—and why? Because 'the Lord God of recompenses will surely requite.'

"In the reign of vainglorious Louis XIV., Alsace and Lorraine were torn from Germany by Marshal de Turenne, whose father was sovereign prince of Sedan. And at Sedan, two hundred years afterwards, France was subdued and discrowned, and was in the course of a few months compelled to restore Alsace and Lorraine to Germany."

The passage alluded to from Bossuet was as follows :—

"Que servirait à Louis d'avoir étendu sa gloire partout où s'étend le genre humain ? Ce ne lui est rien d'être l'homme que les autres hommes admirent : il veut-être, avec David, 'l'homme selon le cœur de Dieu.' C'est pourquoi Dieu le bénit. . . . Ouvrez donc les yeux, chrétiens, et regardez ce héros, dont nous pouvons dire, comme Saint Paulin disait du grand Théodose, que nous voyons en Louis, 'non un roi, mais un serviteur de Jésus Christ, et un prince qui s'élève au-dessus des hommes plus encore par sa foi que par sa couronne."

Mrs. Elliott's sight at this time was growing very impaired ; and in response to frequent invitations from Elton to go there on a visit, she at last made up her mind, wishing at the same time that she could go on from Elton to London to see Dr. Meurer about her eyes. This, however, she found she could not do, as Dr. Meurer would have left town by the time she could get there. To Elton, however, a little later on, she and Dr. Elliott went, and writing of the visit afterwards she says :—

"Our delightful visit to Elton was a great refreshment. Since our return I have endeavoured to surprise my friends and acquaintances by repeating to them separately the same statement, that, 'on the evening of our arrival we had a garden concert.' No one, however, was so astonished as Mr. Hawley. 'On *that* evening?' he said, and then I went on to explain that the concert-room was lighted by the moon, and that the singers were nightingales. This narrative has been followed by different exclamations, among which the very unsuitable word, 'How nice!' has not been omitted. But 'nice' is a poor word for Elton in the month of May— such a paradise of nightingales, cuckoos, and cowslips, to say nothing of the young daughters of Eve in the garden. A fortnight to-night we stood outside your porch with them, and now it is all over, like a dream of moonshine and soft music."

Her remark in the foregoing about the expression "How nice!" is very characteristic. She could not endure any one to make use of the word "nice" as synonymous with beautiful, delightful, &c. "Nice! what is *nice?*" she would say, "why, *nothing*—it has no meaning. Please never make use of a word so absolutely inane. You remember Lord Byron's emphatic reproval of the silly tourist he encountered in the Alps, who exclaimed, when suddenly called to pause and contemplate a panorama of grand and glorious scenery, 'Eh —how nice!'

"'How sublime!' rejoined another tourist.

"'Ah, *that* is the word—*sublime—sublime!*' burst forth Byron, standing by, glancing quickly from one to the other, and darting daggers of reproach at the stupid offender."

It was in June 1876 that Mrs. Elliott was called upon to sympathise with her friend, Miss Marian Bacon, on the occasion of her father's death. The old hero of Waterloo was one morning found dead in his bed ; and she who made the sorrows of others peculiarly her own, was not long in testifying her fellow-feeling for the bereaved daughter : "Grieved

and shocked," she writes, " was I when the sad news came
from Seafield on Tuesday evening.   To you, my dear Miss
Marian, the blow has been sudden indeed ; but to your dear
father who has thus passed away, what a strangely quiet
departure ! more like the shadow of death than the reality.
This will be a soothing thought for you hereafter, and so
also will be the feeling that you were his home-daughter,
the stay of his old age, and his greatest comfort on earth.
How his very heart cried out for you when you were away
in England the last time, and what a touching sight it must
have been to see him go down the pier to meet you on the
day of your return !   You will always be thankful that you
came home that very day and brought gladness to him,
instead of staying away to please yourself and others.   The
thoughts and feelings and prayers of your friends are with
you at this time of trouble.   May the Father of the fatherless be your guide at all times, comforting you by His Holy
Spirit, so that you may feel more and more of the love of
Christ—the love stronger than death, stronger than all our
provocations and perverseness.   In a book of yours there is
an expression to this effect, which was a comfort to me in a
day of depression.   ' God is in your history and in the plan
of your biography.'   As we also learn from the Book of Job
(xxiii. 14), 'He performeth the thing *appointed* for me.'   So
you must believe, dear friend, that your life is an ' earthly
story with a heavenly meaning ' of eternal love.   ' Better is
the end of a thing than the beginning thereof, and better is
the patient in spirit than the proud in spirit.'   If you are
learning these lessons now in the school of Christ, you will
rejoice hereafter in the endless holy days in the light of His
countenance in the home of peace."

Up to July of 1878 the dear subject of this memoir was
unusually well and brisk ; so much so that in June of this
year she, Dr. Elliott, Mrs. Colin Lindsay, and Mr. and Miss
Skottowe (Karine) all went together one lovely day for the
long drive of thirty miles, from Douglas to Kirk Michael

and back—a garden party at Bishops Court being the object
in view—the first given by Bishop Rowley Hill and Mrs.
Hill after the installation of the former as prelate of the
diocese and successor to Bishop Powys.   Our friend had a
peculiar pleasure in garden parties; she rarely declined one.
Conversation of a congenial nature, with fitting accompaniments, was almost a need of her nature.   She had not
words to describe what she felt when in company of her
peculiar choice; she could sit and talk, and at the same
time breathe in the delicious perfumed air of flowers and
foliage and far extending pasture-land replete with a myriad
scents, soothed too with the songs of birds, hum of insects,
and music of soft flowing waters.

And how she did enjoy herself that afternoon at Bishops
Court, walking under the ancient trees or amid the garden
flowers, drinking into her very soul the charm of surround
ing beauty; and as she gazed upon the animated scene of
assembled guests, even though with obscured vision, her
sympathetic heart responded to the gaiety and life of the
hour; and the youngest and fairest there was not more
keenly sensitive to the gratification of the moment than the
gentle, almost blind saint of God.   Then partly for medita-
tation, or to seek the coolness and repose of the spot, she
would enter and linger for awhile within the sacred precincts
of the Bishop's chapel.   And then anon quietly find her
way with some privileged companion into the old mansion,
where upon the walls in one apartment the prelates of
Sodor and Man from remote ages are portrayed in various
degrees of resemblance and artistic merit.   Affixing her
powerful and double glasses, our friend found a keen satisfaction in endeavouring to investigate the old paintings and
engravings of these remote dignitaries, but, little could
she see excepting through the vision and explanations
of others.*   How merciful is our gracious God, who some-

* Since the above was written, a considerable portion of this ancient
and most interesting episcopal palace has been burned down.   The

times, when depriving His creatures of one sense, so quickens
and intensifies another, that the loss of the one is more
perhaps than made up in the additional power supplied to
the other ! Mrs. Elliott, though blind—or nearly so—physically, really saw for her own gratification with a tenfold
intensity, through the mental process of imagination and
delicate perception. Had she been asked to describe that
array of quaint portraits, she would have done so in perfect
good faith that she knew all about them. She would have
also dwelt with rapture on the picture of natural beauty
presented by foliage and flowers without ; the effect of sunlight upon this tree, or that, on yonder slope of grass,
assemblage of flowers, or glinting waters. She would have
described the graceful form and fair features of this young
blooming beauty, or of another, with ecstatic interest and
sympathetic delight. She saw all, and rejoiced in the sight,
with that brilliant fancy of hers, and heart overflowing with
human love and all-embracing tenderness.

Who would have disenchanted her, when often she suf-
fused with imaginary glitter and fictitious *couleur de rose*,
much that was exceedingly dull and commonplace in character and appearance !

Dear, dear friend ! so good herself, she saw goodness
everywhere ; so fair in soul and aspiration, the reflection
of her own being ensued as naturally as object reflects
object in the mirror of a calm sunny lake or beautiful un-
troubled sea. And, with a heart at rest from sin and strife,
how she yearned that each soul with hers should be bright
and free from fret and discord ! One day the impetuous
Karine came to see her, her brow clouded, her temper irate,
some one had offended her, she would not forgive, she would
not relent. "Karine, Karine," said the saint of God, "hush !
my child, *life is too short for quarrelling*." It was enough !

conflagration took place on the night of May 16, 1893. The part
consumed was the central wing, chiefly the erection of the renowned
Bishop Wilson, prelate of Man in 1700.

The words, the tone shot with all their solemn significance into the heaving breast, stilled the tempest, and stamped for *ever* their holy lesson.

On another occasion, Karine again coming to her, sick and sad at heart and very anxious, all seeming dark to her understanding and perception; the way before her blocked with obstacles innumerable; wrong, in the case . that perplexed her, triumphing, and right going to the wall; her friend, instead of reading her a lecture on irritableness, impatience, and want of faith, simply pointedly and distinctly repeated the three words: "Remember, Karine, 'The Lord reigneth.'" And giving her a book, she wrote her name in it, accompanied with Ps. xcvii. 1, 10, 11.

Another instance of the joy she felt, and the endeavour she ever made, to sow and keep peace in the hearts and lives of her associates. One day two of her friends chanced to encounter on her door-step—two, however, who were at variance one with the other—and happening to come out at the moment, she hailed the opportunity of confronting them together, and seizing both their hands, united them in hers in a clasp of reconciliation and renewed friendship. Oh, the beauty, the beauty of holiness, the love of Christ which constraineth! "Blessed are the peacemakers: for they shall be called the children of God."

CHAPTER XXVII.

PITCAIRN.

Mrs. Colin Lindsay, incidentally mentioned in the preceding chapter, was a special favourite of Mrs. Elliott's. She admired her for her amiable disposition and many graceful accomplishments; but Mrs. Lindsay possessed an additional attraction for Mrs. Elliott, in that she was the widow of a naval officer, Captain Colin Lindsay, who was identified with an exceedingly romantic and peculiarly interesting history—that of the Pitcairn Islanders.

Karine first heard the story from Mrs. Elliott. And especially one evening that she and the latter were present at Mrs. Lindsay's was it made the subject of conversation between the three. The evening was possibly the one signified in the following characteristic little note (Karine, it may here be said, was a frequent and ever welcome visitor at Mrs. Lindsay's, which will account, and be ample apology, for the nature of the amusingly worded request made in the note):—

"Chérie,—As there was no positive engagement that you would come to-morrow evening, I have (though not with a clear mind) accepted an invitation to Mrs. Lindsay's for to-morrow evening. If I had the prospect of meeting you there it would be a peculiarly additional attraction. Cannot you come in a promiscuous sort of a manner?— Toujours à vous, Eleanor Elliott."

The history as unfolded in the hearing of Karine, if not

on this, on some other occasion at Mrs. Lindsay's, is one probably familiar to most; but on account of its charm for Mrs. Elliott, its link with her friend, Mrs. Lindsay, and its wider connection with Manxland, it falls naturally in its place, and will bear repeating here.

As early as 1787, in the reign of King George III., His Majesty's ship the *Bounty* set sail to the South Pacific Islands for the purpose of obtaining plants of the bread-fruit tree. Lieut. Wm. Bligh commanded the vessel. All went well with the crew until after their sojourn at Otaheite. Here they were detained for a considerable time; and, luxuriating in the attractions of the lovely island, they became enervated and unfitted for the stern and arduous duties of seamen. A very short time after their departure from Otaheite they resolved to mutiny against the captain. Accordingly, one night they woke him from his sleep with a pistol at his head, and threatened his life if he offered any protest. They then obliged Bligh and eighteen others to get into one of the ship's boats; and flinging them only enough provisions for a limited period, they shoved them off, and left them to their fate.

The chief mutineer was an officer, Fletcher Christian, next in command to Bligh. Christian was connected with the Isle of Man. He is said to have been one of the Christians of Unerigg Hall, and related through that family to the Taubmans of the Nunnery, Douglas, Isle of Man. Counsellor Edward Christian, his brother, was Professor of Law at Cambridge, Chief-Justice of Ely, and editor of "Blackstone's Commentaries."

Those others that remained on the *Bounty* were also more or less identified with Manxland. Captain Bligh himself, it is averred, had been for some time in Douglas, and his sojourn there may have accounted for so many of the crew being Manxmen born, or residents of the island. By far the most interesting of these was Peter Heywood, son of Peter John Heywood, Esq., and grandson of Deemster

O

(Chief Judge) Heywood, then of the Nunnery.* Young Heywood was a midshipman only fourteen years of age, and, it is alleged, much attached to Captain Bligh; and had voluntarily no hand in the insurrection against the commander. Having, however, remained with the mutineers on the ship, he was afterwards brought to trial along with others on the charge of mutiny and piracy.

In the meantime Captain Bligh and the sixteen men that made up his party, deserted by the ship, were exposed for nearly six weeks in mid-ocean, undergoing the most frightful suffering from semi-starvation, cold, and wet. How they survived was well-nigh a miracle. They finally, however, landed at Timar, no one having perished on board. Of the nineteen that had been *forced* into the launch, twelve returned to their native country, the others died soon after landing at the Dutch settlement of Coupang from the effects of the horrors they had passed through.

With respect to Captain Bligh, a distinguished future was in store for him. In 1801, he commanded the *Glatton* at the battle of Copenhagen under Lord Nelson. He was subsequently appointed Governor of New South Wales, and after his return to England from that colony he became Vice-Admiral of the Blue.

As for the mutineers, headed by Christian, they made for Otaheite, where they landed. Fourteen of them remained on the island, amongst these was young Peter Heywood. The others eventually departed and finally settled at Pitcairn, a tiny island, only four and a half miles in circumference, resting on the bosom of the vast South Pacific seas.

On the return of Captain Bligh to England, after his providential escape from death under the most awful circumstances, steps were immediately taken by the Government to send out a ship to discover the whereabouts of the mutineers, and have them apprehended and brought to justice. The

* The Nunnery did not become the property of the Taubmans till some years later.

fourteen at Otaheite were the only ones found; the Pitcairn refugees escaped discovery. Arriving in England, and after due trial, the prisoners were some of them acquitted, some of them sentenced to death. Of the latter was the young Manxman, Peter Heywood, and another officer; they were, however, recommended to the King's mercy.

Peter was fatherless, but he had a devoted mother, loving brothers and sisters, and a most happy home in the Isle of Man. Very pathetic was his case in consequence, and his relations, knowing his fine honourable disposition, could not bring themselves to believe the awful charge against their darling boy. Heywood had especially one sister, Nessy, who loved him with a love the most devoted and intense. When she heard that her brother had been condemned, she instantly determined to cross the sea, and make her way to London to implore his pardon.

When telling this story Mrs. Elliott was overcome with emotion, and her voice almost failed her, as she described (the account of which she had often heard from her mother) the sufferings and endurance of this noble girl making the passage to Liverpool in the dead of winter, in a wretched vessel and in awful weather (a terrible undertaking a hundred years ago), bent on saving her beloved brother from disgrace and death. With the assistance of wise counsellors and kind friends, a petition was at length secured on behalf of Heywood and Morrison, and despatched to King George. The result was the free pardon of both officers.

Nessy, as well as being a devoted sister, was also an accomplished girl. Besides other gifts, she was possessed of poetic powers of no mean order; but in less than a year after her arduous undertaking on her brother's behalf, she died. Her early death was probably accelerated by exposure to cold, and the severe strain upon her delicate organisation during a period of intense mental suffering.

Now as regards the missing mutineers, they met with terrible retribution. Having taken Otaheitean wives with them, and some Otaheitean men from Otaheite, they existed on Pitcairn in broken numbers for some years, until of all the original number only *one* remained, John Adams. The others perished miserably, most of them by murder consequent upon quarrelling amongst themselves.

John Adams (also by birth a Manxman), the survivor of the *Bounty*, was an illiterate seaman. He could merely read and write a little, having taught himself. Left alone with five or six heathen women, and twenty fatherless children, he now realised his solemn and responsible position. Remorse for the crime he had committed, and which had brought him into his present condition, weighed heavily upon his mind. About this time also he had dreams, which greatly agitated him and gave him no rest night or day. In this state of disquietude, not knowing where or how to find peace for his distracted heart and brain, he suddenly bethought himself of the Bible and Book of Common Prayer that had been rescued from the *Bounty*. He began to read the Word of God. In it he soon found light to his path and peace to his soul. He now studied and meditated upon it continually. By the grace of God, Adams became a new man. Under the influence of the Holy Ghost, he set to work to christianise the heathen women and children under his charge. He was a man of mental vigour and resource, and soon also made laws to regulate the little community. Under the godly discipline of Adams the young people grew up; and eventually the Pitcairn community became a people cherishing all that was holy and beautiful in principle and conduct. Many of her Majesty's ships touched at the island during the course of years, and the commanders have but one testimony to bear, that the inhabitants are, of all people they had ever heard of, the most exemplary in morals and piety. Their loyalty to Queen Victoria was, and is, of the most exalted kind; and the whole order of their government, ecclesiastical and civil, is touchingly perfect in its administration and practice. They built a church and schoolhouse. The order of their Church service is that of the Church of England. Divine service may be said to extend over the whole of Sunday, and they have public service also every afternoon in the week excepting Saturday, when the men are engaged in fishing.

One of their distinguished visitors, in writing of them, says: "The week spent at Pitcairn's Island will be looked upon by me as one of the most interesting of my life. A state of society is there beheld which cannot be believed unless seen. In many points, particularly in the culture of their minds, a high state of civilisation presents itself, without vice or luxury, the community living in the most primitive simplicity. But the most remarkable feature in their character is that of earnest and universal piety. And from this fountain springs their brotherly love, so true, so touching, so unlike anything I had ever seen or dreamed of, as animating a whole community, that it can only be likened to the feeling that exists in a deeply religious and united private family in England.

"So earnest is their piety, so directly does it appear to spring from Him who is the Divine Source of all religion, that I almost fancied myself in a Theocracy of the primitive ages."

Surely the God of all grace can make the wrath of man to praise Him. It does seem so incredibly marvellous that such a model system of living should spring out of one of the blackest deeds on record!

About the time that Mrs. Elliott and Karine spent the evening specified with Mrs. Lindsay, a reference to the Pitcairn Islanders appeared in the newspapers; it was to the effect that her Majesty's ship *Opal* had lately visited the island, by the command of Rear-Admiral A. F. R. de Horsey, to deliver an organ, a present to the Pitcairners from Queen Victoria. Captain F. C. B. Robinson reported on the visit in these words: "It is unnecessary for me to do more than allude to the simple piety and moral excellence

of these charming islanders, whose guilelessness and affectionate hospitality must win on the hearts of all who come
in contact with them; it did so with us, and I should be
sorry to lose this opportunity of mentioning opinions so
much in accord with those of previous visitors.   They were
in great distress at having nothing they could think worthy
to offer for her Majesty's acceptance, and we brought off a
model of one of their canoes, which they ventured to hope
the Queen would deign to receive from them.   By sunset
on the 3rd, the supplies we needed were received, and
having landed the majority of our guests, I prepared for
departure.   It was dark before their boat returned for Mr.
M'Coy and Mrs. Simon Young, the pastor's wife, and her
two daughters, who had remained on board till the last.
These also then bid us an affectionate farewell, repeated from
the boat, with hearty cheers and kind wishes.   Cordially
reciprocating these, we steamed to sea, and as we left, we
heard those in the boat once again, with more than loyalty,
singing "God save the Queen.'"

This recent report renewed all the interest of the Pitcairn
story, and the evening that Mrs. Elliott, Mrs. Lindsay, and
Karine met together, the narrative formed the chief topic
of conversation.   Mrs. Lindsay mentioned that on more
than one occasion Captain Lindsay visited the island, and
how enchanted he was with the people.   Amongst their
feats of prowess, what wonderful climbers and swimmers
they were—how even old women could scramble up almost
perpendicular precipices; and how the children gambolled
and dived in the foaming surf—breasting the huge waves
for sheer sport !

But what was most interesting was the description of the
graceful manners and affectionate behaviour of the people,
combined with the most irresistible simplicity.   Mrs. Lindsay told how when Captain Lindsay parted from them, the
women and girls hung about his neck, kissing and begging
him to soon return.   She then offered to read her guests

some of the Pitcairners' letters to her husband. Mrs. Elliott and Karine hailed the proposition with delight. One of them is as follows :—

"To Lieutenant Colin W. Lindsay, R.N.

"Pitcairn's Island, *July* 1842.

"Dear Sir,—I have taken the opportunity of writing unto you such things as have taken place since you left us. The influenza has not left us without her fatal victims, for in the short space of two months four of our friends have died under that most painful disorder; it is with pleasure I tell you that they died with a fair prospect in that Saviour who paid His life a ransom for their souls. Perhaps you would wish to know their names. The oldest of them is Charles Christian, the oldest man on the island, and Edward Quintall, him that was sick when you was here, and to add more to his afflicted family his youngest son is gone with him; only one female is among the dead, and that is poor old Isabella Christian. She came from *Tihiti* in the *Bounty*, and she is supposed to be more than a hundred years of age; she has known Captain Cook in his third voyage. Mr. Fletcher Christian is magistrate of the island at present. We are all in good health; no disorder of any kind has visited us these six months. Since you left us this state of things is much the same. You must write to me, as it will give me great pleasure to hear from you, and believe me, dear Lindsay, your very sincere friend,   Frederick Young."

In another letter from the same writer, in 1849, he mentions that his sister has been married and is the mother of a child who is to be called "after some one who is very dear to you, and indeed to us all"—meaning Mrs. Lindsay, Captain Lindsay's then affianced bride. And reporting of himself the correspondent further says, "I am still single, but by the time this reaches you I may be spliced to one whom I have loved a very long time."

The father or grandfather of this Frederick Young was the mutineer, Edward Young, midshipman, nephew of Sir George Young, Bart.

After listening to these delightful mementos, Mrs. Elliott then, in her inimitable way, alluded to Byron's poem, "The Island," and repeated passages from that imaginative version of the mutiny and Pitcairn settlement. And we think we can hear her as, with ease and softly articulated tones, she said :—

> "And who is he? the blue-eyed northern child
> Of isles more known to man, but scarce less wild;
> The fair-haired offspring of the Hebrides,
> Where roars the Pentland with its whirling seas;
>
> .   .   .   .   .   .
>
> By Neuha's side he sate, and watched the waters,
> Neuha, the sun-flower of the island daughters,
> Highborn (a birth at which the herald smiles,
> Without a scutcheon for these secret isles),
> Of a long race, the valiant and the free,
> The naked knights of savage chivalry.
>
> .   .   .   .
>
> Come let us to the islet's softest shade,
> And hear the warbling birds! the damsel said:
> The wood-dove from the forest depth shall coo,
> Like voices of the gods from Bolotoo.
> We'll cull the flowers that grow above the dead,
> For these must bloom where rests the warrior's head;
> And we will sit in twilight's face, and see
> The sweet moon glancing through the tooa tree,
> The lofty accents of whose sighing bough
> Shall sadly please us as we lean below;
> Or climb the steep, and view the surf in vain
> Wrestle with rocky giants o'er the main,
> Which spurn in columns back the baffled spray.
> How beautiful are these! how happy they,
> Who, from the toil and tumult of their lives,
> Steal to look down where nought but ocean strives!"

CHAPTER XXVIII.

MARIAN.

In July and August of 1878, well as our friend had for a time been before, a great change came over her. It was foreshadowed by a feeling of extreme lassitude ; then a dreadful sort of boil at the back of her neck showed itself. It became worse and worse—so serious in its nature, indeed, that her life was considered in danger. Her niece, Alice Weatherell, was sent for ; and a devoted, patient nurse she proved herself to her poor afflicted aunt.

In September, when she had got over the worst of the shocking suffering, an insatiable desire took hold of her to go to the country and breathe the sweet balmy air. Athol Street, with its dulness and its dark memories of sorrow and death, chilled her, and as a weight pulled her down in spirit more than she cared to allow any one to be aware of.

Alice was sent to St. John's to look for suitable rooms. She fixed upon a sweet cottage embowered in foliage and flowers, and within sound of a running brook, singing for ever a little tune full of music and suggestive of repose.

There the two went, and there Karine visited them. How strange it seemed to the latter to find her dear brilliant conversationalist so changed all at once—become quiet and almost speechless—a sad look of pain and weariness upon her gentle, noble countenance.

The visitor was depressed at the sight, and a crushing feeling came over her. Was the time approaching when she should lose this friend who had become, she believed, essential to her own life and happiness, and certainly to her spiritual well-being?

It pleased God, however, to gradually recover to a certain degree of ordinary health this precious friend. Previous to her recovery, and long before she could barely crawl for weakness, young Alice Weatherell informed Karine that day by day she would venture forth and visit the adjoining cottages, seeking to do good for Jesus' sake. Alice mentioned one instance of a poor woman who was dying of consumption—how deeply touched and impressed she was by the fact that the lady, who was nearly as ill as herself, came. to see and speak to her of the one thing needful for time and eternity. The poor creature was very ignorant, but gratitude to her benefactress quickened her perception and instigated her faith. She made rapid progress in spiritual things; and Miss Weatherell said she believed that through her aunt's ministrations the sufferer at last passed away a peaceful and enlightened soul.

On another occasion, which impressed Alice very much, she and her aunt went together to visit a poor dwelling, where they expected to find several inmates, but where a child alone was to be seen—father and mother and the rest being in the fields, or elsewhere. Instead of a word with the little one, and then coming away, Mrs. Elliott, nothing deterred by the smallness of her audience, sat down, and, drawing the child to her, engaged it in conversation, till by degrees the little one's confidence was entirely won. Then she brought forward in childish language the "Old, old story of Jesus and His love," unfolding the leading truths of salvation in such a way as to arrest and fill the young mind with interest and grave wonder.

How utterly weak she was, and painfully exhausted, her niece only too plainly saw, but it was useless to urge her to desist talking until she was satisfied she had impressed the Gospel message on the youthful understanding, and touched with its sweetness the tender and aroused conscience.

In a letter from the convalescent to her brother, after her return to Douglas from St. John's, we have a picture of her dreadful sufferings in July and August :—

"At the time," she says, "of my great suffering, dear Robert, your sympathy with me was such real pain, such *feeling with* my agony, that now your congratulations are as heartfelt as was then your sympathy. When Doctor Fleming first saw the wound, the day but one after it had been cut open, he had a look of fear in his face, and he said, 'You must have suffered torments; it is beyond all comparison the worst anthrax that I ever saw." Some weeks afterwards Alice heard him say, that when he first saw it, he thought that I never could get over it. However, through Divine mercy, my life has been spared for a season. But this recent bodily trial has given me a fresh experience of the terrible reality of pain, with the oft-recurring thought of the awful goodness of Christ in 'tasting death for every man,' and going down into the depths of agony that He might save us from sin and selfishness, and from ourselves, to be transformed by His Spirit into His own likeness.

. . . .

"My husband is waiting to answer your letter until he can say my wound is quite healed. It was at first wide and deep, about the length of your hand, now it is about the width of your little finger."

When winter set in, Alice Weatherell returned to Douglas, and her sister Eleanor accompanied her. They came to take care of their aunt, not without self-sacrifice, for they left behind them at Elton their dear sister Marian very unwell.

Alluding to some scriptural references made by the Rev. Robert Weatherell, his sister again writes to him in January :—

"Many thanks for your golden letter, full of heavenly wisdom and love drawn from the treasury of Scripture, from things new and old in the books of the Old and New

Covenant. Yours is real sympathy with pain, because you feel with the sufferer. During the time of agony, day and night, for weeks, thoughts on the mystery of pain were often revolving in my mind. The only answer is to be found in the 'Lamb' in the 'heart of the Throne,' and the self-sacrifice in the heart of God, the Creator becoming in Christ the Redeemer, that by the sacrifice of Himself the lost creature might be delivered from the bondage of sin and selfishness into re-union with God, to be made partakers of a Divine nature. The Lord Jesus is the Lamb because He was slain, so ordained before the foundation of the world, and as you justly observe, 'One meaning of the blood surely implies suffering,' and this very pain proves the intense reality of Divine love ; and the Lamb in the heart of the throne is emblazoned in Revelation as the royal coat-of-arms of Heaven.

"How glad and thankful we were to see your dear girls again. What a comfort they are in the house, what a reviving, cheering influence with their pleasant, obliging, thoughtful kindness. Your dear Marian must try to forgive our cruel selfishness in drawing them away from Elton this winter."

1879 was the year of the Zulu war, a time of painful interest for our friend. In June she writes to her niece Marian, of whom she was so very fond, and who was still ill, on the subject of the lamentable death of the Prince Imperial, and the anguish of the Empress, his mother :—

"We are truly sorry, dear Marian, to learn from dear Alice's letter that you have been suffering so much pain and sickness. It is very grievous to flesh and blood to go through these trials, and very saddening to your friends, who feel a loving sympathy with your sufferings. But the most compassionate Friend is the One who suffered most of all, and for all, who is 'touched with the feeling of our infirmities.' In due season He will take you by the hand again, and raise you up to renewed health and strength ; and then you will be glad that He has taught you to endure, as He teaches every one whom He brings into His school and His family. 'Behold, we count them happy which endure,' is the voice of Scripture, but it is not the world's voice, the world counts them happy who enjoy present things. But the present things are passing away, while patient submission to the Father's will is a preparation for pleasures for evermore in the light of His countenance. But it is not easy or natural to bear pain with joyfulness; this is the result of supernatural strength imparted by the Holy Spirit; and the end of such endurance will be endless enjoyment hereafter. You remember the saying of Job, 'He performeth the thing appointed for me.' And a modern has expanded the thought into these beautiful Christian lines :—

> " 'Nay, I endure; but not because
>   The world imposeth woe;
>   But rather that Thine Hands perform
>   The thing appointed so ;—
> Those kindly wounding hands did brave
> Themselves a deeper wound to save.'

"Your pain, dear Marian, hard as it is to bear, may soon through the Divine blessing be quite removed. But it is very different with the afflicted mother of young Louis Napoleon. Hers is an anguish of the broken heart incurable as long as she lives upon this earth. May the Saviour who pitied the bereaved mother at Nain be her comfort now, and draw her nearer and nearer to Himself, who was once pierced and wounded for our sins."

Soon after writing the above Mrs. Elliott was again a prey to dreadful physical suffering—another boil or abscess, similar to the last, made its appearance; and the drain upon the enfeebled constitution of the sufferer was appalling. The anxiety of her friends was great, and many were the prayers offered for the alleviation of the dear one's agony.

It was during this illness that Miss E. A. Moffat, whose

name has been mentioned before, apprised Archdeacon Philpot, Mrs. Elliott's dear old associate of other days, of her illness, and enclosed to him the following lines, expressive of the anxiety and grief that were felt for her :—

DEAR MRS. ELLIOTT.

November 1879.

We brought her before our Father God
    In the loving hands of prayer,
We bore her up to the Mercy-seat
    And we laid the sufferer there :
The answer came down from the Heavenly Throne,
"Fear not, fear not, she is one of Mine own."

Her Saviour suffers each pang she bears,
    Her sorrows are not unknown ;
And every pain that His servant feels,
    The Master has made His own.
And amid the angels' sweet songs above
He hears the cry of the child of His love.

"Fear not, fear not," saith the Saviour's voice,
    "Tho' the furnace heated be ;
I am with thee in the midst of fire,
    And the flames shall not burn thee."
The eternal God is thy refuge found,
And His everlasting arms around.

And He is still as "mighty to save,"
    And oh, it will ever be
The joy of His heart to sing of His love,
    Of His tender love, to thee !
So we pray in faith, and we leave the rest
In the hands of Him who doth love thee best.
                            —ELIZABETH A. MOFFAT.

A keen sympathiser and literary admirer of Mrs. Elliott's was Captain Edward Dumergue, well remembered for his versatile talents, extensive reading, and remarkable memory. He appreciated the sincerity and lofty piety of his gifted friend in no stinted measure.

It was touching to note the kindliness of the act which led this lively talker to secure for her this, or that bunch of choice grapes, flowers, or whatever he thought would please and do her good.

Calling upon Karine with his gift he would say, "This is for Mrs. Elliott—do take it to her," knowing it would gratify the former to be the bearer of the dainty.

This reminds one, *en passant,* of the intense admiration and affection of the once gay, jocose Clerk of the Rolls, Mr. Alfred Adams, for our friend. Many a day he would leave his busy office in Athol Street to come in and have a chat with her of whom he declared that she "already lived half in heaven." Looking around St. George's Church he would say, "There, at least, kneels one in that pew of whose devotion and sincere holiness of life I have not the shadow of a single doubt!"

Once more, before the year closed, it pleased God to raise our dear friend up again.

Her nieces having returned to Elton in the spring, when summer came, she was very anxious to have Alice back, and wrote to ask her to come. Alice was unable, Marian being so extremely ill.

In September of this year (1879) Mrs. Elliott was sufficiently well to be able to be present at the inauguration of the Douglas branch of the Young Women's Christian Association, in which Karine took a special part. This was a delightful and memorable evening when a work was founded and established in the island, the benefits of which are accruing, we believe, more and more to the glory of God and the good of His creatures.

Towards the close of autumn, news arrived that Marian Weatherell was growing alarmingly ill—the beloved niece in whom her aunt was so especially interested, and of whom she had such bright hopes in regard to her intelligence and piety.

The latter's sorrow on receiving the news was intense,

and her yearning for any relief that could be administered to the sufferer urgent in expression. She herself had gone through such agony of body and mind that acutely she could enter into the sufferings of another, especially, too, when they were of the same nature as those she had endured ; for Marian was languishing from the effects of a dreadful abscess.

"Anything," she wrote, "that gives relief for one day, or one night, is a mercy and a blessing."

Alas ! the next news was that the sweet gifted Christian girl was no more. Death had claimed the fair and good— the young life that had for a season sweetened the lives of others, and left behind the perfume of a gentle, saintly memory.

Writing on the sad event to the bereaved father, his sister says :—

"It must have cost you, dear Robert, a great effort to write that sad letter with the grievous tidings which we have been expecting with fear and dread. If earthly love could have kept our dear Marian in this lower world, she would have tarried for many a day. But it is written in the Song of Solomon, 'My Beloved is gone into His garden to gather lilies,' and He has gathered a fair and lovely one from the garden at Elton, to be transplanted into His own Paradise, until the time of restitution, the 'day of respira-tion.' You and Lydia have been allowed to nurse a child for Him, and He will give you your wages when He gives her to you again beautiful with His beauty, lovely with His loveliness—as He put upon her some of His comeliness here below, where the very stamp of Heaven was imprinted on her young saintly face. She used to sing with that pure sweet voice of hers,

'Angels ever bright and fair,
Take, oh take me to your care.'

And now we believe that they are surrounding her with

songs of gratulation on her escape from this evil world, and from the agonised body, and better than all beside, she has a clearer vision of the King in His beauty, and her soul is satisfied with His goodness. When the lull of pain came after the fiery storm, and Marian spoke to you in that delightful manner, looking so happy and glad, and saying that 'God is love,' and that she never expected to feel in that way—it was as a waft of fresh air from the Heavenly country, or rather a whisper of the Holy Spirit coming from the heart of the Good Father, and breathing into her inmost soul a new sense of the blessedness into which she was entering. Now that she has passed over to the other side of the veil, she will know more of the meaning of the mystery of pain as she looks upon the face of Him who once travailed unto death, to bring many children into His everlasting life, and who was made perfect as a Saviour through the things which He suffered. For weeks and months past the thought of Marian's sickness and pain has lain as a weight on one's mind; but now it is changed into a sense of peace—the pity and sympathy are for you, and the bereaved mother, and sisters and brothers."

To Alice she writes :—

"Your dream of the lilies has been sadly fulfilled, as one feared on hearing it told. The meaning was but too plain ; and no wonder that it kept you awake for a long time afterwards. In the Song of Solomon the word is "My Beloved is gone *down* into His garden to gather lilies,"—and so it ought to have been written in my letter to your father. In a spiritual sense it may be said that the Saviour often comes down to gather His own unto Himself. Eighteen hundred years ago, He did actually come down for their deliverance when he left his Throne and humbled Himself to be born into a body of flesh and blood, on purpose that He might die, to descend 'into the lower parts of the earth.' 'He that descended is the same that ascended far above all heavens,'—and why ?—that He might fill all things—that

P

the creation should not always be subject unto the bondage of vanity and corruption, but be brought into the liberty of the glory of the children of God. When Solomon, the 'sad and splendid,' had tasted every cup of earthly pleasure, he recorded his experience after all, that all is vanity of vanities—emptiness of emptiness—*under the sun.* He said also that 'if a man live a hundred years twice told—if his soul be not *filled with good,* I say that an untimely birth is better than he.' But they who are acquainted with Him who ascended far above all heavens, learn more and more that He satisfieth the empty soul and filleth the hungry soul with goodness. This is now Marian's happy experience as she rests in His love, in the haven where she would be. It seems quite natural to think of her there, in her own congenial clime, where she must be more at home than she ever could be in this lower world, though she had a pleasant earthly home with those who loved her so well. Some dreams, which were mercifully given to me last winter, have suggested some faint ideas of her present blessedness. In one of these dreams there was a consciousness of resting in a serene blue ether, with a patch of rippling light in front, while one's whole being was imbued with an intensely calm delight in the sense of God's lovely character; it was indeed a 'rapture of repose'—an ecstasy of peace ineffable and indescribable—the soul was satisfied with His goodness.

"In another dream there was a vision of glorious creatures of gigantic stature, and resplendent with light, on each side of a cloud; those on one side making signals of invitation to the others to come and join them, and the others waving their arms in token that they were coming.

"When one thinks of Marian where she is now, in the upper region above the storms, and of what she sees and hears and feels, it seems that the most loving mother and father would scarcely bring her down again into the waves of this troublesome world, though the heart does cry out for those who are gone. About three years ago, a few days before Easter, Marian and Maude left us to go to their home at Elton. And now Marian is gone to another home for her holy-days, until the great Easter-day of resurrection life, the re-union of spirit, soul and body, when she will come again, clothed with immortality. Who knows how soon it may be?"

CHAPTER XXIX.

EASTER.

A most intense love had our friend for the season of Easter. How she delighted, when the great feast came round to lift not only her whole spiritual being in joyous adoration and thanksgiving of praise for the crowning triumph of the Christian faith commemorated that day, but in her outward garb she manifested her gladness, wearing as much white as she could appropriately do to relieve her usual black attire, deeming its symbol of purity consistent with the spotless glory of renewed, sanctified, and risen life vouchsafed to sinful man through the death, burial, and resurrection of Christ Jesus !

On Easter Day of 1880, was she specially absorbed in wondering and elevating thought, as she contemplated the mystery of the resurrection, and the triumph of Life for ever more over Death and the Grave; for dear Marian Weatherell's recent death gave an additional impetus to her flood and flow of thought.

"At this feast of the resurrection," she says in a letter to her nieces, "one remembers some lines of a Moravian hymn—

> 'He riseth who mankind hath bought
> With pain and grief extreme,
> 'Twas great to call a world from nought,
> 'Twas greater to redeem'—

because the work of redemption involved in it the depth of humiliation and self-sacrifice, the death, burial, and resurrection of the Redeemer, King, Creator, by whom and for whom all things were made. The 'pain and grief,' 'the love and sorrow,' give the moral glory to the crown of thorns—

> 'Did e'er such love and sorrow meet,
> Or thorns compose so rich a crown?'

a crown that fadeth not away.

.   .   .   .   .   .

"What happy Easter holy-days dear Marian is spending now in the calm upper regions above the storm!—

> 'Tell me of that celestial calm
> Each face in glory weareth'—

though the fulness of glory awaits the resurrection morning, when the Saviour and His saints shall appear in the glory of their transfigured bodies."

Alas, this year there is apparent in our dear one's hand-writing a rapid and marked change. At times the letters are only partly formed, and the words occasionally only partly written. Her sight, it was evident, by this and other proofs, was quickly failing her altogether; and it is pitiful to read the following reflections wrung from the shrinking heart incidental to its sense of weakness and helplessness:—

"You must know, my dear Eleanor," she wrote to her brother's eldest daughter, "that for some days I have been in a disturbed and saddened state of mind, in a turmoil of inward vexation, owing to my unruly and morbid habit of self-reproach, spending so much time and thought in vain regret for what I have said or left unsaid, for what I have done or left undone. Your uncle has had notes and cards from London inviting him to vote for Lord George Hamilton, the Conservative candidate member for Middlesex; and at last, on Thursday evening, a railway-pass was sent for his journey to and fro. He suggested at first that I should accompany him, but this I refused at once with hot-headed impatience, because the state of my eyes seemed to make it almost impossible. And my own idea was terror at the thought of his danger in a London crowd, as he is neither quick to see nor to hear. Yet it might all have been easily managed by first driving up in a cab to Guildhall, where the polling was to take place. But this thought did not occur until it was too late. So with my usual rashness I persuaded him to give it up. And after nine o'clock on Friday morning, when the packet was sailing, the keen regret began, which went stinging hour after hour throughout Saturday and Sunday, as I went on saying to myself, 'Only for me, he might have had the satisfaction of voting once for his own city. Only for me, he might have gone on to Elton, and that would have been a refreshment to him who has no refreshment, and we should have been surrounded by the fair young faces. And then on Sunday it was so painful to feel that only for me we might have been at Elton Church, where your father and brother would both be officiating—an opportunity that might never occur again. And then on our return one of you might be induced to come with us. To all these vexatious thoughts I was trying to answer, that if it had been so ordered for our good we should have been compelled to go. But then as no direction had been sought from above, I could only blame myself for stupid obstinacy. However, it is just barely possible that before the end of this month we may (D.V.) perhaps consult two oculists in London, Dr. Meurer, when he arrives from Germany, and Dr. Baden, another German. Dr. Baden is ophthalmic lecturer at Guy's Hospital."

Notwithstanding what the correspondent secretly dwelt upon with fear and anguish of mind, it is marvellous to see from her letters, and it was marvellous to witness at the time, how she contrived by the Spirit of all power working in her to rise above her fears, above her anguish, and above herself. For instance, in 1880, Governor and Lady Loch opened the first Insular Exhibition of Pictures—a choice collection, as before noted, of some of the foremost works of the day ; and Mrs. Elliott, roused to the occasion, was infinitely more interested and enthusiastic over the event than were several of its professedly most ardent supporters and admirers.

This Exhibition was the forerunner of the School of Art, instituted this same year by Sir Henry and Lady Loch, and placed on a sure foundation by the unremitting zeal and concern displayed in its maintenance and usefulness by her Ladyship, seconded by the then talented and enthusiastic Head Master, Mr. W. J. Merritt.

Touchingly, too, is it evident how, amid all loss and involuntary depression, supreme in our dear friend's soul was the love and thirst for the beauties of Nature. How she could enjoy them still, feeling them if she could not see them, and drinking their sweetness into her impassioned being with a yearning responsive enjoyment, only felt and conceived by the soul akin to its God, or the heart aglow with poetic fire and artistic perception !

" Karine walked with me to Pulrose stream," she said in one of her letters, " where we sat beside the quiet waters and listened to their soothing song."

Ah, happy recollection for the younger friend—recalling how that day, when beside her heavenly-inspired companion, she sat on the bank of the Pulrose stream. It was like a foretaste of the joys known to those who have crossed the river, and entered the paradise of the blest, meeting one with another, and basking in the ineffable light of that city which hath " no need of the sun, neither of the moon " to enhance its beauty; and listening to the voice which "is as the sound of many waters" proceeding from the throne of God and the Lamb.

Sweet, passing sweet, were the words uttered and glowing thoughts expressed by one of the friends by the shining stream under the clear blue sky, and within sight of the Nunnery grove in its vesture of tender "leafy June" foliage !

And happy, passing happy (though clouded by transient misgivings) was the attitude of the other, listening, quietly learning, and wondering at what she heard!

On another occasion we have a picture of a visit to Kirk Marown, to the farm of Balla Garey, where Karine had taken rooms in July of this year for the sake of her health :—

"Yesterday," describes the word painter, "I spent some refreshing hours with Karine at Balla Garey. We walked in the green grassy glen, beautiful with green trees, and enlivened with the soft music of a running brook, singing 'a quiet tune,' very different from the noisy bawls and box organs of the town. This calm country retreat seems to breathe balm and health into the very soul of poor Karine.

"After our walk in the glen we had tea in the garden, with such delicious butter and cream as might have been tasted in Arcadia, though the Arcadians could never have dreamed of such scones as were made yesterday by the Scotch landlady, the mistress of the farm, Mrs. Templeton!"

Praise was the natural voice of our friend's soul. In the autumn of 1880 she, as her custom was, was present at the Harvest Thanksgiving service at St. George's, and writing of it she says :—

"The special Psalms were the 103rd and 107th. The first lesson was the 2nd chapter of Ruth—a lovely pastoral scene, always bright with the light of early days, while Boaz and the reapers greet each other with words full of prophetic and typical meaning. The lord of the harvest-field comes forth from Bethlehem, saying to the reapers, 'The Lord be with you,' suggesting the great Emmanuel, who in after days came forth from Bethlehem to be always present with His people, 'God with us.'"

In another letter about this date, she refers to a quotation from Dr. Paysan, to which she alludes in these interesting terms :—

"I send you, dear Alice, a reprint of a letter of Dr. Paysan's, which is well worth reading, though you may have read it often, as it is often quoted. Such heavenly thoughts and feelings as are expressed in those beautiful words are well condensed into two lines of Keble's Evening Hymn—

> 'Till in the ocean of Thy love,
> We *lose ourselves* in heaven above.'"

And now comes the year 1881, and we have the last letter apparently that Eleanor Elliott wrote to her relations at Elton. In it she makes a remarkable reference to the end of this dispensation. As she wrote, it is evident her own soul held out both its arms, as it were, eager to catch the first gleam of the new day, when the saints of God should be safe and glorified for evermore; the glorious blessed day, when the children that God had given her should return again from the land of the evening, and sunlight, and eternal life and joy should be her and their portion for evermore !

"This 1881," she wrote, "has been expected as the probable end of the present dispensation. If so, it will be a glad new year to the redeemed who are waiting for the Redeemer, more than they who watch for the morning.

"But the very expectation makes it somewhat unlikely that so it will be, and at such a time, because the Lord Himself has said to His disciples, 'At such an hour *as ye think not*, the Son of Man cometh.' But still it is well to be waiting and watching, and to be so renewed by the Spirit of holiness as to be ready for the time of regeneration, when the Son of Man shall sit on the throne of His glory."

CHAPTER XXX.

"UNTIL HE COME."

In the spring of 1881 Karine visited Elton, and from there went on to Paris with Eleanor Weatherell. Mrs. Elliott had given the former a special message to M. Bersier, and the young lady had promised to bring back a full and accurate reply.

When Eleanor and Karine started on their journey to the continent, Mrs. Elliott was not well; but before much of their time was over, news reached them that she was very unwell indeed. So saddening was this intelligence that they considerably curtailed their visit, and Karine made haste to return to the island.

During her stay in Paris she had been hoarding up every bit of information that she thought would interest her dear friend at home, especially had she a budget on the subject of Bersier, whose acquaintance she had made, and whose church she had embraced every opportunity to attend.

Alas! when on coming back to Douglas she visited 31 Athol Street, little did she imagine she should find such a change in her beloved Mrs. Elliott. To her disappointment and pain her Paris news met with little, or no interested response. Bersier's kind reply to the message conveyed fell flat. His name—the first golden link of the loving relationship that existed between the sufferer and her companion—had lost all its wonted charm. She was no longer the gay, graceful, intelligent talker—talk was a weariness, and news of even the most interesting and cheering kind was apparently of no moment, and hardly welcome.

Karine was crushed. She was little prepared for such a reception. Half her enjoyment in going abroad was to bring back what she believed would tend to brighten her friend. She could not have conceived that in so short a time such a change could possibly have taken place.

On another occasion she called, and being at that time full of the new School of Art which she attended and was very fond of, she began to expatiate on her love for art and her hope of success in the study of it. Mrs. Elliott sat very quiet as if listening; and then, as the speaker paused for a reply, thinking that she had been interesting her hearer, the latter ejaculated almost petulantly, " I cannot think, Karine, how you can possibly care for such things—how very uninteresting they appear to be ?"

Karine was thunderstruck. Could she believe her ears —her dear Mrs. Elliott no longer interested in her pursuits, voting them even worthless !

Alas ! alas ! it was evident that the brilliant intelligence that once shone with such radiance and beauty was fading away, and the loving heart and gracious manner that had always had such irresistible charm were becoming weary and fretful.

Ah, vain and foolish, indeed, are the things of Time, when Eternity is looming before, with its vast and all absorbing concern !

Karine saw with a flash what she was to expect. She understood that the strings of earth were slackening, and the eternal future was about to claim, unalloyed and unaccompanied by any admixture of Time, all the faculties of her friend's being.

It was a few weeks perhaps after her return from Paris, she called one day as usual to ask for Mrs. Elliott, when the servant said, " Do come in, Miss, my mistress would, I am sure, like to see you—she is lying on the sofa."

And opening a room door the visitor was announced

The sofa was empty, no Mrs. Elliott was there.

"Annie," called Karine, hastening after the retreating servant, "you are mistaken, Mrs. Elliott is not there."

"Dear me!" said the girl, "she must then have got out through the surgery door, and gone into Shaw's Brew."

"Gone out!" said Karine; "and by herself—surely she is not fit to do that?"

"She is *not*, Miss," was the answer; "but she does it—without knowing, I think—whenever she gets a chance, the Doctor or none of us watching her."

Karine was not long in tracing the whereabouts of her friend. She entered the back street, and then from it turned down the wretched alley termed Little Ireland, when lo!—what did she see but her beloved friend kneeling on the cold, dirty, rough ground in the very middle of the alley! She was praying, and entreating of the people—as for a lifetime almost she had been in the habit of doing—to turn from sin to righteousness, and from death to life in Christ Jesus.

"Oh, Mrs. Elliott, dear!" cried Karine, putting her arms round her whom she so much loved; "don't, dear, kneel here in the cold. Come back with me, and get warm, and lie down and rest."

The tender sightless eyes were raised to those bending over her, and the gentle saint rose; and, like a little child, suffered herself to be led quietly away by the hand she had been so long familiar with, and that she no doubt felt was laid upon her in loving compassion.

A smile was on her lips too, though she did not speak, as if she was pleased to be interfered with by one who cared for and loved her.

Days and weeks went over, and occasionally there were gleams of the old brilliant intelligence, the old interest in healthy mundane employment and recreation, the old grace of demeanour and loving winsomeness.

And one day, when the strong will was also again asserting itself, our dear friend made the announcement that she had ascertained there was hope for the recovery of her sight

—the eyes were now ripe for operation, and she was going to Manchester to have them operated upon—the journey to London would be too much of an undertaking.

Her husband and friends were terrified. They represented to her the thought of such a thing was the extreme of rashness, that her strength was so enfeebled that to undergo any such tax upon her constitution was perilous in the extreme. Their words only vexed her—she was resolved to go.

All remonstrances being in vain, the many anxious hearts could only trust and pray for the best. To Manchester the sufferer went, accompanied by Dr. Elliott and a servant; and in course of a few days after her arrival she went through the operation. After which she was kept in a dark room; and finally, at the end of the prescribed term, liberated; and, it was asserted, in a fair way to complete recovery.

When she returned home, though looking dreadfully worn and ill, she certainly gladdened all hearts by assuring them that she could now really see to read.

Alas! it was a fictitious gleam, which almost immediately ended in total and irrevocable darkness.

Oh, blow unbearable! She never recovered the frightful, the overwhelming disappointment!

"The thing which she greatly feared had come upon her." The brave heart succumbed.

Time with all its interests, its joys, its exquisite pleasures of intelligence and heart, was a thing of the past!

Nothing now remained before but the sweep of eternity— the illimitable shore of the future.

And, thank God, she could meet *that*. Though the beautiful mind was a vacuum as regarded the things of this life, it was still clear and unclouded as regarded the things of hereafter.

Miss Alice Weatherell being sent for to remain with her aunt during this trying time, says, she will never forget what her distress was when on arriving her aunt did not recognise her.

In a few days, however, her powers of recognition returned; and Miss Alice Weatherell was with her during six months of a sad and trying time—the mind alternately going and coming, and the physical strength proportionately weak and wavering.

It was about this time when one morning after family prayer, the invalid remained in complete silence as if in deep thought, then all at once suddenly rising, she exclaimed to Alice :—

"Call all the servants. I wish them upstairs again."

Alice did as she was bid, and the household reassembled.

"Let us pray," she then said solemnly.

"In the prayer that then followed," said Miss Weatherell, "the sense of sin was so present, that she cried out again and again, 'Lord, have mercy—Christ, have mercy. Oh, the burden of sin! Oh, to be delivered from *self!* Oh, the *infinite love* of God!'"

Alice and the servants were overawed. The reality—the intense earnestness of that prayer—were overwhelming in their power and startling impressiveness.

Finally the saint of God was altogether laid on one side. For many weary months she lay on her bed—the mind gone —the frail body wasting away.

Gone! do we say—that bright intellect? No, not when it concerned the language of the King. Her lips were always moving in prayer; and any allusion to Scripture would wake a ready repetition of verse after verse and passage after passage. Spiritual things were ever present; and visions of holiness and beauty kept her spirit calm and at peace.

One day when she had been rendered much more comfortable by change of bed, linen, &c., she turned to her niece and said :—

"Do you know I owe all this comfort to a poor beggar, who deprived himself of his cloak to cover me? How very kind it was! Was it not?"

And again and again she spoke of the wonderful goodness of God. The goodness of God and the benevolence of His creatures swelled her heart with recognition even in dying. Thanksgiving was on her lips to the last.

Shortly before the end came, she was evidently visited with some wondrous vision of delight, which we were informed she described in the language of Bunyan's Pilgrim. From the account given we would conclude that the passage repeated, word for word, and with a countenance of calm joy, was the following :—

"I see myself now at the end of my journey, my toilsome days are ended. I am going now to see that head which was crowned with thorns, and that face that was spit upon for me. I have formerly lived by hearsay and faith; but now I go where I shall live by sight, and shall be with Him in whose company I delight myself. I have loved to hear my Lord spoken of; and wherever I have seen the print of His shoe in the earth, there I have coveted to set my foot too. His name has been sweeter than all perfumes. His voice to me has been most sweet, and His countenance I have more desired than they that have most desired the light of the sun. His word I did use to gather for my food, and for antidotes against my faintings. He has held me, and hath kept me from mine iniquities; yea, my steps have been strengthened in His way."

As was her life so was her death—a tribute of praise to Christ her King. "The diamond was cut"—the saint's work on earth was done. She had fought a good fight, and henceforth was laid up for her a crown of righteousness which the Lord, the righteous Judge, shall give her at that day; and to all who, like her, love and wait for His appearing.

The announcement that the loved and gentle spirit had fled was made on Wednesday, May 31, 1882, from the reading desk in St. George's Church by the Rev. Beauchamp George, the vicar, during the evening service.

A solemn hush pervaded the building as the words fell and held every heart in sacred awe, whilst those who loved her best bowed the head and "shed the mortal tear"; but as they did so, they, as it were, beheld as in a passing pageant the glorious entry of that happy released spirit into the regions of everlasting day, amid the angelic throng, and the company of the redeemed: those who, having come out of great tribulation, have washed their robes white in the blood of the Lamb, and are before the throne of God, serving Him day and night in His temple: who "hunger no more, neither thirst any more; neither shall the sun light on them, nor any heat. For the Lamb which is in the midst of the throne shall feed them, and shall lead them unto living fountains of waters: and God shall wipe away all tears from their eyes."

She sleeps in St. George's churchyard, in the family vault, by the principal entrance gate, where too we have seen her mother laid, and her three sons; and where now her husband has joined them. Her dear old friend, the Rev. William Drury, the venerable Vicar of Braddan, Isle of Man, laid her to rest.

A small additional monument was raised to her memory. It is of granite, surmounted by a Bible—the symbol of her strength—on the open page of which are engraved the words, "Great peace have they which love Thy law" (Ps. cxix. 165). And beneath :—

To the Memory

OF

ELEANOR ELLIOTT,

WHO FINISHED HER LIFE-LONG TASK OF
SELF-DENYING LOVE AND
DEVOTED CHRISTIAN SERVICE,
MAY 31, 1882,
AGED 68 YEARS.

"HUSH! blessed are the dead
   In Jesus' arms who rest,
And lean their weary head
   For ever on His breast.

O beatific sight!
   No darkling aught between
They see the Light of light,
   Whom here they loved unseen.

For them the world is past
   With all its toil and care;
Its withering midnight blast,
   Its fiery noonday glare.

Them the good Shepherd leads
   Where storms are never rife,
In tranquil dewy meads
   Beside the Fount of Life.

Ours only are the tears,
   Who weep around their tomb,
The light of bygone years
   And shadowing years to come.

Their voice, their touch, their smile—
   Those love-springs flowing o'er—
Earth for its little while
   Shall never know them more.

But soon at break of day
   His calm Almighty voice,
Stronger than death shall say,
   Awake—arise—rejoice."

APPENDIX.

Page 58.—VICAR OF BRADDAN, 1847–1887.

The Rev. W. Drury will long be remembered in the Isle of Man. He was a magnificent type of the Manx clergyman, of great stature, strength, and bodily presence. But his popularity, not unaffected by these qualities, was mainly due to his untiring zeal, his lovingkindness, and his willingness and desire to pray with all men and sundry, at all times, and in all places. He was the Vicar of Braddan, the parish in which Douglas is situated, and was a much loved friend of Mrs. Elliott's. Beside his labours in Braddan, he did most excellent work in the Town, and was thus brought into close association with the subject of this memoir. She greatly admired and revered his noble character. Douglas people will not soon forget his preaching in Man to the "hobblers" on the Quay, or at the open-air overflow services in the old churchyard of Kirk Braddan. At these services he preached to immense congregations of visitors in the season, and thus became widely known as well as beloved in the north of England. A stone of rough black marble, with an inscription, points out the spot where he used to stand and address the crowds of willing listeners.

Printed by BALLANTYNE, MANSON & CO.
Edinburgh and London

www.ingramcontent.com/pod-product-compliance
Lightning Source LLC
Chambersburg PA
CBHW031429020726
47499CB00005B/1664